CHASING THE MIRROR

DEDICATION

For my wife, Charity

"Audrianna," Kendis said as she knelt in front of her. She took Audrianna's hand, and she immediately noticed the gold band Lorna had put on her finger earlier that day. Kendis looked up with tears in her eyes, and then she offered Audrianna the ring she had made for her more than ten years ago. "I trust there is a good reason you took this off of your finger," she whispered. "If you still wanna wear it, I still want you to have it."

CHAPTER 1

Audrianna tented her hands over her nose and glanced around at the motionless figures standing on the beach. She tried to choke back tears. "Oh my God, Kendis. What have you done?"

Kendis wiped her own glistening eyes with the backs of her hands.

"I've stopped time, Audri," she replied. When she recognized Audrianna's continued distress, she pulled her into her arms and rocked her. "I know you're scared, honey. It's okay. I gotcha now. Everything's gonna be all right."

"Everything's not going to be all right, Kendis!" Audrianna cried. She pushed weakly at Kendis with her forearms, but Kendis did not let go. After a moment, she gave up trying to escape and simply broke down sobbing.

"You lied to me about all of this!"

"I didn't lie to you, Audri," Kendis said, rubbing her cheek against Audrianna's. "I just didn't include you."

Audrianna tore loose from her in a rage. "No, that privilege was reserved for my son! A bootlegger, Kendis? You made Devon a bootlegger?"

"He wanted to be involved," Kendis justified calmly.

"He wants to please you, Kendis! Do you have any idea what I've just been through as a result of his wanting to be involved?" Audrianna took a breath and continued without waiting for Kendis to respond. "Prohibition agents came around to my office yesterday and told me if I didn't help them collect evidence against Hiram Evans, I would never see my son again! I had to join the Ku Klux Klan, Kendis! That was—of course—before I was abducted and terrorized all night by Maria!"

Kendis reached for her again, but Audrianna backed her off with her hands. "Just stop it, Kendis. Stop trying to placate me." She looked around, first at Devon, then Lorna, then Maria; then forced a laugh. "So what? You've frozen time. Now what, Kendis?"

"That depends entirely on what you wanna do."

"You've got to be kidding me, Kendis." Audrianna pulled at her own hair in frustration, dilemma scalding her brain. "You can't really think this is that simple."

"It's just that simple if you'll let it be, honey."

"What about Lorna?" scoffed Audrianna. "What about the promises I made—promises I wouldn't've had to make in the first place if you'd just been forthcoming? My God, Kendis! This goes so far beyond the realm of what I want. Other people must be considered!"

Kendis looked down and sniffed. "If you go with them, you're the only one who's gonna get hurt. Is that what you think?"

"No, Kendis. I—"

"Audri," Kendis said, snapping her head up. "You have a home here, a family. You have a purpose. Now, if that means less to ya than whatever lukewarm promises you were forced into makin' ... all right. I'll put everything back as it was and let ya be on your way. But, before I do, I want you to look me in the eyes," she added, pulling Audrianna forward by the arms, "and tell me that's the life you really want."

When Audrianna hedged, Kendis held out the ring. "Put this back on your hand, honey. Trust me. I will make everything okay. But you gotta trust me."

A glance at Lorna's marred face gave Audrianna a moment of pause. On opposite sides of the same war, he and Kendis were both casualties of love—whether they knew it or not. Lorna would not have endured torture on Audrianna's account and Kendis would not have faced this attack had love not been an issue. It was love that had paved the path to this tragic moment.

She took in the bizarre tableau surrounding them. The massive airship *Die Glocke* loomed overhead, its guns trained on Kendis and her people. Two opposing clans of the Children of Gavrilek facing each other down on the beach. Kiah and his team shoulder to shoulder, their mouths open in mid-song. Maria, tall and regal even in fury, holding a pistol in one hand. Lorna paralyzed with an anguished expression on his face, one hand half-raised. Even the waves were still, luminous and arrested, a pod of dolphins paused upright, their dance interrupted.

Looking back at Kendis, Audrianna suddenly realized that love could not be relied upon when making life-changing decisions: love was undependable. Uncertainty had allowed a rival influence to sneak in and vie for her confidence; she felt her soul exhale. For better or worse, she had moved on. Yes. She and

Devon had made a beautiful life there with Kendis and they had both moved on. The soothing hand of time applied salve to her wounds producing an unfamiliar sensation—resolve. Plucking the brittle ring from Kendis' palm, she pulled Lorna's gold band off her finger and buried it in the sand, replacing it with Kendis'. Instantly the ring rejuvenated, buttressing her decision.

"I trust you," Audrianna whispered.

Kendis cupped Audrianna's face with her hands and pulled her close, touching their foreheads together, allowing the moment of trust to fully resonate. Eventually she said, "I'm gonna negotiate a surrender with Miss Orsic. Stay here. Okay?"

"Kendis?" Audrianna grabbed hold of her hand.

"Yeah, honey?"

"Be careful."

Kendis quickly scanned the area, then checked in with Audrianna again. "Why? Is there something else comin'?" she asked.

"I don't know, but Maria's about the cleverest person I've ever met. Look. See?" She directed Kendis' gaze to the handgun Maria had seized earlier from Lorna. "Look in her hand, Kendis. You've got to get that gun."

Kendis agreed. She slunk over to Maria and pried the pistol from her hand, seating it in her own. She lifted it for a look. "I've never held one," she confessed. "It's sorta heavy."

"Kendis, please." Audrianna sat up on her haunches, gripping her thighs. "Just point it at her when y-you…" she stuttered," when you do whatever it is you're going to do. What are you going to do?"

"I'm gonna release her time warp with harmonic counterpoint in the key of—"

"Yes. Good," Audrianna interrupted, holding her hands up. "That's a good plan, but just make sure you hold that gun on her when you do it. All right? Promise me. Shoot her if you have to—better yet," she added, reaching out her fingers, "give the gun to me."

Audrianna had shot and killed someone once before and she was every bit as ready to do it again. When Kendis did not hand her the weapon, she resorted to manipulation. "Kendis," Audrianna growled. "Give it to me. I've trusted you to handle this. Now, you trust me to back you up."

"You're not trustin' me, Audrianna," Kendis countered in a huff, handing over the weapon. "You're tryin' to control the situation—one is not the same as the other. Do ya hear me? I don't believe in violence."

"Good thing it's not up to you, then," Audrianna replied. She rose to her knees and aimed the gun at Maria. "I'm sorry for being ugly, Kendis," she apologized, though she didn't feel sorry at all "Sing your song. I'll cover you."

Kendis gently shook her head. "Audri—"

"Do it, Kendis," Audrianna snapped. "Just get on with it, please. We'll debrief later." She fought the impulse to squeeze the trigger with a clenched jaw as Kendis reluctantly turned toward Maria. She lifted her arms and raised her voice in song, removing Maria from her trance.

Twisting out of the magic, Maria caught them both off guard, cracking an invisible whip which sent a stream of green energy across the space, dislodging the gun from Audrianna's hands.

"Come!" Maria called, summoning the weapon from the air into her hand then immediately turning it on Kendis. "Another bad move, Miss Lewis," she said. "Always secure the enemy prior to pursuing terms."

She pulled the trigger—Kendis went down with a gunshot to the neck.

———•◦•———

"Kendis!" Audrianna let out a blood-curdling scream. On all fours, she scampered across the sand to help, but Maria intercepted her with another crack of the whip.

"You have absolutely no sense of integrity, do you, Baroness von Traugott?" Maria said, yanking her to the ground, immobilizing her in a tight coil of green. She stood over Audrianna and glowered, hands on hips. Her stance belied her mellifluous voice. "You pledge me loyalty; I reciprocate. The depth of my disappointment is immeasurable." Looking inward with a minute shake of the head, she declared, "You have violated the terms of our agreement and now your lover will suffer the consequence."

"*No!*" Audrianna wailed. "Maria, it's my failure. Not hers!"

"However true that may be, madam, it does not preempt her liability."

"Maria! Please!"

"Quiet," Maria ordered. She snapped her fingers, silencing Audrianna's cries. She turned her attention to Kendis, kneeling beside her and pressing the gun to her heart. The gesture was certain, but not cruel. "Miss Lewis, I have delivered a penetrating injury to your throat, effectively removing the threat of your vocal chords; magnificently you've played, but your foray is finished. The advantage is now mine."

Kendis wrung her hands around the gaping wound in her neck, gurgling and choking on her own blood. Her gaze darted around as she desperately searched the air for a point of reference, trying to speak but managing only bloody bubbles. Her tearful expression gradually turned grim.

Affected by Kendis' distress, Maria glanced at Audrianna wriggling helplessly in the sand. She lifted her face to the sky, hesitant to discharge the final shot. Closing her eyes, she whispered, "Why have I been cursed with such an obstinate mirror?"

After a moment of silence she gently shook her head and looked down, engaging Kendis' eyes. She placed a consoling hand on Kendis' forehead and said, "I can't do this, Miss Lewis. Here is the reason why."

They had a brief telepathic dialogue, after which Maria continued out loud, saying, "If I proffer mercy, you must submit yourself to me entirely. Otherwise, I will systematically eliminate everyone in your group, starting with your partner, Mr. Alan Turing. You will lose your objective and the game: you will *all* be destroyed. Miss Lewis, I'm offering you one last chance. Will you yield?"

Licking her lips, Kendis—on the verge of unconsciousness—nodded weakly and Maria took that as a yes. She quickly tossed the gun aside and called her whip to hand, dragging Audrianna along.

"I cannot save Miss Lewis alone," Maria said. "She must change bodies quickly before this one dies: I must carry her to the original creature she keeps in a spring. What is its location?" She snapped her fingers, releasing Audrianna's seething reply.

"I *hate* you!"

Maria snapped back at her. "Be that as it may, madam, Miss Lewis cannot be saved without *both* our efforts. Direct me to the spring."

"Go to hell! I'm not telling you anything!"

Maria leaned in and narrowed her eyes, laughing at Audrianna's defiance. "You've spent an intimate ten years here with your teacher, snubbing your nose at a far more natural path. What a shame her instruction wasn't retained."

"I hate you!" Audrianna shrieked, but then quickly withdrew. Maria would win *any* argument. She had proven that more than once. The path of least resistance would at minimum buy Audrianna a few last moments with Kendis—small goals, small gains. That felt right. Dropping to the ground, she ripped the sleeve from Kendis' blouse and applied a pressure dressing to her neck, cradling her body with kisses and weightless whispers of comfort. Maria continued to ruffle her.

"Forgive me if I'm not following the drama well enough, dearest," she said, "but isn't *trust* what you were to have learned on this odyssey?"

"Trust of *her*, not you," Audrianna muttered, unable to stop herself.

"I'm fairly certain that's not how the lesson was meant."

"Go to hell."

Maria snorted. "Be original if you insist on being vulgar. There's nothing more obnoxious than a coupling of boring and crass."

Bloody fingers lifted into Audrianna's sight, quashing her response to Maria. A faint, foamy voice reached her ear. "Please," Kendis gurgled, pointing in the direction of the spring, urging Audrianna to go there.

Without hesitation, Audrianna reinforced Kendis' hand, helping her point; she squinted up at Maria and said, "Follow that path. She's showing you the way to go herself."

Maria did not waste any time. She deployed her whip again, this time with an overhead crack that reached across 300 yards to the tree line, anchoring it there. Maria pulled slack on the thong and wrapped it around Audrianna and Kendis in a tight figure-eight, pulling them up with a finger snap, torquing them against her body. She spoke softly into Audrianna's ear. "Miss Lewis is *your* responsibility: take careful hold of her. I have only two hands, one of which will be holding you." She wrapped her arm securely around Audrianna's middle despite her protestation.

Brandishing the whizzing energy of the whip, Maria cracked it sideways, sending them whirling across the divide. It took a mere second to accomplish and Audrianna barely noticed the sensation of dropping in her stomach. A jarring collision with a small pine tree was the highlight of the transit; Maria absorbed the majority of the impact, purposely so.

Hobbling up on one leg, Maria bent over at the waist, breathing hard, saying, "I do apologize, dearest. I meant that to be a gentler…" She stopped talking, diverted by the bleary revelation of a great timbered entryway—Kendis' underground spring. Normally concealed from visibility by Kendis' magic, the spring had materialized as she lost her ability to obscure it. Ashen now, unresponsive and gulping for air, Kendis was barely alive.

"Let go," Maria said, prying Audrianna off and scooping Kendis up in her arms. She rushed through the entryway and down into the hollow, where she was forced to crawl and drag Kendis behind her near the end of the passage. Dropping into the inky water, she took off her glasses and set them on the ground, then pulled Kendis over the lip of the spring and began to submerge, pausing when Audrianna cried out after her.

"Wait! Please. Give me a chance to say goodbye."

Maria glanced over her shoulder and said, "You may say your farewells when we return." Then, she slipped with Kendis below the surface of the water, leaving Audrianna with darkness, dampness and the echo of her reply.

———•◦•———

Heaviness of infinite, indescribable weight brought Audrianna to her knees. Shaking, sobbing, she fell over in the bog and curled up in a ball, trying to think what to do next. Unable to escape the cobwebs of remorse, she simply gave up. Her breath fell in hiccups; her eyes glazed over. Memories of an earlier time with Kendis took over.

"What is this place, Kendis? An old mine shaft?" Audrianna looked up, down, and around. Her wonder at the site eclipsed her anxiety.

"Nope. Try again," Kendis said with a smile.

"A cave?" Audrianna guessed.

"Nah. It's my spring," Kendis replied. She squatted down and motioned for Audrianna to follow suit. "Another one of the reasons that water nymphs aren't overly active in the game is that we are tethered to the water dwelling we live in. This is mine. I can't leave unless I'm in human form, and I've already told you how often that is."

Audrianna smiled warmly, touched by Kendis' gesture of disclosure. She snuck a peek at the shadow of standing water in the hole, cringing at the thought of Kendis being stuck in that murky mess, unable to leave but once every several hundred years.

"Why don't you trust me?" Kendis asked. "Is it because I haven't done enough to earn your trust?"

Audrianna hesitated, caught off guard. "Kendis, I do trust you."

"Do you?" Kendis said. "Let's see." She pulled Audrianna up from the ground and began unbuttoning her blouse with just one hand. Audrianna allowed her to do it, determined to persevere in what was apparently a test of faith. She tilted her head backwards, closed her eyes, and exhaled through her nose, accepting her increased rate of breathing as a natural byproduct of loss of control.

"I prefer to think of it as an exercise," Kendis said, "not a test."

Audrianna wiped her forehead with the topside of her hand as Kendis continued to undress her. "How do you figure?" she said, aggravation brewing in her tone.

"Audrianna, look at me," Kendis said.

Audrianna opened her eyes—difficult though it was in her perturbed state. She tilted her head down to look at her.

"I have no cause or reason to test you," Kendis continued. "That would mean I harbor some sorta disappointment in ya that needs to be appeased." She finished unbuttoning Audrianna's shirt and eased the material off her shoulders, softly kissing her chest. Working her way up from there, she murmured, "I'm not disappointed in ya, honey."

Audrianna gasped as Kendis slowly ascended her neck in a succession of painfully slow nuzzles. As usual, Audrianna found it challenging to maintain close control over her libido. They had been lovers for over six months, but it was still difficult for Audrianna to keep passion from dictating the pace of their sex—if that's what this was.

Kendis whispered, "You want me to believe you trust me, and I want to believe you do. We're not so very far apart, are we?" She laughed quietly into Audrianna's ear, evidence of the playful personality that she never put away. "It isn't fair to ask you for honesty if I don't first have your trust," she continued, unlatching the hooks holding Audrianna's skirt in place. It fell to the ground, followed shortly by her slip. "Maybe by the time we're done here tonight, I'll have earned it." She snapped her fingers and the pool became flooded with white light. Hunching down, she kicked off her shoes and stepped backwards into the spring.

"Is it cold?" Audrianna asked, watching Kendis' face for her reaction to the temperature.

"Nah," Kendis replied. "This is a hot spring."

"A hot spring?"

"Uh-huh. Come 'ere," she said, holding out her hands, helping Audrianna into the water. She pulled her in and held her, giggling a little. "Okay. Ready? I'm hidin' somethin' else way down there." She pointed over the edge to a deeper cavern.

"Are you serious, Kendis?" Audrianna pulled her head back quickly.

Kendis heckled her a little, saying, "Yes, Audrianna, I am serious. What about what we've done together up to this point—has deepened our level of trust?"

"Oh, I don't believe this," Audrianna looked away, vexed.

"Do ya wanna leave?" Kendis asked.

"No, Kendis," Audrianna said, snapping her head back. "I don't want to leave. I wish you'd quit giving me a pass out of everything."

Kendis bit down on her lip; her eyes cackled behind soft, blinking lashes. "I guess I'm just a' softie when it comes to your tantrums," she crooned, slurring her words with a slow southern drawl, tickling her fingernails down Audrianna's back.

Audrianna shuddered. "Well, Kendis. I already put away my panic button, and pouting is the only other way I know how to handle anxiety. What are we working on here, anyway? Trust, or tantrums?" She blew out her breath.

Kendis reached up with dripping hands and cupped Audrianna's face, chuckling. "We're working on trust," she whispered, "whenever you're ready."

"I'm ready." Audrianna answered without another thought. Her voice was a forced calm: she hoped she could stay calm.

Kendis whispered, "I'm gonna hafta swim down and get it. It might be less startling for you if I turned the light off."

"Sure! Go ahead. Why not?" Audrianna laughed, but then recanted when Kendis tried to snap the light out. "No Kendis!" she exclaimed, grabbing her wrist. "I was being sarcastic. I don't know what it's like on Gavrilek, but here on Earth, it's much worse to be startled in the dark."

Kendis rolled her eyes. "Fine, Audri. Suit yourself." She took Audrianna's hands, then released them as she slowly waded to the fall of the next chamber. "I'll keep the light on, but you hafta promise me you'll stay put, regardless of what ya see."

"Oh God, Kendis," Audrianna clutched her throat. "Really?"

"Really," Kendis said, and then she waited for Audrianna to nod her head before dropping down under the water and out of sight. In moments, a moving black flash rose to the surface, blurred by air bubbles. The head of a strange woman with long black hair and the emerald eyes of the Biverse popped out of the water. Audrianna fell backwards screaming, then scampered out of the hole. She wasn't quick enough. The woman grabbed her around the waist and dragged her back down into the water.

"Oh no you don't. We made a deal, Audrianna. You're the one who wanted the light left on. We could've eased into this if you'd just trusted that I had your best interests at heart."

"Kendis?" Audrianna asked, voice quivering. It was Kendis' voice. The woman was Kendis—only she was not. Audrianna started to cry.

"Stop," Kendis said gently, wrapping her arms around Audrianna, fitting her entire frame into her embrace. "I'm not gonna hurt ya, honey, please. Try to understand that the only reason I showed ya this was because it's the very last bit of me there is to give ya." She tilted her face forward and kissed Audrianna on the nape of her neck.

"What do you mean?" Audrianna cried. "What is this? Who are you?"

"It's me, Audrianna," Kendis replied, her lips grazing Audrianna's skin. "I'm in my original naiad body, but it's still me." She pulled Audrianna's hand back and pressed it into her outer thigh, continuing to speak into her neck. "Touch me, it's okay. Please don't be afraid of me. I'm not gonna hurt ya."

The calm Kendis exuded was infectious. She stripped Audrianna of her panic by singing a soft, operatic melody between kisses, tranquilizing her with the potency of her charm. Eventually, Audrianna swept her free hand up from the water and placed it around the back of Kendis' head, exploring her thick, straw-like hair with her fingers. "That's a lovely tune," Audrianna sniffed. "What's it from?"

Kendis spun Audrianna around in a gesture of dance, swaying back and forth. "It's from an opera-ballet I saw once when I was traveling, called Les Indes Galantes."

"What's it about?" Audrianna asked, pulling her opposite hand up to join the other one, completely exposing her breasts, purposely so. She invited Kendis' touch with her thoughts, and Kendis began to fondle her, first with one hand, then with both.

"It's about a man searching the world for his lost love, Emile," Kendis said, nibbling on Audrianna's earlobe. "She's being held captive by another man who wants to be her lover."

Audrianna took a gulp of air. Her nipples turned hard as tacks; her heartbeat began thumping down below. "What happens?" she asked.

"I don't know."

"Why don't you know?"

"Because I wasn't watching the opera. I was watching the woman, Emile. I'm afraid I got lost in her." Kendis reached between Audrianna's legs and stroked her from the outside.

"Are you trying to seduce me?" Audrianna half-laughed, half-gasped, thinking of being touched so intimately by someone she had not even seen properly.

"If ya like. Or maybe I'm just tryin' to get ya to trust me." Kendis replied, sliding two fingers inside of Audrianna.

"Oh!" Audrianna gasped.

"How'm I doin'?" Kendis purred, accent thicker—an obvious indication of her level of comfort.

"Uh-huh, yes. It's good." Audrianna nodded, reinforcing Kendis' hand, helping with the depth of her movements.

"Do ya trust me enough to let me have ya in a way you've never been had before?" Kendis asked.

"Yes." Audrianna began to pant.

"Do ya trust me enough to let yourself fall in love with me?"

Engulfed in the memory, Audrianna murmured, "Yes." She rolled over in the mud, dangling her fingers in the warm water. Slowly, she opened her eyelids.

"Audri! Get up!"

"Ahh!!" Audrianna jumped back as a pair of yellow-brown eyes popped up from the spring.

"Stop it," Kendis said, snatching her into the water with her long naiad arms. She shook her. "Maria's not breathing," she said. "I think she lost her way in the sub terrane. She must be blind as a bat."

Reflexively, Audrianna smacked her hands against Kendis' chest, shouting, "Who cares, Kendis? Thank God! Yes! I'll drag her out before she rots! Don't worry!"

Kendis widened her eyes and Audrianna stopped striking her, embarrassed by her unexpected slip of the tongue. She wrapped Kendis up in her arms and hugged her tight, cupping the base of her skull with one hand, softening her tone. "I mean, good. Thank God we've had one thing go right for us today."

Kendis pushed back with one shoulder and dragged Maria's floating form around to rest between them. "Audri, you hafta save her, honey."

Audrianna shook her head in disbelief. "Kendis! She just shot you dead—your human body dead! Are you crazy?"

"I know. I know," Kendis said, fidgeting a little, clearly wrestling with internal struggle.

Audrianna narrowed her eyes. "Why do you want to save her? What did she tell you? Out there on the beach, what did she say? Why didn't she just kill you right then and there, put you out of the game permanently?"

"Audri, there's no time now."

"Tell me!" Audrianna shouted.

"She said it was because you'd never forgive her," Kendis replied.

"She's got that right," Audrianna scoffed, then she shook her head adamantly. "No. I'm not doing it. If you're worried about her suffering, drowning is a remarkably peaceful way to die. I know. I almost drowned. Remember?"

In actuality, her experience had been anything but peaceful, but Kendis didn't need to know that.

Fed up with Audrianna's stalling, Kendis decisively gripped her chin and pulled her forward, staring deeply into her eyes. "If you don't save her now, you'll never forgive yourself. Trust me, honey—no questions this time. Trust that I have your best interests at heart," she finished. Audrianna vividly remembered the first time Kendis had said that to her. It had an exacting impact.

Her eyes glazing over, Audrianna slowly turned to revive Maria—no questions asked. She lifted her with one hand behind the neck and felt a slow, pounding pulse, negating the need for chest compressions. Placing her lips around Maria's mouth, she exhaled breath into her lungs. She did this several times until Maria's cough reflex kicked in. When it did, Audrianna tilted Maria's head to the side whilst cradling her body, patting her back repeatedly until she spat out a lungful of frothy water. Audrianna's hand movements slowed to comforting rubs, while Maria recovered from the ordeal. "All right, Maria," she said. "Breathe. Breathe."

A moment in that position until she caught her breath, then Maria slowly found her feet and retrieved her glasses. Focusing through muddy lenses, she found Audrianna's eyes; her stare reflected equal parts relief and longing. Confused by the look, Audrianna instinctively backed away. Maria followed her, arms gently outstretched, quietly beseeching, "Dearest. Please. You must ... care."

"Wait a minute. Hang on." Kendis swam between, cutting them off. She nudged Maria backwards, telling her, "Ya can't just come at her like that. She dudn' understand who you are, yet."

"Understand what?" Audrianna slapped at the water, looking back and forth at Kendis and Maria, teeth bared. Her fight or flight response kicked in—she registered the easiest exit, the most manageable rock to use as a weapon.

"Okay, Audri. Just hang on," Kendis said, as she began snapping her fingers. "Be easy. Be easy."

"I do not appreciate your use of restraint, Miss Lewis," Maria quipped.

"Tough."

"I beg your pardon?"

"*Tough,*" Kendis said again, this time with emphasis. "You think ya can handle her reaction to this news without my softenin' the blow? Go ahead and try it. I don't hafta hear Audri's thoughts to know she's thinkin' of a hundred ways to kill ya, right now. I can see it in her eyes. Just let me talk to her for a minute before ya barge in and swoop her off. Okay?"

She turned back and collected an anesthetized Audrianna in her arms, saying, "Honey, honey. Please try tuh' calm down. Everything's gonna be all right. I know you're scared, confused. I'm a little confused, myself—I mean," she hiccupped, "I'm disappointed … I guess." She slowly shook her head, delving into thought. "I shoulda' known, shoulda' seen it—it was *you* she wasn't leavin' without."

Forced hypnotization caused incomplete thoughts and slurring of words. "Known—sooner—confused. Damn!" Audrianna shook her head, trying to formulate a sentence. She pulled Kendis out of her internal process, conveying urgency with a gentle shake. Whimpering, Audrianna pointed over and over again at her own throat until finally, Kendis came around and snapped her fingers, releasing her voice.

Audrianna's panic immediately returned. "What are you saying, Kendis?" she cried. "I don't understand!"

Kendis licked her lips. "She's your mirror, honey: different bodies, different personalities, but *you share the same consciousness.* That's all of it; that's enough," she finished in a whisper.

Audrianna gave Maria a sidelong glance then covered her mouth, her expression blanching. She shook her head, refusing Kendis' revelation. "No. That's not right," she said, her voice strangled. "I am *your* mirror, Kendis—that's what she told me. Why else—oh God," Audrianna whispered as she buried her hands in her hair. "Why else would you be so intimate with me—for so many years?"

Kendis gave her a sad smile. "If I told ya that I've loved you—loved being with you and that's what my motivation has been—would that stretch the imagination?"

"Enough, Miss Lewis," Maria groaned. "Why carry on with this pretense? What purpose does it serve beyond the subversion of my objective?"

Audrianna whirled around to face Maria.

"Shut up!" she screamed, then turned back to Kendis. "You haven't answered my question," Audrianna said. "Who am I to you? Am I your *project*?"

"Yes," Kendis whispered, directly.

Doubling over, Audrianna held her middle, short-winded from the disclosure, as if she'd been punched in the stomach. "Oh, God," she mewled.

"I tried to tell ya a hundred times," Kendis quickly continued. "Especially after Tru admitted he'd tricked ya into it."

"Tricked me?"

"The night you *fell outta the boat*—"

"I didn't fall out. I jumped out!"

Kendis continued, "Two o' my cousins approached ya and asked if you would participate in a project. You agreed to it."

"They asked if they could help save me and my son, Kendis!" argued Audrianna.

"That wasn't how it was put, honey. That was Tru's wording. He didn't wanna be a part of the Incubus anymore." She gestured to Maria. "He saw a way out. He made ya believe that my intentions were entirely benevolent, when they weren't—at least, they weren't at first."

Audrianna shook her head with a pained laugh. "And, what was it you were supposed to have accomplished with me, Kendis?" she asked, falling back on sarcasm because nothing else made sense. "Wait! Let me guess. Trust?"

Kendis quietly replied, "I'm working toward a level of achievement called Master of Human Trust." She cleared her throat. "It's a diploma, of sorts."

Seconds lapsed while silence skated across thin ice; conflicting emotions swept over Audrianna, vying for control. Denial, disbelief, humiliation, and rage suffused her: Audrianna surrendered to the undeniable winner.

"Here's what I think about your project, Kendis!" she bellowed, yanking the ring off her finger and hurling it against the wall.

It shattered into pieces.

"Audri—"

"I don't want to hear it!" Audrianna screamed. Stitches from her recent head wound tore through waterlogged skin, releasing a smeary torrent of blood which ran down her face and into her eyes. It did not stop her tirade. "Trust is not an endowment that goes with a diploma!" She wiped the blood from her eyes with wet fingers. "Trust is," she stammered, "something you earn, Kendis—something you earn!"

"Honey, stop. Please. You're bleedin'."

Maria started her way, but Audrianna slapped at the water sending a splash at her face.

"Don't you dare come near me," Audrianna warned. "Don't you—"

Maria snapped her fingers and Audrianna's hand flew to her mouth, choking back a sudden onslaught of nausea. Dizziness besieged her, then weakness, rapidly followed by darkness. Overcome, she sank into the water, submerging herself. Cleaving to her own resistance, Audrianna swatted at the two sets of hands reaching down to rescue her. Together, Kendis and Maria lifted her from the water and held her between them in a momentary truce, both breathless, both coddling her in their own individual way. Audrianna abandoned her inner struggle, listening to them talk with faraway ears.

"Your tenderness is greatly appreciated," Maria told Kendis.

"It's not a chore," Kendis replied, tugging a piece of green moss from the embankment and sopping up water, applying pressure to Audrianna's still-bleeding wound. "Shh…" she whispered with a kiss. "It's over, now, honey. Let go." After a moment, she asked Maria, "What is your psalm? Perhaps you should call it in now, to help her through this transition."

"The Wind Is My Master," Maria replied wistfully, running her hand through Audrianna's hair, holding it there to give a gentle massage. The ambrosial scent of her breath wafted over Audrianna's face as Maria looked down at her and whispered, "Everything is ruled by change."

Her eyelids fluttered as Audrianna struggled to keep them open and focus on Maria. Her spectacles were foggy but the message of devotion shone in her translucent green eyes. Audrianna whimpered, stung with heartache. Life as she knew it was over— everything was ruled by change. The reality of it finally soaked in.

Maria looked at Kendis and asked, "Since it makes no difference now, will you tell me why you allowed this relationship?

It is a conflict of interest to be intimate with your project. You forfeited any level of achievement you had the moment you touched her."

"Uh-huh."

"Why?" Maria asked, her tone soft, non-accusatory.

"Audrianna was mistrustful in general because of what happened with Lorna. I had tuh' open that channel with love. That was more important than my advancement."

Maria stared at her without blinking—Kendis took the opportunity to finish.

"The Consciousness of Gavrilek is on my side, Miss Orsic. You may take him away from here this day, but his allegiance remains to us: We're *all* goin' home this time. No one is gettin' left behind on Earth, not like they were on Tawn the last time. No one."

Maria took physical control of Audrianna and started out of the spring. This time, she did not argue anything Kendis had said.

"I hope you're right, Miss Lewis," she called behind her. "I really do. I wish you the best of luck with that objective."

Impulsively, Kendis called out, "Good luck to you, Miss Orsic."

Maria twisted and stared. "I beg your pardon?"

Kendis took one more heavyhearted look at Audrianna and replied, "Good luck chasing the mirror."

CHAPTER 2

"Dearest?" Maria called through the closed door.

There was a dainty tap-tap, and the door opened. Maria stepped from the hall into her private library where she'd set up Audrianna's bed. She wore a tailored two-piece chalk-line suit and shiny black pumps, a single cyan blue tulip in her hand. The unusual color complimented her exquisite beauty. It had been five days since they arrived at Maria's primary residence in Berlin, but Audrianna had yet to emerge from the suite. The only other person she had seen was Devon and a few of the servants. Lorna had been absent the entire time. Presumably, Maria's doing.

"I'm sorry you couldn't make it to breakfast again this morning," Maria told her. "Everyone is really quite anxious to meet you, dearest."

Audrianna turned her face away. "Don't call me that," she said.

Maria approached the bed; her delicate perfume drifted into Audrianna's nostrils. She kissed her sweetly on the side of her forehead and said, "*Guten Morgen.*"

"Don't touch me," Audrianna snarled, pulling away from her.

In a soft but determined tone, Maria replied, "You are the dearest thing in the world to me. Of course I'll touch you."

"That wasn't a request!" Audrianna shouted. She held strong eye contact with Maria and watched as her expression changed from adoring to puzzled.

"I don't understand that statement, dearest," Maria said, scrutinizing Audrianna's eyes for the answer. "Will you say it another way?"

"God, just forget it," Audrianna grumbled, falling backwards on the bed, rubbing the backs of her hands into her eyes. "Why are you here, Maria? What do you want?"

Seating herself on the side of the bed, Maria fanned her fingers out on Audrianna's sternum. She placed the tulip on the nightstand. "I've come to wish you a pleasant day and to invite you for dinner tonight. I'd like to take you out to enjoy one of the many gastronomic delights Berlin has to offer."

"Don't you get it?" Audrianna cried, sitting up abruptly. "I don't want to be courted! I hate you; there's no gastronomic delight on the face of the earth that can fix that!"

Maria tilted her head to the side, producing an underbite. "Well, at least you're looking at me today," she said. "I was beginning to wonder if you had somehow broken your neck."

"No, fate was not that kind," replied Audrianna, curtly.

Her response heightened Maria's aggravation. "Audrianna, I'd like to treat you nicely. I'd like to give you nice things, to put you on a pedestal. Why are you perpetuating this friction between us?"

"Maria, you really have no clue, do you?" Audrianna asked, shaking her head in disbelief.

"Dearest, please phrase your question in such a manner which will not require me to infer—"

"Do you or don't you have any clue as to why I am so upset?" Audrianna interrupted her, shouting.

"Yes, of course I do," Maria replied. "I'm insensitive, not stupid."

Audrianna fell back on the bed, laughing despite herself. Elegant manners notwithstanding, Maria was just like every other Gavrilekian—forthright to a fault.

"Now I've gone and made you laugh when you're trying so hard to be cross with me." Maria twirled one of Audrianna's ringlet curls around her finger, lifting it to her lips, lingering there until Audrianna shook her hair free.

"Go away, Maria," she said, hiding her face behind her hands. She took a deep, sniveling breath, then blubbered, "I don't want you near me."

"Yes," Maria softly answered. "You've been perfectly clear about what you don't want. Why don't you tell me what you *do* want, then perhaps we can move forward from this stalemate."

"I want my freedom!" Audrianna cried, slamming her hands on the mattress. "You can't force me to love you!"

Maria withdrew from her and tilted her chin to the ceiling, her jaw jutted. After a moment, she lowered her face and carefully enunciated a reply: "I'm not asking for your love, Audrianna. I'm asking for your help."

"You aren't asking me for anything," Audrianna sobbed. "You're just taking things away from me and expecting me to comply." She grabbed a tissue from the nightstand and wiped the stinging tears spilling out of her bloodshot eyes. She pressed the tissue to her nose.

"You killed Kendis," Audrianna sobbed. "You banished Lorna."

"I did not *banish* Lorna. He left because of you, Audrianna. I'm sorry. But, that's the way it happened."

"What?" Audrianna shouted. "Why? What did you tell him? That I chose Kendis over him?"

"I told him nothing of your betrayal. He drew his own conclusions when he saw you were no longer wearing his ring."

Audrianna sidestepped her defense. "Now, you're driving Devon away, too. You mean to break me at any cost, don't you?"

"No," Maria replied calmly. "Devon came to me on his own with his request to attend University—I didn't command him to go there." She sat silently for a moment. "Should I withdraw my permission and insist he remain here with you?" she asked.

Audrianna found her comeback cheeky. "Don't put this on me. It is painfully obvious that you are eliminating everyone in my support system so that I'll have no willpower left to fight you!"

"Audrianna—" Maria started and stopped. She pinched her eyebrows together while she thought. After a moment she put her hand down and tried again. "Dearest, I wish to cherish and pamper you. That is my intention, nothing more." Scooting closer, she captured Audrianna's trembling hands between her own soft palms, attempting to reason with her. "Miss Lewis engaged me in a battle I tried my hardest to avoid, you know that. Lorna asked for furlough; I allowed it. Once we're regularly bonding, I'll insist he return here to resolve your quarrel. Presently, I prefer not to have him as a rival."

Audrianna forced a bitter laugh. "Once we're bonding. Sure, that'll happen. I thought I was too explosive for your taste! And I thought you didn't sleep with your team members!"

"Dearest, please don't bait me," Maria said. "As thrilled as I am to have finally secured you, I see now that my method was flawed." She unfolded Audrianna's hands and kissed both of her palms, sweetening her apology. "If you had only met me half-way, I would have—"

"You would have what?" Audrianna spat, yanking her hands away.

"I would have been more careful with your heart," Maria said, rising from the bed, and smoothing her skirt over her hourglass silhouette.

"Quite an empty sentiment given that your regret actualized only *after* all your pathetic advances toward me failed," Audrianna said spitefully. "Beyond that you have single-handedly destroyed my life and the lives of everyone important to me, even Devon. Don't fool yourself into thinking that I'm the only one affected by Kendis' loss, or by Lorna's absence. You don't give a damn about me! The only person you care about is yourself!"

"Master?" A man's breathy voice called from the hallway.

Maria ignored him, speaking to Audrianna instead. "I'll ask you not to belittle my sentiments again, particularly as they relate to you. Frankly, dearest, you have no concept of my feelings, the sacrifices I've made, or the hardships I've already endured to gain your favor."

When Audrianna opened her mouth to protest, Maria snapped her fingers. Audrianna found herself unable to speak.

"Master?" the voice called again.

"I am sorry you've been hurt by Lorna going away," Maria told Audrianna. "I am sorry you've been hurt by my putting Miss Lewis back into her water dwelling. Would you have me destroyed over it without first giving me a chance to make amends?"

"Master?" A feral-looking man with stooped shoulders slogged into the room, interrupting them. Still clad in her nightdress, Audrianna ducked beneath the bed sheet, popping her eyes up over to observe; Maria drew the quilt overlay up from the middle and tucked it around Audrianna to protect her modesty. She remonstrated the man over her shoulder.

"Alex, did I invite you in here?"

"No, that's okay, Master. I think you were distracted or something."

The man was a living caricature of the film star Peter Lorre. Peeping around at Audrianna, he added some color to his voice. "Oh, hello, Leyonelle."

Audrianna averted her gaze.

Alex looked to Maria for insight. "Doesn't she speak English?" he asked.

"Alexander, you are dangerously close to spending the remainder of this lifetime on my line. Do you understand?" Maria demanded.

"Yes, Master. The line is a good place for me."

"Please remove yourself from my sight," she said.

"Okay," replied Alex, moving to stand directly behind Maria, out of her sight.

"Alex!" Maria barked, whirling around. "Leave!" She pointed with an authoritative finger at the door and he scurried off without another word.

Maria turned back to Audrianna and quietly apologized, emotional fatigue telling in her tone. "I'm sorry, dearest. Naturally, they're all quite curious about you."

Audrianna felt a surge of sympathy for Maria. She cleared her throat and spoke to her again, this time without malice.

"Who was that?" she asked.

"Alexander is one of my hawks. My other hawk, Tyler, is his twin brother," Maria explained.

Audrianna knew Tyler from their initial meeting in Savannah. His mannerisms were quirky bordering on bizarre. She remembered suspecting he was schizophrenic—a familial trait, apparently. With an upward nod of the head, Audrianna tacitly accepted that theory, saying, "Yes, I can see the similarities. Have they always been so odd?"

Maria saw an opening and took it. "Define odd," she said, reseating herself, reengaging Audrianna with a grin. Her ploy was easily identified and thwarted.

"I don't want to play this game with you, Maria," Audrianna told her. She slid out of the bed and sat down at her vanity to brush her hair, turning away from the mirror to avoid her sallow, tear-streaked reflection. "I simply meant that their point of view is different from that of anyone I've ever known."

"Mutti?" Devon's voice called from beyond the doorway.

"Hold on, sweetheart. I'm not dressed." Audrianna put down her brush and crossed quickly to the armoire, donning the embroidered silk house-robe Maria had given her to wear. All of her own clothes had been left behind on Tybee Island; Maria's offers to take her shopping had been refused. "Okay, Tru," she called, then met him as he came through the door.

He took one look at her face and blanched. Audrianna immediately understood why. "No, no. I'm fine. I'm fine." She gave him a quick hug and pointed to Maria sitting on the bed. "Maria brought me a flower this morning and I'm afraid it has sparked an allergic reaction. That's all it is. I promise."

"Forgive my intrusion, Master. I didn't realize you were here," Devon apologized.

Maria gathered up the tulip and came to where he was, offering her hand to be kissed. She gestured to the flower. "I was just about to remove this offense," she said. "I had no idea anyone could be so sensitive to pollen." Smiling, she then turned to Audrianna with a mischievous twinkle in her eyes. "I'm sorry, dearest. I'll be sure to have the flowers removed from the restaurant prior to our dinner tonight."

Audrianna instantly saw what Maria was up to, and her blood began to boil. In exchange for a dinner date, Maria was playing along with the story. Audrianna could either agree to it and get rid of her for the moment, or decline again and risk another argument in front of Devon. He might not survive experiencing his mother's emotional struggle on top of his own. "I wouldn't want to detract from the dining experience of others," she replied coolly.

"We'll be alone," Maria countered. Catching her by the arm, she pulled Audrianna forward and whispered in her ear. "I'll have someone come by later and help you with something to wear." She kissed her on the cheek, released her, patting Devon on the shoulder and chuckling. "Look after her, won't you darling? I would hate for her to develop a rash."

After Maria left, Devon pulled an envelope from the inside pocket of his blazer and handed it to Audrianna. "I have some enrollment paperwork from the University that I need you to sign," he said.

Audrianna opened the envelope and unfolded the paper. "Tru, sweetheart, don't you want to take a few months to adjust to all of this before you jump right into school? My God! Is this what University costs, now? *Chemistry!*" She looked up at him, confused. "Tru, since when do you want to be a chemist? I thought you wanted to be a doctor."

Devon met her stare with yellow eyes. "I've been a doctor. Now, I want to be a chemist. Now, I *need* to be a chemist. Mutti, emotional distemper is pandemic in the Gavrilekian community. We'll all be destroyed before long if it isn't cured."

"What?" Audrianna scanned the paper again, looking for a clue.

"I have to *finish* what your father, my grandfather started if I am to save the Children of Gavrilek."

"What?" Audrianna jumped into a panic, then immediately she backed down, careful not to upset Devon further. "Okay, okay," she soothed, dropping the letter on a table, pulling him back into her arms. She rubbed his back, though she still didn't understand. "I'll find some way to pay for it. Just calm down, sweetheart."

"I am calm, Mutti," he said.

"What day is it?" Audrianna thought quickly, then answered her own question. "Tuesday. Okay, well no matter. Catholics are always praying somewhere." She knew she needed to get him to church where he could absorb the energy from prayer: Gavrilekians survived on human energy, with praying crowds providing one of the few ways to access it without taking life. Over at her armoire, she flung open the doors. "Just give me a moment to get dressed and then we'll go find a cathedral to sit in for a while. Okay?"

"I'm all right, Mutti," Devon insisted.

"Clearly you're not, son," she snapped, pulling one of the two dresses off the hanger. She started into the bathroom with it, tilting her head back to keep the tears in her eyes. "I understand that you're used to Kendis helping you with these things, but I'll have to be the one to help you now."

She opened her lingerie drawer, pulled out a pair of nude stockings, and put them on, slipping into the dress. Afterwards, she brushed her teeth. When she came out of the bathroom, she wrapped herself up in a wool polo coat, and wound her hair into a low loose bun.

"Okay sweetheart, I'm ready," she announced, slipping on her shoes "Do you know the way out of this imperial palace?"

Devon cracked a weak smile. "Yeah," he laughed, casting his eyes down. "It's a different world, isn't it, Mutti?"

"Quite a different world, sweetheart," Audrianna replied. She forced a thin-lipped smile for his sake, then started out the door.

The four-story mansion was a Neoclassical design, laid out with east-west corridors, and geometrically shaped rooms. Elaborate plasterwork ornamentation and mahogany sideboards complimented the graceful interior. Cream and sage walls were decorated with large mirrors in elaborate gilded frames; a double-curved mahogany staircase bisected the house from the main floor up.

Housemaids zigzagged from wall sconces to sideboards, to Grecian pedestals, polishing Ginger Jars and precious pieces of Wedgwood Jasperware. They stopped and stared with surprised expressions when Devon and Audrianna approached; none of them had green eyes.

"*Guten Morgen*," Audrianna greeted a maid in German as she passed.

"*Guten Morgen*, Leyonelle," the maid sheepishly replied.

Audrianna drew herself up and stared at the young lady.

"What's the matter, Mutti?" Devon whispered in a hush.

The maid was clearly intimidated by her stare. After a moment, Audrianna shook her head. "It's nothing," she smiled, and resumed walking. Audrianna had no idea why she was being called Leyonelle but it was nothing to worry Devon with. She quickly changed the subject. "Where is your room, Tru?"

"I'm underground," Devon replied.

Audrianna yanked on his arm to stop him.

"What does that mean, underground?'" she asked, giving him a heated look.

Devon was tickled by her response. "It's not a dungeon, Mutti," he said. "There's another world underneath the house, filled with people just like me: generational Gavrilekians. It's a much easier environment to live in than this stiff place, I can assure ya."

Instead of making Audrianna feel better, his remark shattered her fragile mental fettle. Grief for what they had both lost rushed upon her in the form of memories of a simpler life: seaside sing-alongs, lightning bugs, gentle island breezes. She crumpled, face in hand, thumbs pressed into her eyelids, damming the tears inside her eyes.

"Mutti, what's wrong?" Devon asked, reaching out to gently jostle her.

"I would call that *remorse*, son," said a familiar voice.

Looking up, Audrianna audibly choked, her heart hammering in her chest. "Niklas," she gasped, clutching her breast.

He had aged in the many years since they had seen one another, yet was still recognizable. She swallowed the lump in her throat.

"What are you…" she faltered.

"What am I doing here?" he laughed, flipping his hat in his hand. "I'm not looking for you, if that's what you think. I gave up looking for you a while ago. Hello, Devon." He held his hand out. "Aren't you the spitting image of *my brother*."

Audrianna watched her husband discover his son to be the spitting image of another man: something she had intended to discuss with him, but never had. Devon gingerly shook Niklas' hand, greeting him softly, with suspicion.

"Hello, sir."

"This isn't the best time," Audrianna addressed Niklas, her anxiety building.

Niklas cracked his knuckles. "When is the best time for a reunion, wife?" he scoffed. "Ten more years? You'd probably need ten more years to concoct a tale to excuse this breed of cruelty."

Audrianna took it, wincing and nodding. He deserved his say, but not in front of Devon. Although Devon had played an instrumental role in her decision to remain on Tybee Island, *she* was the adult. She had made the decision. "Niklas, let's speak in private, please—"

"You willingly allowed me to suffer the grief of losing my heir!" Niklas cut her off, eyes narrowing. "My heir! Yes!" he barked. "You never permitted him to be my son. Now, I know why."

Audrianna touched Devon on the arm. "Go on to the church without me," she said. "I'll be right behind you."

"No," Devon countered.

"What?" Audrianna asked, with a grimace of shock. It was the very first time he had openly disobeyed her.

"Is it a wonder you can't discipline your son?" Niklas asked with a laugh. "You've been missing a crucial dynamic, I think—a removable phallus, a man does not make."

"You son of a bitch!" Devon raged.

He lunged forward, drew his arm back, and punched Niklas full in the face. Father and son flew at each other.

"Stop, Devon!" Audrianna implored.

She jumped in between them, sustaining incidental blows. She dropped to the floor, head oozing again.

Niklas pounced on her, taking hold and shaking her. "Where is Lorna?" he growled. "What have you done to Lorna?"

"Get off!" Devon bellowed, aiming a kick at Niklas' stomach. As Niklas staggered back, Devon kicked him again sending him flying into the wall. He was wild with rage. He could not sustain the emotion for long. Stumbling to her feet, Audrianna grabbed hold of her son, imploring him to stop. When her pleas fell on deaf ears, she turned elsewhere for help.

"Maria!" she cried.

In an instant, a green apparition of Maria appeared next to Audrianna, observing the violent scene. Pulling out her whip, she cut targets in the wall, then yanked a glowing fence of green energy around Audrianna; she threw an overhead lasso around Devon, yanking him out of the fight and into his mother's arms. She positioned herself in front of the fence.

"Please leave my house, Baron von Traugott," Maria commanded.

From the landing of the grand staircase, Hannah, Maria's first officer, called, "Master, I'm here!" She rushed into Maria's image and took up her stance, protesting against Niklas. "This is a most inappropriate intrusion, Baron von Traugott. I'm sure—"

"Give me your hand, Audrianna," called Maria, reaching through the fence with her ethereal body. "I need your help to save your son."

Audrianna extended her fingers, taking Maria's astral hand. By way of a back staircase, Maria led her into a wide arched passageway running against the grain of the house. She stopped at a set of distressed double-doors, inlaid with a Gavrilekian ruin fashioned from gray and white Tiffany glass. "This is my bedroom," Maria said. "Please close your eyes until I've said you may open them."

Audrianna raised an eyebrow, but complied, forcing herself to keep her eyelids shut, despite her curiosity. The doors squeaked open and she felt herself being dragged along a smooth, polished path. The climate inside the room was crisp and clean. The entire space was alive with aromas of lavender, eucalyptus and mint.

After a moment, Maria stopped and guided Audrianna's hand across a series of tiny glass vials. "Take hold of this one please," she directed and Audrianna closed her fingers around the ampule, tucking it in her palm.

Maria retraced their steps, shutting the doors behind them. "You may open your eyes. Thank you for honoring my request," she said.

Audrianna opened her hand for a look. "What is this?" she asked.

"Now is not the time for explanations," replied Maria. "My astral body is fading. Return to your son and instill two drops in each of his eyes. Quickly."

"Fine, okay. Just show me the way back," Audrianna snapped. But Maria had already disappeared. "Damn!" Audrianna hissed, sprinting back through the passageway, sliding, hooking the railing with her hand. She flung herself up the stairs, finding Devon still curled up behind Maria's magic wall, Hannah still arguing with Niklas.

"Mutti," Devon murmured, opening his dark brown eyes. "I can barely see you."

"Here. Look up." Audrianna unscrewed the dropper and instilled two drops from the mystery vial in each eye. Within a few seconds, Devon's eye color became reinvigorated, as did his fury. He perked up and sat up beside Audrianna, nostrils flaring; she held him back by the collar of his coat.

Maria arrived in person with Alex, Tyler and a full entourage of armed Nazi Brownshirts, relieving Hannah from her position. Snapping her fingers, Maria picked Niklas up by his lapels and held him at arm's length whilst Hannah, Alex and Tyler dragged Devon into a nearby bedroom, shutting the door. Audrianna was too stunned to move.

"No matter what she does, you welcome her with open arms," Niklas said to Maria. He wiped his bloody nose, chuckling. "I'm not sure whether to laugh at you or feel sorry for you. Your mirror is a mentally deranged ice queen. Watch out. She'll destroy you if you let your guard down."

"Perhaps," Maria responded. "Happily, that day has not yet come."

"Maria, she's done something to Lorna," Niklas said, feet dangling. "Please. I know things haven't been well between you and Lorna but you can't want this."

Maria sat him down and brushed the lint from his jacket. "I sent Lorna away while Audrianna settles in here, *Leyonelle*. My instructions, however, did not include his staying away from you. I apologize for his inconsiderate behavior."

"He *wouldn't* stay away from me, Maria," insisted Niklas. "There is something wrong. Guaranteed, it has something to do with her!" He pointed at Audrianna.

Maria appeared annoyed. "My own understanding of what happened is far less diabolical," she said. "I'll recall Lorna to appease your paranoia, *sir*. Please return to your villa and wait for him there. Neither of you will set foot on my property again until summoned. Guards." She nodded to the Brownshirts and they took Niklas away.

Once they were gone, Maria stood over Audrianna, hands on hips, speaking with visible compunction. "I have the disquieting sensation that I'm caught up in a war, the causes and objectives of which, I can only guess at." She nodded to herself, then vocalized her thought. "Cannon fodder. Yes. That's the appropriate term."

Audrianna scoffed at the idea. Numb from the encounter with Niklas, she felt obliged to explain the situation. "I never told him I was alive, Maria; I never told him Devon wasn't his child. Every bit of what he just gave me I deserve, and more. Well, anyway," she shook her head with a little snort, "thank you for trying to shelter me from the blame. I don't think he believed you, but still."

When Maria remained quiet, Audrianna scrutinized her visage, finding a dangerous species of affinity lying in wait for her there. A restless tingle stalked her; a shiver clawed up her spine. She shuddered, then looked away, unnerved by both sensations.

"Dearest, why you are avoiding my eyes?" Maria asked.

"Well, I, um..." Audrianna stammered, fiddling around in her coat, stalling while she concocted a bluff. She discovered a handkerchief in one of the pockets and took it out. "I don't like looking at you," she eventually said, forgetting that her thoughts were no longer protected by Kendis' magic.

Maria reached down and pulled her up by the elbows, keeping hold of her while she spoke; her beautiful intonation tickled Audrianna's marrow. "Why are you lying to me?" she asked.

"I'm not sure. I just am!" Audrianna snapped, pulling away from her, wiping congealed blood from her head with the lightly perfumed handkerchief. "God, don't you have anything that doesn't smell like you?" she complained, then she muttered an apology, embarrassed again, but unsure why.

"It must be very frustrating not to understand yourself well at times," said Maria sympathetically.

Audrianna wanted to find fault with that statement, but her temper would not ignite. Instead of dissecting her embarrassment, as Kendis would have done, Maria simply acknowledged it. Her mild-mannered reticence was welcome at that moment when Audrianna already felt like a horrible human being.

"It is frustrating," Audrianna acknowledged quietly. "Thank you for saying that."

The bedroom door opened; and Alex and Tyler crept out. Hannah reported directly to Maria.

"Master," Hannah said, "The Consciousness of Gavrilek is much improved. I have counseled him—" she stopped. Eyes bulging, she mouthed "Quit it," to someone standing behind Audrianna.

Slowly, Audrianna turned to investigate; she found Tyler looming behind over her, sniffing her hair.

"Tyler!" Maria whirled on him, finger raised. She pointed down the hall, silently commanding him and Alex to leave.

"What's wrong with you?" Alex scolded his brother as they left. "You can't just smell of her like that. You have to ask permission first, or you have to do it discreetly—"

"I counseled Tru on excessive indulgence of emotion," Hannah talked loudly to cover their conversation. "I directed him to submit a corrective action strategy to me by week's end; he didn't know what I meant, so I said, 'okay.'"

Maria turned and faced her, smiling weakly. "Thank you darling. Please return to your flight plan. We'll meet in my office this afternoon to discuss an alternate disciplinary method for the Consciousness of Gavrilek." She glanced at Audrianna. "He is fragile and unaccustomed to our ways. A better idea, I think, if we let the blows fall by degrees, rather than all at once."

"Yes, Master," Hannah replied, looking genuinely relieved.

"Oh, and Hannah?"

"Yes, Master?"

Maria lowered her voice. "Lorna's leave is canceled. Issue the proper order. Send a man to find him if he fails to report in a timely manner."

"Yes, Master," Hannah said. She squeezed Audrianna as she moved to go, whispering, "It's wonderful to see you. I'll be back later."

After she was gone, Maria made a quick pivot to face Audrianna, taking a worried look at the wound on her forehead. She said, "I'd like to have my personal physician attend you, if you'll allow it."

"Oh, for this?" Audrianna asked dismissively, blotting her head again. "No, that's unnecessary; there's a limited window of time to repair an injury such as this, so I'm stuck with the outcome. But, thank you."

Maria lifted Audrianna's chin and examined her eyes, accentuating the awkwardness with silence. After a moment, she gave her an uncertain nod, then let loose of her chin. "Thank you for the invigorating interlude," she said, turning to go, "but you must forgive me: I have another matter which requires my attention."

Audrianna snagged her arm, releasing it just as quickly. "I'm sorry. That was rude," she said, wiping her hands down her sides. She felt herself beginning to waffle. "I would really appreciate it if you would do that thing that Kendis did with me—I mean… no, that's not what I meant—I mean, it *is* what I meant, it just came off badly as it was … said."

A smirk spread across Maria's face. She took Audrianna's hand, lifting it to her lips, kissing her bare ring finger. "Are you concerned that I'll contrive a script based upon your thoughts?" she inquired with a laugh.

Angered by the banter, Audrianna yanked away and turned around. Realizing nothing would be gained by animosity, she quickly changed her attitude. "Anyway, if it isn't terribly inconvenient," she said lightly, focused on controlling her tone, "I would prefer some other form of ornamentation rather than a ring: a necklace or earrings, or something I can wear to bed." She closed her eyes and swallowed hard. "Something comfortable enough to sleep in is what I intended to say."

"Very well." Maria agreed to it. "It will take some time for me to construct. You will not replay Miss Lewis' folly with me."

"What is that supposed to mean?" Audrianna turned back around, questioning indignantly.

"It means I have no intention of embedding my biverse code into anything that might touch your hands, be it a ring, a necklace, earrings or anything else. A device must be commissioned to protect your thoughts. *That* takes time."

"You have some nerve speaking to me that way," Audrianna spat.

"My nerve pales in comparison to yours."

"What?"

"Do you truly imagine I'm that easily manipulated?" Maria asked.

"I wasn't trying to manipulate you!" Audrianna shouted, which, of course was untrue. The realization splintered itself into Audrianna's soul and bled into her voice. "I don't want my thoughts eavesdropped on, Maria. That's all I'm saying." She lowered her eyes.

"Forgive me. It had the look of provocation," Maria said, speaking more gently now.

"I'm sure it did."

"I will have something for you by this evening," Maria said, turning to leave. "In the meantime, I'll abstain from listening to your thoughts." She walked down the hall and stopped at the top of the stairs, glancing up and catching Audrianna's gaze on the way down. "Good morning, Leyonelle," she said.

"Harrison Steede, that's right," Audrianna grimaced, straining to hear the answer on the other end of the line. "What do you mean the account has been frozen? I was just about to make a withdrawal." The voice on the phone droned a generically bureaucratic response as Audrianna hung her head, covering her eyes with her free hand. "But I *am* the trustee on the account," she argued. "There must be some way around the injunction—Yes, okay. I understand," she said, nodding, rolling her eyes. "Thank you very much for your assistance." She hung up the phone.

So the federal authorities had stopped access to Devon's trust fund, pending the outcome of their investigation into his illegal whiskey trade. It would be months before his case came to trial—even then—he would be found guilty. The money would be confiscated; a sentence would be imposed. The only person who might have saved him from those charges was Kendis. Audrianna was going to have to ask Maria for the money he needed to pay for school. She dared not bother Niklas.

"Baroness von Traugott," a tall sleek female said, as she entered the library. She had bourbon colored hair and a narrowed jaw. Stopping in front of Audrianna, she stared at her for a moment, then said, "There you are, darling. I was worried when I couldn't find you in your room." She shifted her gaze to Audrianna's festering head wound. "Heavens. What a brutal life you've been rescued from."

Audrianna flicked a little eye roll. "No, I did this to myself."

"Oh, I see." The woman nodded her understanding. She picked up a book next to the telephone, chatting offhandedly as she thumbed through the pages. "Shock Therapy, Baroness von Traugott. Have you heard of it?"

"No."

"It's all the rage in this part of the world. I prefer psychotherapy, myself, but should my thoughts turn toward self-harm, as yours have, I would consider it. I know an excellent psychiatrist. Shall I make an appointment for you?"

"What?—No," Audrianna balked. "I wasn't *trying* to hurt myself, I just—"

"Is this your book?" she interrupted with a laugh.

Chafed, Audrianna stood up and sighed. "No. It's probably Maria's. Why?"

The woman closed the book and admired the spine. "*Lady Chatterley's Lover*," she said. "This book enjoys worldwide notoriety due to the rampant descriptions of physical love. Maria probably left it out for you—to help move things along."

"I don't believe this." Audrianna mumbled, fanning herself. She tried to formulate a rebuttal but the woman simply talked over her again.

"Shall we have some coffee, Audrianna? May I call you Audrianna?" The woman asked.

"Okay," Audrianna agreed to it, grateful to be excused from the conversation, whatever the price. She looked around. "I'm not sure how to order it."

The woman sat uninvited on the chaise lounge, taking a cigarette case from her bag. "Don't worry yourself, darling," she said. "I've already asked one of the maids to have it prepared and sent in."

Audrianna narrowed her eyes. "I thought you didn't know where I was."

"That's a very good observation, Audrianna," the woman remarked, removing a cigarette and tapping one end on the lid. She offered the case to Audrianna, but Audrianna declined. "I was told you were quite the naïve little thing, but it seems I've been misinformed—at least in that regard." The lady lit her cigarette with an ivory-handled lighter and took a leisurely drag.

Audrianna felt her temper begin to simmer. "Is that right? You were told that, were you? Who *are* you?"

"There's no reason to be irritable with me, Audrianna." The woman exhaled smoke as she spoke. "My name is Princess Stephanie von Hohenlohe—Steffi to my friends. I am Magda

Goebbles' human mirror, so I would have to be told *something* about you. We'll all be bonding together very soon, so it's only right that I should have some idea of your character."

That statement hit Audrianna squarely in the stomach. "I'm sorry. *Bonding together?*" she sputtered.

"Ha!" Stephanie laughed. "So you are a bit of a prude. Guess they got that one right." She kicked her feet up on the lounge and leaned against the backrest. "You and Maria have that in common."

"What do you mean?"

"Oh yes, the vestal virgin, Maria Orsic," Stephanie replied with a smirk. "Also the whip master, the oenophile, and the serial novel reader—but those are just random tidbits about her. It's her self-imposed abstinence that has really driven her popularity in the community. Privation can be very alluring, I suppose— as long as it is someone else who is being deprived." She took another puff and laughed it out. "I wonder—are you impressed, Audrianna? She claims to have maintained her virginity all this time as a gift for you."

Audrianna felt the blood drain from her face. Nauseated, she eyed the exit.

"Forgive me Princess von Hohenlohe. I'm not feeling well."

"Oh, hooey." Steffi smashed her half-smoked cigarette into an ashtray, catapulting herself up. She corralled Audrianna by the shoulders and brought her back to sit on the couch. "You're just a little shell-shocked by what I've said. Let's fix that. Callum?" she called loudly to someone outside the library.

A squatty, redheaded dwarf with bright green eyes and a toothy grin waddled into the library with a serving tray of champagne. Stephanie grabbed both glasses, putting one on the table, offering the other to Audrianna.

"I was going to wait until after the first cup of coffee to break this out, but why delay the inevitable? Do you know Callum, Audrianna?"

Audrianna ignored the champagne, staring straight ahead, eyes protruding. This might be at a real live Leprechaun she was looking at.

"This is your butler, darling." Stephanie said, nudging her with the glass. Again it was not accepted.

Callum folded the empty tray underneath his arm and scraped Audrianna's white-knuckled hand off her knee, planting a kiss on it. "*Hallo*, Leyonelle," he said, glancing back and forth between ladies.

"She's all right, darling," Stephanie reassured Callum with a nod. "Why don't you come back in a half hour and we'll try the introductions again." She took Audrianna's hand away from him and put the champagne glass firmly in her grip. "Have a drink," she told her. "You're frightfully uptight."

Having had a number of alcohol related catastrophes in the past, Audrianna knew she should not imbibe. Had her nerves not been so completely raw, that reasoning alone would have stopped her. She tilted the glass to her lips and swallowed hard.

"*Prost!*" Callum clapped his hands together, then bowed and marched out the room. Steffi picked up her champagne glass and took a sip.

"Was that a Leprechaun?" Audrianna whispered.

"Heavens, a Leprechaun? Wherever did you get that idea?" Steffi laughed. She took another sip of champagne and replaced her glass on the table. "No—Callum is a *cambion*, just like all of the other generationals in this group."

The term generational was derived from cross-bred Gavrilekians and humans—any being carrying less than one hundred percent biverse energy was considered a generational.

"One thing you must know about Magda, Eva and Maria," Stephanie explained, "is that they are elitists—all of them. They do not mingle with other creatures, and they certainly don't contract to play with them. The notable exception being," she snapped her fingers, "that clown. What is his name?"

"Hiram Evans," Audrianna replied.

Stephanie rolled her eyes and groaned. "Oh yes, that's just awful business—Mr. Hiram Evans. Have you met him, yet?"

"Yes," Audrianna whispered, not caring to elaborate.

"And how is he?" Steffi asked.

Audrianna took a sip of her drink, swallowed, then took another. "Awful," she said.

"I knew it," Stephanie complained. "Magda told me he was backwards, but I knew it was more than that. Is he a slob? We already have one fat slob in the group; two slobs will make group bonding simply unbearable."

Her comment came just as Audrianna began swallowing another sip of champagne. She inhaled half of it, retching in the throes of an intractable coughing fit.

"Oh dear." Steffi took the glass out of her hand and percussed her back. Callum stuck his head into the room.

"Soll ich den Arzt holen?" he asked.

Stephanie waved him off. "No doctor, Callum. Thank you. She's just swallowed her beverage the wrong way. Come on, darling. Get yourself out of it. That's right."

Audrianna cupped her hand over her mouth and nose as slime oozed from her nostrils. She looked around for a tissue.

"Here," Steffi said, reaching around in her purse, pulling out a small caliber pistol first, then a handkerchief for Audrianna. A rolled up magazine fell out on the floor.

"I'm sorry," Audrianna wiped her eyes and her nose with the handkerchief. Reaching down with her other hand, she picked up the magazine to give back, but Steffi refused it.

"No, no," she said, replacing the pistol in her bag. "I brought that for you to have. You've made the front page of *GSpot*. I thought you'd like to know."

With a final cough, Audrianna absent-mindedly replied, "Oh, thank you—What!?" She dropped the handkerchief and unrolled the magazine; her eyes stretched open. "Oh my God! What the hell is this?" she shouted.

Spanning the entire front page of the magazine entitled, *GSpot*, was a photograph of Maria leading Audrianna into the house by the hand. Superimposed was a menacing picture of Eva Braun, Maria's business partner—the Gavrilekian master Audrianna had slain many years ago when fleeing Switzerland with Lorna. The headline read: "Lost Innocence; Broken Empire. The Maiden of Gavrilek Cashes In With Her Partner's Killer".

Gesturing at the magazine, Audrianna turned to Stephanie for an explanation. "Please, tell me this is some kind of sick joke! I really don't think I can take one more shock today."

Stephanie raised her eyebrows, minutely shaking her head. "I know. I'm absolutely appalled, too. I instructed them to publish the most alluring photo. They've made you look quite plump, here." She tilted her head to the side. "Hmm, maybe that's their angle: contrasting Maria's elegance against your ... frump."

"*You* did this?" Audrianna cried.

"This is humiliating for you, I know, darling," Stephanie tut-tutted. "Believe me, you're much more attractive in person."

"Mutti?" Devon walked into the library and looked around, settling his gaze on Audrianna's face. "Mutti, I—" He noticed Stephanie. "Oh, excuse me," he said.

Quickly rolling up the magazine, Audrianna wedged it between the cushions of the couch, and stood up, forcing herself to appear calm.

"Hi, sweetheart," she said, softly, reaching out and brushing the hair from his forehead. "You look like you're feeling better."

"Uh-huh." Devon nodded; his green eyes were brighter than any moment she could ever recall. Audrianna wondered again what had been in that vial.

Stephanie bolted from the couch and grasped Devon around the waist, twirling him around to sit down next to her.

"Hello, Tru," she said. "I am Magda's mirror, Princess Stephanie von Hohenlohe. Call me Aunt Steffi—do. I would prefer that." She patted his hand.

Audrianna fixed her eyes on the fringe of paper jutting out between two cushions. Devon had nearly perished from his emotional surge this morning. There was no telling how he would react to seeing his mother plastered all over a tabloid magazine like a Hollywood floozy.

"Aunt Steffi, yeah," Devon laughed, enjoying her personality. "Um, excuse me for interrupting. I was lookin' for…"

"Here I am, Tru," Hannah called as she skipped playfully into the room. She pulled a squirming red dachshund puppy from underneath her aviator's jacket and handed it to him.

"Thank you, Hannah," Devon beamed.

Momentarily distracted by Hannah's gift, Audrianna touched her hand to her heart, then went over and sat next to Devon while he and Steffi fawned over the puppy.

"You're welcome, Tru," Hannah giggled. "But it wasn't my idea. It was Maria's. I'm simply following her—Oh!" She popped her hand over her mouth, eyes widening. She turned to Stephanie and said, "I beg your pardon, Leyonelle. Good afternoon." She reached for her hand and kissed it.

"Good afternoon, darling," Stephanie warmly reciprocated.

Moving to Audrianna, Hannah issued the same courtesy she'd given Stephanie. "Good afternoon, Leyonelle," she said, kissing Audrianna's hand.

Audrianna needed to know why both she and Stephanie were being called,"Leyonelle." "What are you calling us, Hannah?"

"Hannah, darling, I cannot carry all of your makeup and the dresses, too," a woman with a French accent called from the hallway. "Won't you come and help me, please?"

"She's early!" gasped Hannah. She wheeled about just as an exceptionally dressed, green-eyed brunette entered the room, juggling an armful of dresses and a sizable leather case. Hannah jumped up and took the case from her so the woman could use both hands to manage the dresses. A footman followed her in, pushing a rolling dress rack and a portable sewing machine.

"Heavens!" Stephanie exclaimed, looking up from petting the puppy. She eyeballed the lady with derision. "Madame Coco Chanel. Maria is pulling out all of the stops, isn't she?"

There was an awkward silence in the room that everyone but Devon seemed to notice. Audrianna looked at Hannah; Hannah looked at Coco; Coco and Stephanie glared at one another. After a moment, Steffi lifted her hand to Coco and smirked. *"Bonjour madame."*

Coco draped the dresses over the back of the couch and quickly moved to kiss Steffi's hand. *"Bonjour, Leyonelle,"* she replied in a cool tone of voice. *"C'est un plaisir de vous rencontrer."*

"I know you don't mean that," Steffi patronized, "but you shouldn't let my presence ruin your little fashion show. Callum?" She picked up her champagne glass and drained it.

Callum walked into the room and bowed. "Darling, won't you be a jewel and fetch us some more champagne?" Stephanie asked him. "We're having a dress party in here. Did you know? Audrianna, may I stay for your fitting?"

The demon alcohol influenced Audrianna's response. "Yes, I guess so. If that's what's happening," she said, looking around, playing dumb. She knew perfectly well what was going on. Maria told her earlier she would be sending someone by to dress her— Coco Chanel was clearly that person. Clearly, she and Stephanie disliked each other intensely. Audrianna was curious to know why.

"Would that be okay?" she asked Coco.

"Your pleasure, madame," Coco replied. She scooted past Devon and planted a soft kiss on Audrianna's hand. "*Enchanté,* Leyonelle," she whispered, looking deeply into Audrianna's eyes. "Aren't you lovely?"

Audrianna thought the woman seemed sincere and felt badly for being disingenuous.

"Wonderful!" Stephanie clapped her hands; she turned to Devon. "Are you staying for our little *soirée*, Tru?"

Audrianna started to object but Devon made up his own mind. "I don't think so, Aunt Steffi," he said. "I'm gonna take Rodney down to the lake."

Steffi drew back at his thick Southern accent, replying, "Forgive me, darling—you mean to do what? With whom?"

"Rodney." Devon pointed down at his tiny dog. "He wants to go to the lake. So do I."

Frowning at the thought of Devon walking alone outside, Audrianna got up and held out her hand. "I haven't seen the lake either," she said. "Why don't we all walk together?" She didn't want Maria's dress, anyway.

Devon pulled Rodney into his cheek and met the puppy's sideways kisses. "Nah, don't bother, Mutti," he laughed. "I think you'd be lonely."

Audrianna was stung by his words. He was as candid at times as the rest of them were; sometimes it hurt.

Stephanie picked up on Audrianna's wounded feelings. She rose and joined Audrianna where she stood, giving her a little comforting back rub, encouraging her to let him go. "Of course you must have your own quiet time to get to know Rodney."

Audrianna nodded, but she was obviously not at ease.

"Don't be worried, Mutti. I'll be all right," he said. He gave her a peck on the cheek, then waved goodbye. "See ya later."

"Heavens, that diction is impossibly adorable," Stephanie said, escorting Audrianna back to her seat. "What a refreshing change of pace to our aristocratic elocution."

Callum reentered the room with a dripping bottle of Krug Brut, and moved to refill their glasses. Stephanie stopped him. "No, no darling. Throw that out. Go down to the cellar and bring up a bottle of 1928 Chèvre de Montagne. If Maria went to such an effort to bring Coco here, it stands to reason she would want the appropriate champagne served."

Callum did not move. He stared at Audrianna while Stephanie lit up another cigarette. "Oh," she blew out her smoke and turned sideways to Audrianna. "I've spoken out of turn. Callum is waiting for your permission, darling. Only you can make decisions about the dispensation of Maria's property."

Sensing a trap, Audrianna looked to the only person in the room she trusted—Hannah. "Why me?" she asked.

"Maria views you as an extension of herself, Audrianna," Hannah answered, clearly on edge but deliberate in her reply. She took a seat next to Audrianna and engaged her in a look "Feel free to enjoy anything of Maria's as if it were your own. She wants you to be happy."

"Does she?" Audrianna snorted.

Instantly, Hannah's expression turned worried and Audrianna regretted her response. She switched her position, reinforcing the sentiment with a smile, "That's lovely. Let's have the champagne suggested by Princess von Hohenlohe. I would like that very much."

The champagne was obviously quite valuable, likely one of Maria's prized possessions. Perhaps her frivolous consumption of it would make Maria angry. Audrianna would like that very much, too.

Callum raised his eyebrows at Hannah, then shuffled out of the room to retrieve the champagne. Stephanie reached across Audrianna and offered Hannah the case of cigarettes. "Hannah, would you like one of these?" she asked.

Hannah shifted her gaze to Audrianna.

"I'm not being rude, darling," Stephanie told her. "Audrianna doesn't smoke." Maria doesn't smoke either" she added, directing the remark to Audrianna. "Another thing you two have in common."

Hannah smiled and said, "What other likenesses have you identified?"

"They're both prudes—"

"Prunes!" Audrianna blurted over Stephanie's voice. She stuffed the magazine deeper into the innards of the couch. "Neither of us like prunes," she insisted.

Hannah took a stick of tobacco from the case and accepted a light from Stephanie. Guilelessly she replied, "But, Maria has prunes with her breakfast every morning." She blew out her smoke and handed the cigarette to Coco who was busy hanging dresses on the rolling rack.

"Why would she eat prunes if she didn't like them?"

"That question is self-answering, darling," Stephanie told her.

Hannah looked embarrassed. "Oh, I'm sorry, Leyonelle. Let me see." She contemplated momentarily then guessed out loud: "She's constipated?"

Stephanie burst out laughing and Audrianna chuckled, too. How could she not?

"Constipation. That's it. I agree," said Stephanie. "That's a brilliant diagnosis for Maria."

"Baroness von Traugott," Coco called. "I'm ready to get started—that is, unless you would prefer to wait for your champagne."

"No." Audrianna rose from her seat and fidgeted for a moment. "I'm sorry, Ms. Chanel. I'm not sure of the etiquette. It's been a very long time since I've been fitted for a dress."

Coco came forward and collected her with a smile. "Do not distress yourself, Leyonelle," she said. "This is very informal. Should you have a need for my services in the future, we can meet at one of my shops in Paris. Maria is very keen on fashion; I stoke her enthusiasm as often as she permits."

"Maria is also a bit shortsighted in that regard," Stephanie offered. She flicked her ashes in the ashtray, continuing, "Madame Chanel is not the only reputable designer in Paris. I shall take you there myself and show you a broader point of view."

Stephanie was meanly exploiting her rank; and Audrianna hated bullies. Fingering through the garments, Audrianna demonstrated her understanding of the balance of power by using Stephanie's nickname. "How kind, Steffi. But, with clothes as stunning as these, I can see why Maria is disinclined to shop elsewhere. This one is very pretty." She pulled a one-shouldered, floor-length dress of red crepe romaine off the rack and flashed it at Hannah. "What do you think?" she asked.

Hannah housed her cigarette in Stephanie's ashtray and got up, taking the frock out of Audrianna's hands and holding it up against her. "I think it's lovely," she breathed. "What a striking contrast with your eyes."

Callum came in with the bottle of champagne. He offered Audrianna a look at the label, uncorking it after she nodded her approval. She disguised a bitter face with the first taste. "Thank you, Callum. It is spectacular," she said, secretly preferring the taste of the cheaper bottle.

Pleased, if not a little surprised, Callum smiled and said, "I am very glad you like it, Leyonelle. Please enjoy your afternoon."

⁂

"One hundred and twenty marks for breakfast; one hundred ninety marks for lunch." Audrianna followed the sound of Alex's voice down the grand staircase of the house. A message had come from Maria at six o'clock to meet her downstairs for their date at eight. Audrianna was ten minutes early.

Stepping lightly through the reception hall to the parlor, she eavesdropped on the conversation, concealing all but one eye behind the door. Standing over Maria, Alex read from a ledger while she lounged on a couch reading a book. "Eleven hundred marks for electricity," he continued.

"That's outrageous," Maria remarked, flipping the page without looking up. "What *is* the problem?"

Alex casually looked around the room. "I think someone is stealing from you, Master," he said.

"That's ridiculous. I constructed the security pattern, myself. Are you suggesting it has been breached?"

"Yes, Master."

"Ridiculous, as I've said. Please have the department heads meet me first thing tomorrow morning so we can identify the source of the hemorrhage." She flipped another page and said, "Next."

"1928 Chèvre de Montagne."

Maria looked up. "Who ordered that?"

Alex ran his finger across the page and tracked the answer with his eyes. "The authorization was made by Baroness von Traugott at three o'clock this afternoon."

Maria adjusted her glasses and said, "Please ask Callum to come here and see me now. Hurry up, I don't want my evening delayed by this issue."

Thirty seconds later, a dwarf-size door disguised as one of the wall panels opened. Callum rushed through it, wrought with worry.

"You summoned me, Master?"

Maria folded the corner down on her page and set her book to the side. "Callum, please provide me with an explanation as to why you served a bottle of Chèvre de Montagne to my leyonelle."

Audrianna huffed. Now she was Maria's leyonelle—whatever the hell that meant.

"The leyonelle asked for it," Callum said.

"She asked for that particular bottle? By name?"

"No. The bottle was first suggested by Princess von Hohenlohe, and then ordered by Baroness von Traugott."

"I see." Maria raised an eyebrow. "Firstly, why was I not made aware that Stephanie was in my house? Secondly, was Coco present at the time?"

Callum nodded. "Yes, she was tending to the leyonelle's garment as you ordered, Master. I've never reported any of Princess von Hohenlohe's visits to you in the past. I didn't think you would care."

"In the past," Maria snapped, "my very vulnerable leyonelle has not lived here." She narrowed her eyes to slits. "In the future, you will clear everyone entering this house with me. Also in the future, you will never serve that drink to Audrianna again—even if she asks for it. Tell her you're out of it or some other such absurdity. Have I made myself clear?"

"Yes, Master," Callum replied.

Maria got up and patted his head. She donned a set of opera gloves, adjusting the backings on her earrings one at a time. "We'll return around ten. I'll let you know if it is to be any later than that."

"Shall I have your room prepared for company?" Callum asked.

Maria laughed. "That's kindly optimistic of you, darling, but unless our dinner has been prepared with some kind of mystical aphrodisiac, I'll be sharing my bed with only my pillow. Have cognac decanted for us in the library. If luck prevails, I might convince her to share that with me." She turned to Alex. "Is the car warm? I don't want her shivering."

Audrianna looked down at her bare arms and realized she had forgotten her coat. Tip-toeing around, she lost her balance in her heels, tapping off-kilter along the slippery white marble. The train of her evening gown finally overcame her momentum, sending her face-first to the floor. "Damn," she whispered, angry rather than hurt.

A scramble of frantic feet scurried from the parlor. *"Mein Gott,* dearest. Have you fallen down the stairs?" Maria asked.

Pushing herself up on her forearms, Audrianna tapped her fingertips on the floor, responding, "Yes, Maria. I missed the last stair." She shoved herself back on her knees, then started to rise. Alex and Callum rushed to help her but she swatted them with her hands. "I'm fine, I can do it," she said, brushing herself off. "I'm sorry but I've forgotten my coat. I'll need to go and get it."

"Nonsense." Maria took off her fur-collar wrap and draped it around Audrianna's shoulders. She looked down at Callum and said, "Please have Kuniko fetch my black sable. Alex," she turned to him, "we're going now. Please prepare the car."

After both men were gone, Maria examined Audrianna from head to toe. "Have you always found it difficult to remain upright?" she asked, grazing her thumb over Audrianna's head.

Audrianna pulled back, cupping a hand over the wound. "Yes. Sometimes I have problems with my footing when my mind is not on walking," she replied.

Kuniko, a petite Asian maid in her early 20s, ran into the reception hall holding Maria's coat. Helping her into it, Kuniko held on a little longer than necessary, laughing something into the back of Maria's hair. Maria engaged her over the shoulder with a smile—there was a clear sense of familiarity between them.

Audrianna tried to walk away, but Maria quickly broke from Kuniko and took Audrianna's hand. "Let me assist you," she said. "There is gravel in the driveway. If you fall down, you'll injure yourself further."

"Master?" Alex opened the front door and poked his head inside.

"Yes, I know. We're coming out right now," Maria said. She led Audrianna forward, stepping outside, drawing up with a gasp.

Parked in the driveway was a four-door Isotta Fraschini—the only legitimate competitor to Rolls Royce. The original finish was a green-grey livery but garish crimson stripes had been crudely brushed onto the paint. Tyler stood outside the back door; he held a motorcycle helmet beneath one arm.

"Alexander, come before me this instant and explain what has happened to my car!" Maria demanded.

Rushing to heed her call, Alex slipped a little on the gravel as he reported in front of her, saying, "Master, I have placed safety markings upon the vehicle for the leyonelle. I assumed you would be pleased."

"You assumed?" Maria asked, fire in her voice. "I am not sure which part of that explanation is more remarkable, the fact that you assumed I would want my vehicle defaced, or that you had the gall to act upon that assumption. Never assume anything, Alexander! I grow weary of having to revisit this subject with you over and over and over."

Noticing his brother's distress, Tyler came forward with an untamed, almost animalistic expression. "Master, I agreed with him about the safety markings," he said.

"You agreed—well, that does influence my understanding of the issue. Thank you, Tyler. I now know, I have not one imbecile representing me, but two."

"Master," Tyler objected defensively, "I don't think you know just how many crazies are on the road these days." He tried to put the helmet on Audrianna's head, but Maria shooed him back.

"Thanks to you and your brother," she said, "I am now fully aware of the *crazies* on the road—Stop." She held up her finger when Tyler tried to respond. "You," she pointed at Alex, "open the door. You," she pointed at Tyler, "drive the car." She wagged her finger back and forth at both of them. "Neither one of you say another word to me for the rest of the night. Is this in any way unclear?"

"No, Master," they replied in unison. Then they hastily complied with her orders.

Maria closed her eyes and took a deep calming breath through her nostrils. She then turned to Audrianna with a forced smile and said, "Shall we go?" They walked together to the car and climbed into the backseat. Alex and Tyler took the front; they both donned helmets

"Should we be wearing those, too?" Audrianna whispered to Maria.

"No, dearest. The helmets are unnecessary. They often do things that are nonsensical. I pray you pay them no mind. Tyler," Maria leaned forward to speak to him, "please get—ohhh!" Her voice jounced as the car took off, sending her careening along the slick leather upholstery into Audrianna. She pushed herself away and smoothed out her evening gown. "I beg your pardon. I wasn't expecting that impetuous acceleration."

"Yes, those impetuous accelerations get me too." Audrianna made fun of Maria, but she seemed not to notice. Instead, Maria started up a conversation.

"Dearest, I gather you've had a visitor today."

Audrianna rested her elbow on the cushy seam of the window and traced the overhead upholstery with her forefinger, masking a smile. "I've had several visitors today," she replied.

Maria tried again. "I hear Princess von Hohenlohe was over to see you."

"Yes, she came by," Audrianna answered, then immediately changed the subject for fun. "What part of Berlin is this?"

"This part of Berlin is called Grunewald. Dearest—"

"In what part of the city is Grunewald?" asked Audrianna.

"In the western part of the city. Dearest—"

"What does Grunewald mean?" Audrianna persisted, determined to get on Maria's nerves. It worked.

"Audrianna, I am trying to discuss something with you."

"Yes, Maria. I know."

Maria shook her head, confused. "Why are you toying with me, then?" she asked.

Leaning into the leather seat on her knuckles, Audrianna returned Maria's gaze with an angry look. "So you can see what it feels like to be toyed with," she spat. There was a prolonged silence between them while they left each other to think. Eventually, when she felt the punishment enough, Audrianna spoke again, this time in a softer tone of voice. "What would you like to discuss, Maria?" she asked.

Maria adjusted her glasses and said, "How did you find your visit today with Stephanie?"

"I found it full of surprises," replied Audrianna.

"What surprises, specifically?"

"Why does it matter?"

Clearly unaccustomed at having to work so hard for answers, Maria sharpened her voice. "It matters," she drew the word out, "because the woman has a penchant for mischief and I don't want you caught up in her antics."

Audrianna purposely redirected the conversation. "Maria, what does leyonelle mean?"

"Dearest, may we please remain on topic?"

"No, I don't want to," Audrianna replied, simply. She repeated her question. "What does leyonelle mean? Why does everyone keep calling me that?"

The car stopped along a row of painted concrete buildings, commandeering Audrianna's curiosity. "What's this?"

Elaborate mosaic courtyards with wine barrel planters brimming with African Violets abutted the buildings. Vertical trellises were festooned with glowing red grapes. Mismatched street lamps provided an expansive umbrella of artificial light for everything. Delightfully eccentric, the entire place felt like a scene from a comic book.

"I thought you might like to inspect Devon's quarters," offered Maria. "There was some question of appropriateness, I believe."

"Are we underground?" Audrianna peered through her window at an upward angle. Twenty feet high, the ceiling was supported by immense concrete columns and reinforced with exposed steel beams. "Devon told me it was a different world, but I had no idea it would look like this," Audrianna marveled.

Maria seemed pleased with her response. "Yes. We've taken great pains to enrich this living environment for our players. They live active and fulfilling lives, every ounce the experience of their above ground counterparts."

"What do you mean? Aren't they permitted above ground?"

Maria shook her head. "Not generally, no. An overt public presence is not in our best interest, and therefore, is restricted to those generationals who have proven their competence with emotion." She laughed a little. "Also, the Consciousness of Gavrilek—your son—may leave anytime he wishes. There is no mechanism in our contract to restrict his comings and goings, or anything else, for that matter. He is his own entity."

"So, everyone else is trapped here," Audrianna said, meanly.

"I offer you transparency and you turn it into something tainted!" Maria snapped. "Our city is intended as a safeguard against embroilment. Consider my efforts to rescue your son from emotion today, then imagine the impossibility of my providing that help to a thousand people at the same time."

Audrianna empathized with the desire to institute overly protective measures—she had locked Devon away from the world the first eight years of his life. For that reason, if no other, she apologized. "I'm sorry. I didn't think about it that way."

Maria cleared her throat and nodded, indicating she was ready to move on.

"Would you care to look around?" she asked.

Alex opened the door and Audrianna could not resist the buzz of the thriving young adult community. The crowd stopped and gawked as she and Maria emerged from the car.

"Have we interrupted something?" Audrianna asked.

"Yes," replied Maria. "Ordinarily I would not trespass upon their social hour. Obviously, they've been caught unawares."

"Are they startled or enraptured?" Audrianna asked her.

"How would I know, dearest?" Maria was authentic in her reply.

When the group began applauding, Audrianna turned to her and chuckled. "Aren't they used to seeing you?"

"They are used to seeing me *alone*," Maria blushed. Unaware, or unconcerned with her physical response, she gestured to the crowd, continuing, "Loyalty binds people like no other cause, but it can take courage. If just *one* person fails to meet the requirements for winning," she touched her hand to her breast, engaging Audrianna's eyes, "if *one* person fails to bond with their mirror, the entire group endures the loss. Loyalty is nothing if it is not absolute."

Before Audrianna could compliment her eloquence, Maria quickly added, "I owe you the courtesy of kindness. You owe me no such consideration, but I would be grateful for your forbearance."

"What does that even mean?" Audrianna grimaced, exhausted by the effort of constantly translating Maria's pedantic language.

"If you're determined to impose a death sentence upon me," Maria rephrased, "so be it. But, these people are innocent of my crimes. Please do not dash their hopes of going home by making a scene."

Audrianna gently rolled her eyes. "I wasn't planning on announcing it, Maria. I wouldn't do that to … you." She lost her voice as another realization forced itself upon her. "Just take me to see Devon," she whispered. "I'll act like we're together."

They moved through a brigade of well-wishers, all vying for a chance to kiss Audrianna's hand and welcome her to their group. It was difficult not to feel flattered by their attention. She felt important, admired. It had been a long time since she had been admired, if ever.

After entering the building, they proceeded to apartment 420. Maria rapped once on the door, then opened it slightly, saying, "Excuse me, Devon, but you mother—"

She stopped at the sight of bottles tipped over on the floor. *Bark, bark, bark …*

Instantly on alert, Audrianna pushed past Maria into the room. She braced herself on the doorjamb as a progress of naked men jumped up from their sexual entanglement and slipped by her, begging her pardon between giggles.

"Mutti, get out!" Devon shouted, shooing at her from the bed where he lay beneath another man. Rodney jumped on the floor. *Bark, bark, bark …*

Mortified, Audrianna turned the blame on Maria, saying, "Is this what you came up with as an alternate disciplinary method? How can you allow this kind of depravity to go on?"

It was clear from Maria's expression that she, too, had been caught off-guard. Eventually she managed, "I am the Master Protector of the Consciousness of Gavrilek—my mission is to keep him alive, not to command his social activities."

Bark, bark, bark …

"Mutti, I said *get out!*"

"Are you kidding me, Maria?" Audrianna cried, ignoring him. "You don't think his social activities—*these* social activities," she gesticulated with her hands, "pose any threat to his existence? He is drinking alcohol and having group sex in here!"

"Thank you, dearest. The agenda was unclear," Maria quipped.

The last naked man pulled the door closed, leaving just Devon and his male lover in the room with Maria and Audrianna.

"This is super awkward, Maria," the man said, getting up. He was slim with effeminate features, chestnut hair and a cleft between his teeth. He wrapped a towel around his waist and walked up to Maria, hands clasped underneath his chin. He spoke to her with genuine kindness. "I know you're very new to socializing with other people, but it's considered impolite to just drop in unannounced. Often, it engenders unpleasant feelings for those involved."

"I beg your pardon, Leyonelle," Maria said, adjusting her glasses. "I didn't realize that tenet applied to immediate family members." She was serious.

"Immediate family members are really the most relevant class," he said, nodding. Hand to shoulder, he steered her gently toward the door. "These human codes of conduct are a lot to keep up with, I know. Just remember, no one wants their mother sprung on them."

"I'll come here anytime I want to!" Audrianna exclaimed, leaping forward, jamming a finger in his face. "Now, who are you and what are you doing here with my son?"

The man drew his head back with a started look, eyes wide like he had encountered an exotic toad. He glanced back at Devon saying, "Oh, dear. She's away with the fairies."

Devon fell back on the bed, laughing hysterically. "Oh my God, Jörð!" he cried, placing a pillow over his face, shaking his head. "Mutti, I didn't invite you here," he playfully screamed. "I don't want you here. Please go away!"

Bark, bark, bark …

The wind left Audrianna's sails. Now that she was the object of his ridicule, she cringed at this very adult sight of him, here with his lover. When had he grown up? Why hadn't she seen it?

"Come, dearest." Maria collected her by the shoulders and escorted her out the door. Audrianna did not resist.

Back in the car, she sat staring out the window, while Maria attempted to offer her comfort. "I don't doubt you've endured the destruction of your dreams; we have that in common, at least." How elegant she was with her incantations.

"This isn't about you," she whispered, in a weak attempt to fight her.

"Yes, it is," replied Maria. "It's about *me*, because it's about *you*. We share the same consciousness. I wish you'd see that."

"Don't put that on me right now, Maria. Please. If you had *any* understanding of my consciousness, you'd see I am at the end of my rope."

"I'm sorry, dearest but I am unfamiliar with that saying," Maria said. "If you would like to avoid using idioms in the future, our communication will be much improved."

Audrianna held her skull between her palms, laughing in disbelief at Maria's clueless response. It felt good: the laughter; laughing at her; making fun of her. It melted away the other emotions: anger, sadness, if only for a little bit. She turned back out the window, giggling through her nose. For some inexplicable reason, she thought of her mother.

Her mother had perished in Berlin many, many years ago, but somehow, she still felt ... here. Her mother's memory belayed Audrianna's smile and she began to wonder. With their overwhelming presence in Berlin, Maria's group was suspect in her mother's death—Maria might know the details of what happened to her. A new objective settled into Audrianna's mind—she would find out what Maria knew.

The car pulled up in front of a deserted, fully lit restaurant. When Audrianna did not stir, Maria tested her temper. "We've arrived, Leyonelle. Are you amenable to dining?"

"What does leyonelle mean, Maria?" Audrianna asked, turning toward. "Why does everyone keep calling me that?" It wasn't just her. It was Niklas, Stephanie *and* Devon's lover. All of them had been called leyonelle that day.

Maria took off her glasses and rubbed her eyes, resetting herself before speaking again. "It means place of refuge, and its use means you are being paid homage," she said. She snuck her hand over to touch Audrianna's while she talked; Audrianna pretended not to notice. "The Leyonelle is a Gavrilekian flower that forms a bond with just one pollinator. If the pollinator becomes sick or wounded or needs shelter from the elements, the Leyonelle closes its petals around the pollinator and keeps it safe until such a time when the creature is ready to fly again."

Audrianna tried to resist the obvious interconnection, but the beauty of the story weighed on her heart. She pulled her hand away and rubbed her face until the feeling faded a bit. "God, just let me hate you. Won't you?" she croaked.

Maria swallowed. Her eyes turned glossy. "Leyonelle, are you amenable to dining?" she asked again.

Before answering, Audrianna cataloged two important things from Maria's telling of the Leyonelle story: Niklas was probably Lorna's mirror and the man she had just encountered was obviously Devon's mirror: Jörð, The Consciousness of Earth. Maria would not have capitulated to a lower rank. That notion soothed some of Audrianna's hurt and much of her worry about Devon. With his mirror, Devon *should* be safe.

Yes, she decided. She *was* amenable to dining.

———•◦•———

Alex opened the door and Audrianna absentmindedly got out, lost in another world. Maria slithered around the back of the car to catch up with her, eyes brightened. "This is my favorite restaurant," she said with an eager smile.

Audrianna looked right and left replying, "I'm surprised you would come here. It seems a little common to me."

"It is the very opposite of common." Maria defended the place. "The food is excellent, the service is extraordinary," a doorman opened the restaurant to them and they stepped inside. "And the atmosphere is charming," she finished.

"*Guten Abend, Frau Orsic,*" the maître d' greeted Maria with a kiss on both cheeks. Maria introduced Audrianna as her companion and the maître d' acknowledged her with a bow of his head "Baroness."

He made small talk with Maria whilst escorting them to a simply prepared table in front of the fire. Seating Audrianna first, he handed each of them a menu before excusing himself to retrieve a carafe of water.

"Would you like wine?" Maria asked over the top of her menu.

Back on point, Audrianna replied, "I prefer champagne," though the statement was untrue. She simply meant to provoke Maria again and was willing to drink whatever she had to in order to accomplish that task. The maître d' came back over with the water and Audrianna delved further into her scheme. "Might we have a bottle of 1928 Chèvre de Montagne?" she asked him. "I find I've developed quite a taste for it."

The maître d' stared at her, speechless. He flipped a set of questioning eyes to Maria, and Audrianna inwardly giggled at the thought of Maria having to pay another extravagant sum of money for something as frivolous as a bottle of champagne.

"*Bitte entschuldigen Sie uns,*" Maria excused him, then adjusted her glasses saying, "What do you enjoy of the taste, dearest? I'll see if I can't think of a suitable substitute."

"Suitable?" Audrianna laughed. "By suitable, do you mean less expensive?" She put her menu down on the table, and leaned forward on her elbows. "I enjoy it because I enjoy it," she said. "You live in a mansion, you ride in a luxury automobile, you have a world famous fashion designer at your beck and call. Am I not worth the price of even the most expensive bottle of champagne?"

"Certainly you are," Maria said, leaning forward, nodding her head once. "Are you sure you've ordered one?"

Audrianna hedged and Maria jumped on her uncertainty; she signaled to the maître d'. "Please bring out and uncork your five most expensive bottles of champagne for Baroness von Traugott to taste; whatever she doesn't care for, you may share with your staff."

Suspecting she had just been caught in her own trap, Audrianna cursed under her breath, "No, Maria—Goddammit." She twisted in her chair and held up her forefinger to the maître d', saying, "Just wait a minute, please." To Maria she continued in a whisper. "Chèvre de Montagne isn't going to be one of those bottles, is it?"

"Crass language is extremely distasteful to me, Audrianna."

"Your pretentious babble isn't that great, either," Audrianna rebutted. "What's the deal with the champagne? Is it super cheap, or something?"

Maria slid her menu onto the table and stood up. She walked around to the back of Audrianna's chair and whispered in her ear. "You've made a mistake. Let's correct it." She helped Audrianna up from her chair and kept hold of her hand while she spoke to the maître d'. "Baroness von Traugott has confused the name of the drink she would like to have with our dinner. Might we have a look around in your wine cellar? She feels certain she can identify the bottle by label."

"*Ja, ja,*" the stunned maître d' agreed. He rustled in his pocket for a set of keys, then led Maria and Audrianna to the back of the restaurant and down an unlit set of stairs.

"Wait," Maria said, stopping Audrianna with her hands. "It is dark. You'll fall." She asked the maître d' to hand her up the first bottle of wine he touched; he did. Maria rolled the bottle between her palms until the liquid inside began to emit a glowing green light. She held the bottle by the neck like a lantern, then backed down in front of Audrianna, lighting the way for her.

Once solidly on the ground, Maria handed the bottle back to the maître d' and steadied Audrianna by keeping hold of her arms until a kerosene lantern was struck. Afterwards, she took the lantern from the maître d' and said, "Thank you, you may go now. We shan't be long."

After he was gone, Audrianna asked, "Are people always so accommodating with your requests?"

"Yes. Money and power assures you those things."

"I guess you're very proud of yourself, aren't you?" Audrianna sneered, angrier at herself than Maria.

Maria hung the lamp on a protruding rod and calmly replied, "I am proud to have remained kind in the face of such corruptible influences. Let's look here and see what we can find for you." She twisted individual bottles in the wine racks to view the labels. "Do you really prefer champagne or was that a ruse?"

"I prefer whiskey."

Maria stopped perusing the store. She turned around and stared at Audrianna, her head slightly tilted. "Why would you not say as much?" she asked.

"I wanted to hurt you," Audrianna replied, looking down. "I overheard your conversation with Callum and I assumed the bottle I ordered was quite expensive. I meant to insult your generosity." She paused. "I take it this charade, this bringing me down here to show me other bottles, is your attempt to spare me embarrassment in my mistake. Is that right?"

"Yes," Maria replied.

"What is Chèvre de Montagne?" Audrianna asked. "Will you tell me the truth?"

"I will always tell you the truth if you have the courage to ask me for it," Maria patiently replied. "We've discussed this, I know."

Audrianna nodded her head.

Maria continued, "Chèvre de Montagne is by far, the cheapest sparkling wine sold in Europe: it is not true champagne. The only place it enjoys notoriety is in houses of ill repute and amongst the women who are employed by those houses. I keep a small stock of it on hand for those of my players who must replenish their energy from prostitutes."

Audrianna dropped her head in her hand and closed her eyes. She had two options: admit defeat with honor, or drown herself in a pathetic display of self-pity. There was no choice. "I'm sorry, Maria," she said, and she meant it. She looked up. "It was Princess von Hohenlohe who suggested the champagne. I assumed that it was the most expensive bottle of champagne in your cellar and that is why I agreed to it. I had not the first inkling she was labeling me a whore."

"She wasn't," Maria replied. "The insult was meant for Coco, not for you. You were simply the vehicle for her discourtesy." She pulled Audrianna in for a one-sided hug and rubbed her back. "Still, the offense was made. I shall speak with Magda about it." She said nothing of Audrianna's offense.

"I'd rather just forget it," Audrianna told her. "It was a game of spite and I lost. The punishment is fitting." She freed her arms and returned Maria's embrace, contrite for her childishness, and willing to sacrifice her pride to convey that message.

Maria abruptly stepped back.

"What's wrong?" Audrianna asked her.

"Wrong? In what context?" Maria replied.

Audrianna shifted her gaze. "We had a moment of connection; you pulled out of it," she said. "Why?"

"It felt strange," Maria replied.

"It felt strange."

"Yes."

"Would you care to elaborate?" Audrianna asked.

Maria's eyes fell out of focus. "I felt *fearful* of you."

"Oh," Audrianna said. She was curious, of course, but not enough to inquire further. Patting Maria on the shoulder, she drew her back into the moment, saying, "We should get on with choosing something to drink, don't you think? These poor people will want to get home some time tonight."

Maria quickly selected a bottle of red wine, then helped Audrianna climb out of the cellar. Upstairs, they were reseated and their food orders were taken. A jazz quartet emerged from the shadows, playing "Mood Indigo" by Duke Ellington; Audrianna guilelessly resumed conversation at an easy pace. "Why do Steffi and Coco dislike each other so?" she asked.

Maria replied, "Stephanie and Coco have history together."

"They were lovers?"

"Yes."

A waiter came from the kitchen with wine glasses, decanting the bottle for them. After he poured it, Audrianna rolled the stem between her fingers and watched the liquid swirl inside the glass. It was clear Maria intended their relationship to be monogamous so she was confused why Stephanie was permitted a lover outside of her mirror, Magda. "But I thought Stephanie and Magda were, ahem, bonded mirrors." She took two big gulps of wine. It had been eighteen years since her induction into the world of Gavrilek, but she still found their concepts awkward to discuss.

Maria leaned forward. "Dearest, are you trying to ask me a question?" she said.

Audrianna bit down on her lower lip, looking away with a laugh. "Sort of. I think your translation skills are worse than Kendis' were."

"I'm sure they are," Maria replied, softly. "The humans of my acquaintance are paid to speak to me without making inferences. I haven't much practice with humans outside that fold."

"I heard you had no practice," Audrianna retorted. Surprised by her own coarseness, she instantly apologized. "I'm sorry, Maria. I'm not sure why I just said that."

Removing the glasses from her face, Maria laid them on the table and took a sip of her wine. She tapped her fingertips lightly on the tablecloth and said, "I see Stephanie has taken it upon herself to apprise you of certain details of my private life. I intended to have that conversation with you myself, when the time was appropriate. My celibacy is meant as a gesture of devotion to you. I am sorry if you were embarrassed by it."

Butterfly wings swatted the inside of Audrianna's stomach; her mouth turned dry. She guzzled more wine to mitigate both afflictions, eventually replying, "Clearly it's not as you had planned, but that's not your fault. I was embarrassed, yes, but I'm often embarrassed, so there's no harm done there, either—I guess."

"Dearest?"

Audrianna glanced at Maria but found she was unable to maintain eye contact. Every lesson she ever learned from Kendis on how to remain engaged was forgotten. She finished her glass of wine.

"Dearest, why were you embarrassed?" Maria asked. "Do you imagine I won't be able to please you when the time comes?"

Audrianna squirmed. "God, Maria. Can we just not talk about it anymore?" She fanned herself. "What is it with you people? Why do you all insist on discussing what goes on in the bedroom like you were discussing the weather? You all do it!" She grabbed the decanter and poured herself another glass of wine, continuing, "I don't know why I was embarrassed. I shouldn't be embarrassed, because to answer your question—no! I don't imagine that you'll be able to please me—not because you haven't the experience, but because I don't intend to give you the chance!"

Maria tilted her head, considering Audrianna in a whimsical manner. She then swept her up by the hand and led her to the dance floor. "Come dance," she said.

"Dance?" Audrianna looked around. "That's a bit suggestive, don't you think?"

"I'm not sure what you mean," Maria replied, twirling Audrianna into her arms. She moved with the grace of a swan, the agility of a leopard. Her body was hard; her skin was soft; her scent of perfume and perspiration was hypnotic.

"Suggestive of impropriety," Audrianna said. "Two women dancing together to soft, romantic music. It might bring some stares, you know?"

Maria laughed. "You worry too much what others think," she said.

"Really, Maria?" Audrianna asked in a hush. "You're going to accuse me of being worried about what others think after the trip we just made to the wine cellar? What a clever plot hatched by you to keep me from being labeled lover of the whore's champagne!"

"Sparkling wine."

"Sparkling wine." Audrianna corrected herself. "Don't you also worry too much what others think. What if I really liked it? What would you have done then?"

"Did you like it?" Maria asked. She gave Audrianna a little dip.

"Well…no."

"Then, there's no point in arguing that question, is there?" Maria laughed.

Audrianna stopped dancing and pulled away from Maria, the effects of alcohol rapidly manifested. "Maria, I want you to admit that you, too, worry with appearances—or you can just take me home right now," she said, pointing to the front door for emphasis.

"Fine." Maria surrendered with her hands. "I *do* consider appearances when fashioning the makeup of my ability to influence people. Yes."

"Really?" Audrianna laughed. She pulled one fist to her lips and emulated a microphone. "Now, for the common translation of the Queen's English." She presented her imaginary microphone for Maria to speak in. When Maria did not understand what she was supposed to do, Audrianna tapped the imaginary microphone with two fingers and pulled it back to her lips. "Testing, testing," she mimicked.

Maria looked over at Audrianna's wine glass, then back, brows drawn inward.

"Dearest, are you drunk? How can you be so drunk from one glass of wine?"

Letting go of her imaginary microphone, Audrianna stomped her foot, angry at the accusation, though it was true. "Something happens to me when I drink alcohol, Maria! I told you that before!" She made a dismissive gesture with her hands and that simple shift in momentum brought with it a subsequent loss of balance. She began to stumble.

Maria rushed forward to catch her. "Weightless, weightless," she said, snapping her fingers twice, giggling as she swung Audrianna back into her arms, continuing the dance. "Yes, I think you did mention something about that. It turns you into Ginger Rogers. Right?"

For once, Audrianna was not being made to feel ashamed of her drunken behavior, and that, in turn, did make her a better dancer. She moved more and cared less. She let pain go and succumbed to the pleasure of pure motion, enjoying being led by a woman who had absolutely no reason to exude such confidence.

"Do you enjoy being a tabloid star?" Audrianna asked her.

Maria laughed. "We did cover quite a few topics in our luncheon, didn't we?"

Audrianna would not be put off. "Do you?"

"No," Maria replied. "Had this catastrophe not befallen us, I would still be happily ensconced in the forest of Aldebaron, tending to my garden, moon bathing by the lake."

"What is Aldebaron?"

"Aldebaron was the name of my estate on Gavrilek," Maria explained with a shy little smile. That was something Audrianna had not seen from her before—*vulnerability.*

"Who lived there with you?" Audrianna asked

"Just me."

"You lived there by yourself?" Audrianna asked, shocked at the idea of Maria living alone, without servants, without *Lorna.*

"Oh—I had my books, of course." Maria nodded, misinterpreting Audrianna's reaction. "How clever of you to feel an injustice for the characters; they *are* amongst my closest friends." She flashed that girlish smile again.

Audrianna blinked. "What about Lorna?"

"Let me know the intent of your question, please," said Maria, gently.

"You've said you were lovers. Didn't Lorna live there with you?"

Maria studied Audrianna's eyes, taking her time to answer. "We were estranged when Gavrilek fell," she eventually divulged. "Excuse me for a moment, dearest. I've forgotten something." Maria doubled back to the table then returned to Audrianna with a small silk sack. Grinning, she held it out.

"Your request," Maria declared mysteriously. "I hope you find it satisfactory. My craftiness is quite stunted when I work within the confines of a such a strict deadline."

Audrianna emptied the contents into her hand: a simply constructed braided leather thong in the style of a dream catcher. Inlaid with crystals and emeralds still crusty with dirt, it was the image of the Gavrilekian rune branded into Maria's skin: The Wind Is My Master. Audrianna tuned into that wavelength.

"Thank you, Maria. You made this, didn't you?" she said, turning it over in her hands and admiring it.

"Yes, is it so obvious?"

Audrianna scoffed. "On the contrary, if you hadn't handed it to me with such enthusiasm, I never would've known you were the craftsman. It's um," she lifted her eyebrows, searching for the right words, "not very fashionable," she finished with a chuckle.

"I apologize. I didn't realize fashion was such a serious consideration," Maria replied, laughing along with her.

"No, no. It isn't. Not for me—for you. I think it's..." Audrianna swatted her hand down, abandoning the rationale. "I think it's great. Put it on me, please."

She handed Maria the necklace and turned around, lifting the back of her hair.

Maria fastened the clasp and fixed Audrianna's hair over her dress. "There," she said.

The beat of the song slowed and she reengaged Audrianna in the slower dance. Their connection was palpable again; but this time, neither resisted it. Audrianna let her hand drift to the nape of Maria's neck while they danced, searching with her fingers for her branding—the same Gavrilekian rune which Audrianna now wore around her neck, the device protecting her thoughts. Once touched, Audrianna traced her fingers around the design, questioning Maria with a whisper. "Is this so important?"

"Yes," Maria answered, softly.

"Why?"

"Because it is the psalm of our spirit, dearest," Maria replied, pulling Audrianna closer, pressing their cheeks together. "It is the psalm to which we were created. The Gods sire children through song. They create a verse together and transpose it into their individual dimension. Discarded notes and passages: mistakes—they put into the Biverse. The result is you, your tawn, and me. We are the psalm entitled, The Wind is My Master. It is a unique expression of our identity."

Men with trays came forth from the kitchen, forcing Audrianna to reorient. "It's time to eat," she said.

"Hold please." Maria caught her by the hand and Audrianna turned around. "We can disagree on a great many things," she said, "but on this particular issue, we cannot. Please tell me you know what I've said is true."

"It makes no difference whether I believe you or not, Maria," Audrianna quietly replied, conflicted.

"It makes every difference." Maria insisted. "If you know I'm telling the truth, then you can never hate me. You can be very, very ill with me, but you can never hate me." They stared intently into one another's eyes and Maria lay down her cards. "Do you really hate me, Audrianna?" she whispered. "Or are you just trying to make me pay for the pain I've caused you?"

Audrianna's head wound suddenly began to pulsate, and the pain was incapacitating. She staggered, dropping first to her knees, then to all fours. Blood drops spattered on the floor. She reached up for Maria but shadows snuffed out her vision. She quickly sank into unconsciousness.

CHAPTER 3

Audrianna jerked awake in complete darkness; her sweaty, naked body was stuck between two sheets. The gentle sonance of someone sleeping next to her elevated her state of panic. Holding her breath, she inched her fingers over and touched a woman's soft thigh. *God!* Audrianna flogged herself internally. All right—fine. She had obviously gotten drunk and slept with Maria, but that did not mean she had to stay overnight in the bed with her. She would find her clothes and somehow get back to her own bed unseen.

"Audri, where are ya goin' honey?" Not Maria's voice.

Kendis.

Audrianna let her breath escape. She was still intoxicated—that must be it. Her mind was playing tricks on her. A localized headache pounded the front of her skull; she reached up and touched the tender, uneven tract of skin on her forehead and winced.

"Audrianna?"

Again. Kendis' voice.

"Yes?"

A slender set of arms wrapped her up from behind, falling backwards and giggling. "Come'ere. It's not time to get up yet. Or don't cha wanna make love anymore?"

Untrusting of her ears, Audrianna stretched out her hands in the direction of the voice. Her fingertips delved into a curtain of coarse African hair. "Oh God, Kendis. Am I dreaming, or are you really here?"

Kendis gently nibbled the nape of Audrianna's neck and said, "You know I wouldn't go into your dreams."

"No, you wouldn't, would you?" Audrianna choked, sounding the alarm of her distress. Kendis rolled over on top of her, lighting her face with lustrous green eyes.

"What's wrong, honey?" she asked, stroking Audrianna's hair. When Audrianna failed to reply, Kendis repeated her question. "Audri, what's wrong? You know I can't hear your thoughts, so you're gonna hafta tell me what's goin' on."

Audrianna let out a sobbing sigh of relief. "I thought you were dead, Kendis!"

"Oh, honey. You've had a nightmare, that's all," Kendis murmured, gently helping her sit up. "Shh, honey, shh ... Nobody's dead." She smothered Audrianna's face with soothing little kisses. "You've just had a nightmare. Everything's okay now."

Audrianna took a deep sniveling breath. Through chattering teeth she said, "It was so real, Kendis. All I could think was—" She stopped chattering. Suddenly, it did not matter. None of it did. The only thing real was the lessons she had learned. Tightly wound tension released a sudden surge of warmth beneath her breastbone. She cupped Kendis' face in her hands. "I love you," she said, then pressed her finger to Kendis' lips when she tried to respond. "Don't talk. Just listen for a second. Okay?"

The sound of their breathing enhanced the amity, and for several moments that was all Audrianna wanted to hear. In stark contrast to her usual behavior, she rolled over on top of Kendis. Drawing tiny breaths, she lingered on her exhalations. "I love you and I trust you, Kendis. Please always talk to me about what is going on in your world—even if you don't think it is something I'll want to hear. Promise me that you will."

Kendis nuzzled Audrianna's neck. "Sure, honey. If that's what you'd like."

Hearing flippancy in her voice, Audrianna responded, "I'm serious. Is there something you need to tell me, Kendis? Right now? Is there something I need to know?"

Kendis looked up at her, licking her lips. "Like what?"

"Are you doing something with Devon behind my back?"

Kendis hesitated for a moment, then replied, "He told you, didn't he?" She shimmied out from underneath Audrianna, and sat up against the headboard with a sigh.

Audrianna rolled onto her back. In a way, it came as a relief to know her nightmare had some basis.

"You tell me, Kendis," she croaked. "I want to hear it from you."

"We've been dabblin' in the illegal whiskey trade in America. Prohibition agents busted us a few months ago. For the time bein', the federal government has frozen Tru's trust fund, but don't worry, Audri. Prohibition has been repealed now, so we're gonna get the money back. We'll hafta wade through the process, but we'll get it back." She cleared her throat. "What happened to your head?"

Audrianna's fingers brushed her forehead, and she winced. She had no idea what had happened to her head. "Don't change the subject," she said.

"I'm not, Audri. I've been worried about you. I really thought you weren't comin' back? What changed your mind?"

"What?" Audrianna sat up slowly next to her.

"Oh, I'm not complainin', honey," Kendis told her. "You had a right to be angry with me. I shoulda' told ya about bein' my project from day one. I'm sorry 'bout that."

Audrianna's heart began to bump against her ribcage. "That, too," she scoffed. "That's great. What else? How do you know Maria Orsic?"

When Kendis stayed quiet, Audrianna asked again. "Do you know her?"

"I know *about* Maria Orsic because she's famous, honey. I've never actually met her. You know that."

"I don't know what I know, right now." Audrianna stumbled out of bed, kicking over an empty whiskey bottle. "Christ," she cursed, dizzy from rising. She sank back down, quickly realizing that she must've gotten into a spat with Kendis over these very issues and had some sort of drunken psychotic break. Audrianna had not done that in years. What to do now?

She turned her face to observe Kendis' dimly lit profile. The details of their argument would have to be explored, but right now, convalescing from the trauma of such a horribly vivid nightmare was at the forefront of Audrianna's mind. They could talk it out, sure, but sex was a far more compelling authority.

Kendis laughed. "Ha," she said, "Audrianna, I recognize the way you're breathing."

"Do you?" Audrianna tickled her fingertips across Kendis' bare leg.

"Yeah, but it's not gonna work this time. It's my turn to go first. You fell asleep earlier."

"What?" Audrianna withdrew her hand, laughing at her very unromantic, yet Kendis-like response.

"Kendis, Kendis," she teased as she wrenched herself over and straddled Kendis' legs, dragging her downward by the waist. When her head hit the pillow, she leaned over her and said, "That's a deeply scandalous accusation. Where is your proof?"

"That empty whiskey bottle over there on the floor," Kendis replied, interlacing her fingers around the back of Audrianna's neck and pulling her down for a kiss.

"That's circumstantial," Audrianna crooned. "What else do you have?"

"How 'bout that mysterious cut on your head," Kendis offered, running her fingertips across Audrianna's head. "How in the world did ya do this anyway, honey?"

"I don't know," Audrianna grumbled. "Does it look that bad?"

"Yeah, it's pretty bad, honey."

"Kendis, why do you let me drink that much?" Audrianna smacked her playfully on the bottom. "That's probably why I'm having nightmares, too."

"It wasn't my fault, honey," Kendis said. "I came in here and you were passed out cold. I dunno when ya got here, or where ya got the whiskey from."

"Where I got the whiskey from, phish. Really Kendis? I didn't write myself a *prescription* for it if that's what you're implying."

"Huh?" Kendis asked, with an innocent giggle.

"You've just forfeited your turn," Audrianna growled. "I am no longer aroused and therefore you must act quickly to regain my interest."

"Uh-oh. Lemme see what I can figure out," Kendis purred, tracing a circle around one of Audrianna's nipples. "How's that?" she asked.

"That's a good idea."

"Oh, yeah?"

"Yes." Audrianna dangled her head.

"How 'bout this?" Kendis caught Audrianna's face between her palms and met her forehead-to-forehead. She made an energy exchange from there: a bit of her biverse energy for Audrianna's soul. The detonation produced an aphrodisiacal high known as a *headgasm:* that's what Audrianna called it, anyway.

"Oh!" Audrianna crumpled on top of Kendis, wrapped in goosebumps. Mouth hanging open, she pushed herself up and positioned herself between Kendis' eager legs, both of them wet and ready for sex. They ground against each other, groaning. Audrianna's accelerated pace became an issue.

"Too fast," Kendis panted.

The only way Gavrilekians could safely make love was in slow motion, otherwise they risked using up all their biverse energy. At that moment, Audrianna didn't care. "Let me have you however I want right now. You can take whatever you need of my soul to help get you through."

"Whoa, whoa," Kendis said, trying to sit up. "Slow down, Audri."

"Why?" Audrianna became more aggressive. "Why can't we be just a little bit reckless, Kendis?"

"Because it's dangerous, that's why, honey," Kendis replied. She overtook Audrianna with a deliberate snap of the fingers, crawling back on top of her and whispering, "Come back to me, Audri. Wherever you've been, come back to me." She kissed her sweetly on the nose. "I wanna make love as badly as you do—but not like this, honey. If I get lost in this darkness, I'll never find my way out. Do ya understand? Come back to me, okay?"

Audrianna reset herself, embarrassed, but Kendis did not allow her the feeling for long. "There," Kendis said. "I feel ya." She moved over her with slow sensual kissing, moving downward at an excruciating pace. Hiding behind her hands, Audrianna fought closing her legs against Kendis as she hovered on her core with balmy breath.

"Please." She shifted a hand to the back of Kendis' head. "Either do it or don't. Please don't tease me."

"I haven't even begun to tease you," Kendis replied, then she continued her sensual kissing down below, her mouth opening gradually after each kiss. When Audrianna tugged on her hair, Kendis trapped both hands to the bed. "If you lift another finger to rush me," she said, "you'll be very, *very* disappointed."

Frustration tamed Audrianna's immediate sense of urgency and she propped herself up to watch as Kendis opened her folds and licked with one long, slow tongue-stroke.

"Mmm..." Audrianna moaned, gripping the sheets, head dangling backward as Kendis pressed forward with her expert repertoire of cunnilingus. Eyes closing, she imagined Kendis was Maria, tasting her for the first time. Guiltlessly she did it: guiltlessly she muttered, "Make me come with your mouth."

Kendis groaned but her voice was Maria's.

"Oh!" Audrianna let out a shriek of pleasure, falling backwards in the bed, tossing her head side to side as she climaxed to Maria's image. Afterwards, the disgust of what she'd imagined seeped in. A longer than usual silence prompted Kendis to creep up to her face.

"What's wrong?" she asked.

Audrianna rested her arm on her forehead, exhaling. "Nothing. That nightmare really got to me. That's all," she said.

Kendis accepted that, rolling over onto her back and asking, "Did you get things settled with Lorna?"

Audrianna felt her heart stop. "What?"

"Something about your mother? You were meeting him tonight."

"My mother? What!? Oh God." Audrianna stumbled out of bed and searched in the dark for a lamp.

"Audri, what are ya lookin' for?" Kendis asked.

"I'm looking for the light," Audrianna replied. She continued to prospect, finding that none of her paraphernalia was where it should be: her lamp, her pictures. Her entire nightstand was missing.

"Here." Kendis snapped on a light.

Immediately her eyes took in the filmy amber glow of a frosted shade floor lamp. Navajo stitched rugs and Hollywood movie posters hung on the walls. A medium sized metal-framed bed occupied most of the room. Audrianna staggered at the sight. "Where are we?" she asked.

Kendis got up slowly like she was uncertain of the situation and wrapped herself up in a robe. To Audrianna, nudity between them was second nature but Kendis' modesty had a contagious effect. Audrianna looked around for a covering.

"Here." Kendis pulled a sheer costume garb from a dressing screen and threw it over to Audrianna. Audrianna wrapped herself up in it.

"Master?" came the voice of Kiah, Audrianna's adopted son, as he rapped on the door. "They've opened the salon. Thirty minutes 'til show time."

"Thank you, Kiah. I'm up," Kendis replied. To Audrianna she whispered, "I've gotta get ready, honey. You should go home, ya know? Isn't Maria comin' in this evening? I'm sure ya told me that." She walked behind the dressing screen and began sorting through various hanging garments.

Audrianna watched her, unblinking. Her mind seemed frozen. She waited for insight; but none came.

"Audri, I'm worried about you." Kendis glanced over the top of the screen. She unsnapped an iridescent blue gown and pulled it off the hanger asking, "Are ya sick, honey?"

Audrianna sat back down on the bed. "Kendis, I'm very close to coming completely unglued," she said, repeatedly looking around. "Why are we not at home? Have we taken a vacation or something?"

Kendis narrowed her gaze, staring. She pulled on a lamé shawl.

"Kendis!" Audrianna shouted at her. "Please talk to me. Can't you see I'm on the verge of a breakdown? I don't understand what's going on here!" She tented her hands over her nose and mouth, searching inward with her eyes. Still, no theories came to mind as to how or why she had come to be in this unfamiliar situation. She started to hyperventilate.

"Okay, okay." Kendis rushed around the screen and sat down next to Audrianna, wrapping her arms around her. She said, "I'm gonna call Stephanie to come get ya."

Audrianna shook her head. "Stephanie who?"

"Oh my goodness." Kendis rose and retrieved a black rotary telephone from a small cabinet next to the bed, dialing a series of numbers. Holding her hand over the receiver, she whispered, "Audri, I'm not puttin' ya in taxi like this—yes, hello?" She pulled her hand away and spoke into the receiver. "Princess von Hohenlohe, *bitte*—Kendis Lewis—*danke schön.*"

Stretching the telephone cord out so she could stand over Audrianna, Kendis waited for Stephanie to come on the line. She lifted Audrianna's chin with her forefinger and took a very serious look at the injury on her head. "Hi, Steffi," she said, dropping Audrianna's chin and pulling her face into her tummy, stroking her hair. "Will you come and get Audrianna? I hafta be on stage in fifteen minutes and she isn't actin' herself at all. I don't wanna put her in a taxi: there's no tellin' where she'd end up at." Pause. "Yeah, she's been drinkin' but I think it's more than that. It looks like she's taken a good whack on the head from somethin'—I came up here after rehearsal this afternoon and found her passed out in my bed. She woke up a little while ago and can't seem to remember anything about anything." Another pause. "Okay, just a second." Kendis handed Audrianna the telephone and whispered, "Here, honey. She wants'tuh talk to you."

Audrianna reluctantly accepted the phone. She pressed it to her ear and swallowed. "Hello?"

"Audrianna, what *is* the matter, darling?" Stephanie's voice said. "You know they're all coming in tonight. If this is another one of your schemes to get out of group bonding, it won't work. You know what a bitch Eva is when protocol is broken."

Audrianna felt sick. She glanced up at Kendis, slowly handing back the telephone. She looked around for something to throw up in.

"Hello?" Stephanie called through the earpiece. "Audrianna, are you there? Hello?"

Kendis took the phone and replied, "Nah, it's me again. She handed me back the phone."

A knock came at the door. "Master, can I come in? I need to discuss some changes I made to tonight's score."

Kendis dropped the receiver to her shoulder and turned her head. "No, Kiah. I'm still gettin' ready. Send me the changes telepathically and I'll look'um over."

Unable to formulate an alternate plan, Audrianna dove into the corner of the room and pulled a trashcan to her face, vomiting mouthfuls of putrid whiskey.

Kiah knocked more forcefully. "Master, are you all right?"

"Oh my goodness," Kendis muttered in a rush. "Yes, Kiah, please. Just send me the changes and I'll see ya downstairs in a few minutes. Go on now."

Kiah's hesitant footsteps fell away and Kendis spoke quietly into the receiver. "Stephanie please come here and get Audrianna. I think she might need a doctor." She hung up the telephone and grabbed a hand towel off a pedestal sink, wetting it and wiping Audrianna's mouth. She took the trashcan out of her hands, then dragged her across the room and laid her on the bed.

"Kendis," Audrianna panted, weakly. "Please don't send me away with that woman. I barely know her."

"Barely know her?" Kendis sat down with a laugh. "Honey, you've known her a lot longer than you've known me. She's your best friend." She pressed the towel into Audrianna's hairline, absorbing the perspiration.

"Kendis, stop," Audrianna whimpered. "What about the children, the distillery and this ring?" She held her hand up in the air, but there was no ring. Her hand flitted to her neck where there *was* a necklace. "Oh my God. This is her doing," she choked. "She's playing a trick on me! Kendis, she's playing a trick on us!"

Kendis shook her head. "Who? What are ya talkin' about, Audri? You know I hafta be downstairs in justa minute. What is this tantrum all about?" she asked.

"Downstairs for what?" Audrianna cried.

"It's ten o'clock, honey—my nightly performance. I can't cancel now. The audience is already seated."

A knock came at the back door, drawing Kendis' attention. "Kendis let me in! There's a pile of spectators out here!" Stephanie's voice called.

"Kendis." Audrianna clung to her. "Please don't send me away. Whatever has happened, we can work it out. Please let me stay here with you."

Kendis pulled her in and held her tightly, whispering, "Oh my goodness, Audri. You're breakin' my heart. You know ya can't stay here with me—at the island, either. I know Maria is a generous mirror, honey, but frolickin' with another Master Gavrilekian would test the limits of her understanding. We need her! If she finds out about us, our chances of succeeding become much more difficult."

"Succeeding at what!?"

"Kendis!" Stephanie knocked more frantically.

Tugging herself out of Audrianna's clutch, Kendis walked over to the door in her flowing blue show gown and opened the room to Princess von Hohenlohe. Parading inside, Stephanie walked straight up to Audrianna and grabbed her chin, smoothing her hair back, examining her injury. "Gracious, this takes the cake," she muttered, disbelievingly. "I left you alone for three hours. Three hours! How could you have gotten into this much trouble in such a short amount of time?" she demanded.

"You left me sitting alone at the Adlon Hotel so you could sneak off to bed with Fritz!" Audrianna shouted. She had no clue who Fritz was or how she knew that, but it felt like the right thing to say.

Stephanie laughed. "Really darling, and where are you right now? If you insist upon playing the role of the prude, perhaps you should take care not to end up hoary-eyed drunk in the bed of your undercover lesbian lover." She pulled on Audrianna's arm and forced her to stand, "Get up," she said. "We have twenty minutes to make you presentable—Heavens! What are you wearing?"

"That's mine, Steffi," Kendis explained. She scooped Audrianna's bloody dress and undergarments off the floor and handed them to Audrianna. "Just bring the other thing back next time you come honey, okay?" She asked, caressing Audrianna's cheek.

"The next time she comes?" scoffed Stephanie, dragging Audrianna by the hand toward the door. She turned back and said, "Kendis, you do realize that as soon as Maria takes one look at her, she'll probably never be permitted out of the house again?"

Kendis did not reply.

"Maria has no say in my comings and goings," Audrianna snarled.

"Oh that's right, you rebel," Stephanie snorted. "Maria simply provides the roof under which you live, the food that you eat and as much money as you care to spend—not to mention the exorbitant payoff she's made to your husband to keep you from being a source of ridicule, or the comforts and protection she has provided for your son. You're absolutely right—how dare she expect to have any say in your comings and goings?"

Audrianna was so concerned about her own predicament that she had not thought of Devon. She had not thought of

Niklas either, but she was thinking of them both now. She took one last glance at Kendis' encouraging smile.

The door slowly closed.

———•◦•———

Snatching Audrianna's clothes out of her hands, Stephanie wadded them up and jammed them under her arm.

"Give me your other hand," she commanded. "This is very steep here; if you fall you'll break your neck." She helped Audrianna navigate the stairs in silence. When they reached the street, she opened the passenger door to a yellow convertible and Audrianna got into the front seat. Stephanie circled around to take the driver's seat, cranking the engine and starting off down the street.

"All right," she said, momentarily taking her eyes off the road to look at Audrianna. "We're alone now. Please tell me what has happened to you. What are you going to tell Maria? Eva and Hermann will have a field day with this."

Audrianna felt nauseated again; she closed her eyes and became dizzy. "I'm so sorry, but I need to throw up," she said.

Stephanie pulled the car off the road and held Audrianna by the back of her garment while she opened the door to vomit. After a few rounds of retching, Audrianna closed the door and sat back in her seat, head throbbing. She shivered; her respirations became labored. Something was wrong with her body, but she didn't know what it was.

"Audrianna." Stephanie reached over, touching her arm, then her cheek. "Oh darling, you're burning up with fever. My God. Tell me what happened to you. Did Lorna hurt you?"

"I don't know," Audrianna whispered. "I don't remember what happened, but I'm very sick, and it's from more than just alcohol."

Stephanie put the car into gear and spun back onto the road, provoking a series of honks from other vehicles. "I'm stopping at Eva's house. It's much closer than Maria's or Magda's."

"Eva would just as soon see me dead, wouldn't she?" Assuming any of her memories were correct, Eva Braun was the same Master Gavrilekian Audrianna had killed eighteen years earlier when she and Lorna were escaping from Switzerland.

"I'm not leaving you there alone," Stephanie told her. "I'm stopping there for help. She keeps half a dozen physicians on hand at all times to treat Hermann's illnesses—or feed him—or wash him—or who knows what else."

Audrianna felt herself slipping towards unconsciousness. "Who is Hermann?" she mumbled.

"Hermann Göring: Eva's mirror." Stephanie pulled the car to a stop in front of a solid stone mansion with Corinthian columns, adding, "Truly you must be very ill not to remember that fat lug. He is completely unforgettable—in an abhorrent way, of course."

Servants converged on the driveway as Stephanie opened the door. "I'm here for help," she shouted, pointing to Audrianna. "Quickly, get her into the house and call whatever physician is available."

A muscular middle-aged man with a prominent gray mustache rushed from the house and reached over the car door, lifting Audrianna with a groan. He carried her into the house to an elevator, then a dark cold bedroom. Stephanie came in behind him and told him to leave, shutting the door on the remainder of the staff.

"Darling, sit up," she said as she helped Audrianna sit up on the side of the bed. She pulled her soiled dress from underneath her coat. "We have to get you back into this before they all get here. If you're found in that outfit, everyone in the theatre district—all of our friends—will be in Sachsenhausen Concentration Camp before sunrise, including Kendis."

Audrianna tried to lift her arms but found a deficit in her fine motor skills. Her instinct was to panic but she felt too ill manage it.

"Never mind," Stephanie told her, maneuvering Audrianna into a one-armed embrace. She pulled her out of Kendis' costume gown, then yanked the other dress over her head and edged her back into bed, pulling the covers up to her chin.

"Princess von Hohenlohe?" A man's voice called from outside the door. He rapped a couple of times.

Stephanie kicked Kendis' dress under the bed and replied, "Yes, come in." She straightened her outfit, and smoothed her hair.

A green-eyed *SS* physician in full dress uniform entered the room. He took Stephanie's hand and kissed it. "Good evening, Leyonelle. I am Dr. Grawitz, the senior medical officer on duty. How may I help?"

"Thank you, Dr. Grawitz." Stephanie gestured to Audrianna. "Baroness von Traugott is unwell. Will you attend to her please?"

Dr. Grawitz pivoted quickly, giving Audrianna a startled look. "Forgive me Leyonelle," he exclaimed. "I did not recognize you!"

Audrianna blinked, but gave no other response.

The doctor bellowed over his shoulder for someone to bring his medical bag. "Baroness von Traugott, how have you been hurt?" he asked, flipping on a light.

Audrianna could not talk. She quickly lost interest in trying.

"Baroness?" he repeated, glancing at Stephanie. "Can't she speak?"

"I don't know Dr. Grawitz!" Stephanie threw her hands in the air. "I don't know what happened."

Two more green-eyed SS doctors came into the room with medical bags, followed by a team of nurses. The physicians examined Audrianna with various medical instruments, conversing amongst themselves. Audrianna felt oddly disconnected from her body.

"Temperature: 38.9; heart rate: 45 beats per minutes. May I have some ice and 650 milligrams of aspirin, please?" one of the physicians asked a nurse.

"Leave the aspirin," Dr. Grawitz countered. "Bring ice."

"She's burning with fever, Dr. Grawitz," Stephanie shouted. "Surely a dose of aspirin is called for."

Dr. Grawitz gave her an annoyed look. "Forgive me, madam, but Baroness von Traugott has a traumatic injury to her head and now exhibits signs of bleeding inside her brain. Aspirin is contraindicated where bleeding is suspected—as I'm sure you remember from your work as a nurse."

Stephanie covered her mouth. "Bleeding inside her brain? Will she recover?"

Dr. Grawitz smiled thinly. "Leyonelle, this conversation should be postponed until after I've completed my examination. Don't you think?"

Nodding, Stephanie pushed her way through the crowd of caregivers, making her way to the head of the bed. She kissed Audrianna on the cheek. "I'll be back, darling. They'll be arriving soon; I should meet them at the door."

Not wanting to be left alone in a room full of Eva's players, Audrianna tried to reach for Stephanie, but her arms felt like lead—too heavy to move. Lifting her head, she tried to speak but became dizzy and started to vomit. Stephanie quickly turned her head to the side to keep her from choking, holding her hair away while she heaved. She whispered, "Poor, poor darling. I should never have let you go alone."

"Princess von Hohenlohe, if you please," Dr. Grawitz urged her out of the way. After she was gone, he directed the nurses to undress Audrianna and tidy her and change the bed linens while he spoke to the other physicians. Audrianna strained to hear them, but like everything else, it was too much effort to maintain. She had never felt so ill in her entire life and tried to deal God her dwindling life for a few last minutes with her deceased mother. It didn't work. Audrianna remained alive and her mother remained dead.

"Dr. Grawitz." One of the nurses looked up with a dire expression. "She isn't wearing any undergarments."

Dr. Grawitz came over to the bed. With an angry edge he said, "Baroness von Traugott, have you been violated?"

Unable to mount an understandable reply, Audrianna simply moaned.

"Will you examine her, Doctor?" the nurse asked.

Considering for a moment, Dr. Grawitz replied, "No, I will wait further instruction from Maria on this matter. Let us get on with our other treatment. Put the ice bags underneath her arms and bring me a basin with saline and some gauze." He gently inspected Audrianna's cut with his fingers, accepting the basin with saturated gauze when it was offered to him. "This is a mess," he grumbled, wiping the bloody crust from Audrianna's head. He called behind to one of his colleagues. "Dr. Rascher, I'll have the top plastic surgeon here. Please arrange it."

"Dr. Zeitfeld is a pioneer in the field of facial reconstruction," Dr. Rascher replied.

"Fine, summon him at once before the wound festers. What toxicologist do we know?"

"Bruno Tesch."

Dr. Grawitz nodded. "Fine, and what neurosurgeon?"

Dr. Rascher's expression became pained. "Dr. Guttmann is Germany's top neurosurgeon, but he is a Jew. I cannot, in good conscience, summon him here to care for one of our masters' mirrors."

Dr. Grawitz stopped cleaning Audrianna's face and tossed the bloody gauze back into the basin. Wiping his hands together, he slowly turned around. "I would not impose my rank upon your conscience, Dr. Rascher—but consider this. If one of us can't make it home—none of us will. That is the troth we've pledged to one another." He gestured to Audrianna. "Here lies one of our master's leyonelles, gravely ill, and I have not the expertise to treat her—do you?"

Dr. Rascher shook his head and Dr. Grawitz continued in an icy tone of voice. "How, then, shall your conscience fare when she dies and we all *lose this game*, Dr. Rascher?" He punched his fist into his palm, shouting, "You will bring Dr. Guttman here with the utmost haste and I will hear no more about who is or isn't a Jew! That is not our concern!"

Multiple pairs of heavy boots came clomping down the hall. The floorboards vibrated with their approach. An armed guard of four Gestapo in black trench coats blitzed the room, positioning themselves in four corners, weapons drawn. A separate party came in shortly afterwards: Maria, Stephanie, Magda Goebbels, Eva Braun and an obese man in formal Nazi dress whom Audrianna recognized, but couldn't say from where.

Maria rushed to the bed, climbing onto the mattress. She collected Audrianna in her arms, fretting over her. Her beauty was ennobled by her true state of worry. "Dearest, say something, please." She intertwined their fingers, pressing Audrianna's palm against her face. When Audrianna said nothing, she looked to Dr. Grawitz. "Why doesn't she respond to me?" she asked.

Dr. Grawitz bowed his head. "Master, Baroness von Traugott has neurological deficits consistent with either a traumatic brain injury or poisoning—perhaps both. Also," he lifted a finger, "I suspect the possibility of a sexual assault: she wasn't wearing any undergarments upon her arrival."

"Absolutely barbaric," Eva Braun calmly said. She called one of the guards over and told him, "I want the exact whereabouts of Ernst Röhm, Gregor Strasser and Kurt von Schleicher. This was a bad move, and it's their final one. Prepare the Führer's plane for Munich and place the *LSSAH* on alert. I want a regiment of fifty men guarding this house and another fifty patrolling the grounds. Update me on the status of all our people within the hour and *find* the Consciousness of Gavrilek!"

"The Consciousness of Gavrilek is my jurisdiction, not yours," Maria said without looking at Eva. "I'll not have him witness his mother in this state." She smiled at Audrianna. "Close your eyes, dearest. Rest. Tru is safe."

Audrianna closed her eyes but dizziness overwhelmed her. She heaved and wretched in Maria's lap. "Towel, please," Maria ordered, clapping her hands for emphasis. She wiped Audrianna's mouth, then cleaned herself off. Afterwards, she handed it back to a nurse and lowered Audrianna gently to the bed. Audrianna dared not close her eyes again.

"Go and find Tru." Eva placed her hand on her man's shoulder, muttering under her breath.

Maria snapped her head around. "I am the Master Protector of the Consciousness of Gavrilek. I make the decisions regarding his welfare."

"Tell him to come here," Eva said. "He need not see his mother or even know that she is here."

"No," Maria replied, simply.

"He needs to be under guard," Eva growled. She looked to Magda. "He must be here."

Considering for a moment, Magda said, "Maria, your leyonelle has been viciously beaten and raped. It is conceivable that—"

"She hasn't been raped," Stephanie interrupted Magda, shaking her head. "That's not true." She ran her hands nervously down her sides, searching the room with her eyes. She needed a cigarette. Somehow, Audrianna knew.

"How would you know she hasn't been raped, Stephanie?" asked the obese man. "You weren't with her."

Stephanie narrowed her eyes. "I beg your pardon, Hermann?"

"Stephanie, please consider your company before you engage yourself. We must present a unified front to our subordinates." Magda leaned in with a warning.

Stephanie bit the inside of her cheek and Eva used that brief abeyance to dismiss her entire troupe from the room. After they left, Hermann walked over to the telephone and dialed a series of numbers. He took another jab at Stephanie while waiting for someone to come on the line.

"I know you and Audrianna were at the Adlon Hotel this afternoon. You were off spooning with the Führer's adjutant and Audrianna was sitting at the bar going blind on whiskey. What a perfect disgrace the pair of you are."

"Not now, Hermann, please," Eva pleaded, jiggling his arm.

"Oh, let him gab, Eva," Stephanie laughed. "He's clearly very proud of his surveillance, rightfully so. It must have been sheer torture to leave the comfort of the refrigerator to gather intelligence on us."

Magda touched Stephanie on the wrist and said, "Please stop."

"I may be fat," Hermann barked, "but you're a slut!" He then pointed at Audrianna. "And she's a drunk!"

Maria's posture stiffened.

"You pompous pig!" Stephanie shouted. "I *enjoy* pleasures of the flesh—yes. That does not make me a slut! Audrianna has an unpleasant personality when she drinks—yes, but that *hardly* makes her a drunk!"

"*Hallo*," Herman averted his eyes, speaking into the telephone receiver. "Assemble the leaders of the *SA* rampage at the Bavarian Interior Ministry along with the chief of the Munich police. Wait for Hitler and Hess to arrive: this is Operation Hummingbird." He hung up the phone and continued to berate Stephanie. "Neither of you are deserving of your stations. If we lose this game, it will be because of the both of you!"

Maria spoke up. "You are out of line, Hermann."

"Indeed," Magda agreed. "Not only is that statement insulting, it is also incorrect."

Dumbstruck by the reproach, Hermann fell silent.

"Hermie, it's okay. Come for a hug." Eva outstretched her arms. "We'll discuss it later in private," she said.

Stephanie fluttered her eyelashes. "Yes, Hermie. Come for a hug. I have a *strudel* in my pocket for you."

Magda latched onto her arm and pulled her out of the argument. "Darling, I asked you to stop. Our group is under attack; we cannot afford to squabble amongst ourselves." She opened her tiny designer handbag, extracted a cigarette case, and placed a stick of tobacco between Stephanie's lips, igniting the end with a lighter. "There," she said. "That's better now, isn't it?"

Anchoring the cigarette between thumb and forefinger, Stephanie took a long, deep drag, replying, "No—it's—not." She exhaled smoke between each word. "Please don't placate me." She took one more drag and flicked the cigarette at Hermann.

"*Autsch! Autsch!*" Hermann jumped back. He brushed the ash from his uniform and lunged at Stephanie, his hands reaching for her throat.

Eva and Magda snapped their fingers simultaneously, shouting in unison: "Be still!" At once, Hermann and Stephanie both fell stiff and silent. Eva and Magda started into a tense discussion regarding which of their mirrors had started the fight.

From where she lay, Audrianna could see Maria's eye color had begun to fade: her biverse energy was being depleted by emotion. Strangely, she was frightened for Maria's loss. She tried to speak again, to alert her, but still, she could not formulate words. She tried moving her arms and legs: that didn't work either. Audrianna was trapped in her body. She could shift the position of her eyes, but nothing else.

A forceful knock came upon the door. "Master?" called a deep voice urgently. "Master, I must see you!"

"Not now," Eva snapped. The door opened anyway and Eva turned on a hulking, snub-nose man in a rage. "I said, not now! Are you deaf, Oskar?"

Oskar. Audrianna's eyes widened in terror. Oskar was Eva's hawk: her assistant. He was the man who had brutalized Devon's father at his refugee hospital in Switzerland 20 years ago; he'd brutalized Lorna in her home her that last fateful night—the night Audrianna had slain both him and Eva. Here he was again: another body, another lifetime.

"I'm sorry, Master," Oskar rushed in panting, "but I have news to report that cannot be delayed."

"What is it?" Eva turned to him and asked.

Oskar licked his lips, glancing at Maria, then engaged Eva in a telepathic conversation. Afterwards, he burst into tears.

"All right, all right." Eva shoved him towards the door. "Take him to quarantine." She directed the guards. "If you see anyone else crying, take them, too."

After the door closed, there was a long-winded lull that came to an end when Magda lit up a cigarette and said, "Really, Eva, the drama of silence only works on humans—none of whom are currently conscious." She exhaled a stream of smoke, looking around at Stephanie, Hermann and Audrianna. Nobody appeared alert, but Audrianna was at least listening.

Eva fingered an etched crystal vase on a nearby pedestal, calmly replying, "I'm not being dramatic, Magda. I'm resisting the influence of anger." She seized the vase and flung it into one of the oriel windows, splintering the glass. She turned around and pointed her finger at Maria. "You!" she shouted. "What a stellar job you've done at *making Lorna behave!*"

The cords in Maria's neck stood out. "Please explain that statement," she said, slowly standing up.

"I've just received my personnel report," Eva spat. "Lorna is absent without leave."

Maria took a step forward. "I do hope you aren't suggesting culpability on my part," she said icily. "I've provided Lorna with the only shred of contentment he's had this lifetime. If he has abandoned his duty as you say, it will have been because of the despicable way he's been treated by you."

Magda stepped between Eva and Maria, widening her arms to keep them apart. "We don't have time to indulge this ridiculous rivalry. I am sorry to tell you both, but neither of you has the authority over Lorna you believe you should have. Lorna does whatever appeals to Lorna at any given time—that's it." She wagged her finger to the side. "If Lorna has run off again, he likely has his own agenda in mind. Now, we'll have no more of this. My agency will assume responsibility for investigating this attack and for locating Lorna; when he returns, he will be placed under my command. Maria," she turned to her, "I would prefer it if you brought The Consciousness of Gavrilek here, and you, yourself remain here until Operation Hummingbird is complete. But that is your decision."

"The Consciousness of Gavrilek will stay where he is," Maria whispered. "And *we* certainly will not remain here." She turned around, snapped her fingers, and lifted Audrianna into her arms, heading for the door. "Good evening," she finished.

The door opened from the outside and Maria stepped into the hallway. Dr. Grawitz bowed his head. "Master, I've arranged the top physicians to care for her."

"Thank you, sir. Please direct those you've summoned to my estate—"

"Wait, wait. Hold up, hold up." A pear shaped man in casual civilian clothes ran down the hall. He did a quick pat down of Audrianna and said, "Master, put her down for a minute. Trust me on this one." He encouraged Maria and Audrianna to the floor, then doffed his rucksack. He pulled out a palm sized quartz crystal and flourished it over Audrianna's head. "Her energies are unequal. She's broken a chakra. It must be quickly identified and repaired."

Oh, brother. Who was this quack? Audrianna wondered.

Maria elbowed him out of the way. "Not now, Rich," she groaned, lifting Audrianna up again with a snap.

"There. There!" Rich pointed to Audrianna's face. "See that? An exaggerated nystagmus is a definitive presentation of a broken crown chakra—There! She did it again."

"She's rolling her eyes," Maria told him. "Likely at you, Dr. Curtis. Lest you forget, my mirror is also a physician and not at all inclined toward heretical medical practices. Dr. Grawitz," she nodded at him, "please direct the physicians you've summoned to my estate. We'll be waiting for them there. Come along, Rich."

"Yes, Master," Dr. Grawitz bowed his head. Then, Maria took Audrianna home to begin a new, tortuous existence.

"What is the prognosis, Doctor Guttman?" Maria rose from her desk chair, wringing her hands. Twelve hours after awakening in Kendis' bed in a state of confusion, Audrianna was now completely paralyzed except for her eyes. At times she wished to sleep, but the impulse was overridden by ongoing nausea, dizziness and pain: Maria had nursed her through the night. Now, Audrianna was as just as anxious to hear her prognosis as Maria seemed to be.

Dr. Guttman washed and dried his hands. "I'm afraid my exam supports Dr. Grawitz's preliminary diagnosis. Baroness von Traugott has suffered a traumatic brain injury that has rendered her virtually comatose." He removed a radiological film from his briefcase and held it up to the light. "She has a metal object—presumably a bullet—lodged here," he pointed to a bright white spot in the film, "very close to the surface of her forehead. It was unloaded with only half of a charge, I think: a dud, in other words. If the bullet had struck true, Baroness von Traugott would certainly have perished." He put the film down and shrugged. "Perhaps it would've been better that way, because now—"

"Sorry I'm late." Rich bumbled into the room, planting a kiss on Maria's hand. Taking off his rucksack, he leaned against the wall and propped his hands on his considerable hips. "So, uh... What'd I miss?" he asked.

Dr. Guttman stared at him first, then gave Maria a questioning look. After a moment, a light went off in Maria's head. "Forgive my manners, Dr. Guttman," she said. "This is my personal physician, Dr. Richard Curtis. I've asked him here; he'll be in charge of Baroness von Traugott's care after you've gone."

Terrific. Audrianna wasn't sure whether to laugh or cry—not that she was currently able to do either.

Dr. Guttman stroked his beard, examining Rich with curiosity. "Extraordinary. What school did you attend, sir?"

Rich scratched his head. "Yeah, there're a number of ways to answer that question, Dr. Goodson."

"Gutt—man." He hyper-enunciated his name. "It is Dr. *Guttman.*"

A colossal smile spread across Rich's face. "Dr. Guttman, I'm sorry. Which specific school are you inquiring about? I've been to a several of them."

Dr. Guttman looked down at Rich through his spectacles. "Medical school, sir."

"Oh, right, medical school. That would be *Stanford.*"

"I see." Dr. Guttman replied.

Snapping his fingers into his palm, Rich winked at Dr. Guttman and said, "California, U.S.A. That's what you were asking in your mind, right? Where Stanford was?"

Dr. Guttman appeared fascinated. "Yes—California—simply extraordinary. Well, Dr. Curtis, I was using this cerebral angiography to illustrate the extent of Baroness von Traugott's injury." He held the film back up to the light and pointed at various sections of the brain. "As you can see in this example, the bullet is restricting blood flow to the area of the pons. Because the pons is considered the message center of the brain, damage in that area will prohibit the body from receiving messages sent by the conscious mind—if the conscious mind is still being employed. There is no way to truly quantify consciousness, especially when a person is in such a state as this." He gestured to Audrianna.

"Will she recover?" Maria asked.

Dr. Guttman put the film back into his briefcase. "People *have* come out of these states," he said. "But it isn't likely."

"Is there nothing to be done?" Maria pressed, urgency building. "Can the bullet be removed?"

Dr. Guttman sighed. "Presently, the bullet is acting as a plug. If the plug is pulled a hemorrhage will occur, undoubtedly hastening her demise. I am sorry Frau Orsic, but I have no advice to give other than keep her as comfortable as you can."

Rich held his chin, thinking. "She'll need a feeding tube placed, I'd think."

"Of course. Of course," Dr. Guttman readily concurred. "Afterwards, I wouldn't shy away from administering a glass or two of wine through it on occasion. Wine does have the uncanny ability to produce the drillings of one's soul." He patted Maria on the shoulder, finishing, "It would be nice if we had a way to teach the healthy areas of the brain tasks which have been lost by the others. The brain is quite adaptable. I feel certain if new neural highways could be formed, injuries such as this could be overcome."

He gathered his belongings and Maria went to her mahogany roll top desk. "What is your fee, Dr. Guttman?" she asked.

"I would suffer the trials of Job before collecting money on the information I've just delivered." Dr. Guttman put his hat on and turned around at the door. "Goodbye. God bless you both."

"That's very kind, Dr. Guttman, but we are not recognized by God." Maria sat in the desk chair and opened the tambour, revealing small drawers, compartments and an extended writing surface with a pullout ivory slide. She took out a piece of paper and a fountain pen and inkwell, saying, "You are Jewish, are you not, Dr. Guttman?"

"Yes."

"If you are unwilling to accept money for your time, I insist you have this." Maria dipped the pen in ink and scribed a short notation, then fanned it dry. "Sometime in the near future, you will want to leave Germany. This document will allow you and your family safe passage." She folded the letter by three and sealed it with a green wax seal, impressing her signet; she rose and handed it to Dr. Guttman. "God bless *you*, Dr. Guttman," she said.

Slow to respond, Dr. Guttman slipped the letter into is inner pocket, then doffed his hat as he left. Afterwards, Maria went and sat down on the bed facing Audrianna. She took her hand. "I don't believe it, Rich," she said. "She's here. I don't have to hear her thoughts to read those eyes."

Audrianna blinked a couple of times to indicate conscious effort. It was an idea with only a remote chance of working, of course, communicating through eye blinks, but it was the only thing she knew to do. It was the only thing she *could* do.

"There's an idea," said Rich. "Why not take her necklace off and see if she'll talk to you telepathically."

"I can't take it off, Richard." Maria sounded annoyed. "That's something only *she* can do. She has to make that decision. No one else. That's how the device was crafted."

"I never understood those devices."

"It's fortunate you don't have the power to construct one, then."

Rich nodded in agreement, saying, "You're right. If my mirror were in this situation, and I had constructed the device, which kept us from communicating, I'd be a complete basket case by now. I'm glad I don't have that power."

Eyes cast downward, Maria jutted her jaw and said, "I'm not sure what *basket case* means. It sounds eerily akin to American slang, Dr. Curtis. Are you speaking to me in slang?"

Rich walked over to the window and peeped down. "Yeah, it means unable to function normally due to overwhelming anxiety."

"That's absurd." Maria minutely shook her head. "It's a wonder the entire group isn't infected with emotional distemper—what with a concept like that polluting your minds."

"Some say it is."

"I beg your pardon?" Maria snapped.

"There are those who say our group *is* infected with emotional distemper—and not just the group, either—the entire community. Some say if we don't act quickly to find a cure, our species will soon be extinct."

"Darling, I must insist you limit your choice of periodicals," Maria grumbled. "Although Princess von Hohenlohe would have it differently, *GSpot* and *Contempo* are unreliable news magazines. Have you insufficient medical journals to read? Should I order you some more?"

Looking over his shoulder, Rich laughed and changed the topic. "I was told that Hitler and company left early this morning to eliminate Ernst Rohm and the other top *SA* officials. General Göring—I hear—is out rounding up the stragglers here in Berlin to execute a similar play."

Clearly exhausted, Maria closed her eyes and massaged her temples. "I am unconvinced that Ernst Rohm and his team were the perpetrators of this attack," came her level response. "Eva was looking for an opportunity to destroy them. This was it."

Rich turned around. "You think Eva did this?"

"Don't be daft," replied Maria. "It is no secret that Eva desires satisfaction from Audrianna's notorious insult, but she wouldn't act on that impulse—harming a leyonelle in our group is an excommunicable offense—you know that. She would lose everything she has. No, I'm simply saying that she has monopolized on this strike."

"Yeah, well, let's get to this." Rich clapped his hands together, heading to his ruck sack. "So, I've given this some thought and I think instead of using a feeding tube made out of traditional materials—rubber for instance—we might try an organic apparatus like this." He held up a shoot of bamboo. "It came to me in a vision this morning during *shavasana*: I think that I shall never see, a poem, as lovely as a tree. A tree whose hungry mouth is pressed, against a precious leyonelle breast." He smiled at Maria. "I made that last part up. But, you probably knew that."

Audrianna felt sweat pooling in the sheets. He meant to impale her with that branch. Surely, Maria would intervene. Surely.

"What are the advantages of using bamboo?" Maria asked. She was seriously considering it.

"Lots of advantages," Rich said with a shrug. "Digestion, spiritual healing, mental alertness." He walked over and handed her the shoot, then nudged her with his elbow, winking. "It's an aphrodisiac. Eh?"

Maria took her glasses off, holding her forehead. "You haven't sold me, Rich. How long can she be without food?"

"Food?" he laughed. "Food is not the problem—it's water. Baroness von Traugott has a sufficiently ample weight to be able to forgo a few meals."

Audrianna felt ashamed and Maria seemed somehow to recognize it. Slowly, lifting her head, she stared at Audrianna, then turned to Rich and said, "Is there another mechanism for her to receive water?"

"Well, sure. I can give her intravenous fluids, but—"

"Let us proceed in that manner, please. No feeding tube, for now."

"Master, I was teasing about her weight. She will need sustenance beyond water."

Maria nodded. "Thank you, darling. I am acquainted with human physiology." She got up and positioned herself behind Audrianna, adding, "I intend for her to eat on her own."

"But, she can't chew. She can't swallow."

"She will learn," Maria countered. "I'll remap the neural pathways of her brain with my biverse energy, just as Dr. Guttman conceptualized." She ran a soft hand over Audrianna's skull, then looked up at Rich. "She needs a new message center. Which part of the brain should I employ as a replacement?"

Rich caught on to what Maria was getting at, but he was not convinced. He softened his voice. "Master, I think it's a long shot."

"Another figure of speech, I presume," Maria said, almost resigned to hearing American slang.

"Yes. It means I don't think it's going to work. Even if it does, you put yourself at great risk by utilizing such a vast amount of your own energy for this venture."

Maria was indifferent to his warning. "You forget yourself, Dr. Curtis. I do not seek your counsel beyond the pathology of the brain. Please be so kind as to provide me with an answer."

Sighing, Rich thought about it a moment, then said, "The Temporal Lobe. Here." He gently poked the side of Audrianna's head, continuing, "It's already responsible for language and general understanding, so a control center function would be a natural evolution to—"

Bark, bark, bark.

Maria looked up, and Rich turned around. Jörð was in the doorway, and standing beside him was Devon, holding Rodney in his arms. Both men were visibly worried.

Bark, bark, bark.

Maria got up and greeted them. "Devon, Jörð—come in, please." She kissed Jörð's hand and he gave her a little comforting back rub.

"How are you?" he asked.

"I've had better days," Maria replied.

"I'm sure."

Devon scooted by them and went to his mother, sitting down next to her with Rodney in his lap. He took her hand. "I can't believe this. What did the neurologist say, Rich?" he asked, looking up at Dr. Curtis.

"It's not good news, Tru. I'm sorry," Rich told him. "Good morning, Leyonelle." Rich turned to welcome Jörð to the discussion, kissing his hand.

"Good morning, Dr. Curtis. What have I missed?" Jörð held Devon from behind, running his hand through his hair and keeping it there. His presence was imbued with sentience.

"I was just updating Tru about his mother's condition," Rich said. "There's a bullet lodged in her brain—"

"A bullet!? I was told this was an accident!" Devon cried.

"Easy does it," Jörð soothed him. "Accommodate the impact. Let it settle."

It felt strange—seeing two men act that way together. However, a new appreciation of their bond had changed Audrianna's perspective beyond her initial judgement. She grasped the importance of their relationship: Jörð was Devon's much-needed safeguard. She loved him for that.

Rich tentatively continued. "The bullet appears to have been either poorly charged, or poorly aimed. It would've killed her, otherwise."

"I'll speak to you outside, please." Maria crept up and whispered in Rich's ear. To Jörð, she bowed her head and said, "Excuse us, Leyonelle. We'll wait in the hall while you visit."

"Thank you, Maria."

"Master?" Devon called to Maria as she was leaving. When she turned, he said, "Thank you. She hasn't been very nice to you, I know. Thank you for not holdin' it against her."

Clearly taken aback by his statement, Maria simply nodded. She took another look at Audrianna before leaving the room; after she did, Devon spoke to Jörð. "I can't do this without her, Jörð. I know you can find out what happened. Why won't you?" he asked.

"I am *mystery*, you are *truth*. If we start trying to change each other, our union is doomed."

"And where is Lorna?" Devon demanded. "Look!" He lifted Audrianna's hand. "She's not wearing his ring, anymore."

Jörð kissed the top of his head. "I'm not getting involved in this, Tru. What's between your mother and Lorna, is between your mother and Lorna. It makes absolutely no difference now—there's nothing you can do. That helps a little, doesn't it?"

Devon's eyes watered. He petted Rodney's head. "I guess so. I just don't know what to do, now. She was the drivin' force in all of this—the chemistry, I mean. I'm not talented enough to keep goin' on my own."

"Yes you are," Jörð disagreed. "All this time you've been secretly playing for Kendis' team, working toward her objective, hoping that eventually she and Alan Turing will get you all home. Tru, that's fine, but right now, you're stuck on this planet. It may be another hundred years before enough robots can be built to pull this thing off. You have to find a way to help your people survive until then."

Robots? Audrianna had no idea what they were talking about, nor why *she* had been involved; she had no means to procure the answers, either. All she could do was pay close attention to their dialogue—to everyone's dialogue. She must play Sherlock Holmes if she wanted intelligence on the situation.

Devon abruptly turned around. "You know what probably happened," he said, wiping his nose. "She tried to kill herself after I told her about losin' the trust fund: it was such a huge loss of revenue for us, she probably figured there was no point to any of it, anymore. Her disappointment triggered some kinda flare up of her mental illness, I bet."

"Tru, you can't know that."

"Yeah. I do." Devon turned and looked at him. "Kendis told me she'd been acting crazy, ever since she moved in here."

"Crazy like how?"

"Crazy like always talking about my grandmother and how it would be when they were together again in Heaven."

"Oh, dear. She's away with the fairies."

"Yeah, and that's not all of it," Tru said. "Kendis told me she thought Mutti was up to something underhanded regarding Maria."

"Like what?" Jörð asked.

"I dunno—she never said. But, none of us felt right about her suddenly moving in here. I mean, come on, Jörð: she can't stand the sight of Maria one minute, next she's left Niklas and moved in here to begin their bonding courtship. Meanwhile, she's sleeping with Kendis on the side. Uh-uh." Devon shook his head. "There's something more to it—and now Lorna's disappeared, too."

"Lorna has been absent without leave before, Tru."

"Not without telling me, he hasn't," whispered Devon. He pulled a folded paper from his pocket, and handed it to Jörð. "Mutti came by my apartment yesterday and shoved this under the door without knocking. I didn't understand it then, but now I do."

Jörð scanned the paper, then he looked up. "Is this the chemical equation for…"

"Yes. I think it is. She wouldn't give it to me unless she was finished working on it. I think she was trying to tell me she was *finished* with everything."

CHAPTER 4

Curtains were flung open; sunlight flooded the room. Audrianna opened her eyes to Kuniko's brusque introduction of the morning. Three weeks into the attack, Audrianna was still trapped inside her mostly unresponsive body. Thanks to Maria's tireless efforts, she could now chew and swallow on her own, but that was about it. All other voluntary functions remained absent.

Still nestled against Maria's chest, she gurgled on saliva as Maria slowly sat up. Kuniko marched over to the bed, her demeanor frustrated. "You stay out here all night again? You can't keep doing it. You make you-self sick."

Maria reached for her glasses, settling them on her face. She slid out of the bed; her nightgown was soiled with the product of Audrianna's incontinence. "She sleeps when I hold her. When

I put her down, she wakes. I have other bodies to use, should this one fall ill," Maria whispered.

"I'm not talking about body." Kuniko followed her into the bathroom. Noise from the faucet drowned the remainder of their conversation. Audrianna presumed it was more of the same—Kuniko begging Maria to rest, Maria allowing her that say. Occasionally, Maria would pacify her with a gentle touch or a kiss on the cheek. In public, their employer/servant roles were distinct, but here in Maria's suite, the boundaries were quite blurred.

"Something must be done about the eggs." Maria came back to the bed and peeled back the cover; sour odors permeated the air. As usual, she pretended not to notice. She gave directions to Kuniko over her shoulder. "Please tell cook they must be finely minced—and leave off the pâté. She doesn't care for it. I can tell."

That was understatement. The only thing worse than the taste was the aftermath.

"Ma'am," Kuniko stopped Maria as she scooped Audrianna from the bed. "I notice you eyes." She knew Maria's vulnerable areas, and landed the blow accordingly: "If you care nothing for you-self, consider team. No other leaders walking around like this." She gestured to her face.

Drab—not quite yellow, not quite gray. They faded day by day. Audrianna had noticed, too, but there was absolutely nothing *she* could do about it.

Moved at last, Maria nodded and said, "You make an excellent point. Thank you, Kuniko. Please see to the food and the linens. We'll dine at half past seven. Remember, I'm hosting the leaders' luncheon here today."

She carried Audrianna into the bathroom and placed her into a specially constructed seat within the tub, removing her filthy nightgown afterwards. She placed her hand over Audrianna's, closing their fingers around a sponge. Maria began to wash her, branding the know-how into her brain. Afterwards, she dried and redressed her. Once finished, Maria placed her back in the clean bed and disappeared into her own bedroom to bathe and dress. This had become their morning ritual.

On the day after the injury, Maria had relocated her entire command post to her private library so she could work with Audrianna at meal times and between meetings. Audrianna now had a healthy understanding of the Incubus and their objective: Magda, the group's administrator, dealt primarily with finances, fundraising and global propaganda for the Nazi regime. Maria oversaw cultivation of the grape vines fructifying the group's secret weapon called the Vril. In tandem with that occupation was the construction of a spaceship called *Die Glocke*—both were Maria's responsibilities. Eva was responsible for military operations, both earth-based conflicts and scrimmages between major groups in outer space, the purpose of which was still unclear. Hiram Evans, the clown, a Master Gavrilekian from the States who bought into the group for 30 million American dollars commanded German Military Intelligence—the Abwehr.

Evenings, Maria played records on an antique Victrola and danced around the library, practicing whip tricks on the floor. Dressed in a virginal white nightgown and cowboy boots from the American West, this nightly ritual was her method of decompressing, and provided amusement for her. She was a stunningly complex creature, beguiling in every sense of the word

At ten o'clock on the dot Maria climbed into Audrianna's bed with a glass of wine, reading aloud from one of her novels, attempting to teach Audrianna to speak again by branding each individual word into her brain. Despite having her own separate bedroom, she routinely stayed overnight with Audrianna. Those were the only nights Audrianna felt safe enough to sleep. She had no idea if she'd attempted suicide, or if she'd been attacked. From listening to Maria's reports and conversations, neither did she. But it had become clear that Maria was the innocent party in this horrifically confusing turn of events.

Maria stepped through the doorway, now fully dressed in her typical elegant business attire. She held a freshly cut cyan blue tulip—she brought one to Audrianna every morning. Bathed, made up and smelling divine, she leaned over and kissed Audrianna on the temple, as if they were meeting for the first time that day.

"Good morning, dearest," she said. Her eyes were now a radiant emerald green. Audrianna wondered how she had managed such a quick, inconspicuous refuel.

With a disgusted glare at Audrianna, Kuniko walked in with a tray of mushy food and situated it in front of Audrianna, then tied a bib around her neck. She turned to Maria and immediately softened her expression. "Will you join for breakfast today?" she asked, hopefully.

Maria slipped the tulip into a black Wedgwood bud vase and replied, "No, I'm sorry, darling. I haven't the time. Princess von Hohenlohe is due here any moment and I simply must make an appearance at morning formation before they forget who I am."

Kuniko gave her a disbelieving look. "You have to eat," she said.

For once, Audrianna agreed. Maria's beauty was eternal, but she did look gaunt.

"I'll eat this afternoon," Maria said.

But Audrianna knew she wouldn't. She would forget again, just like yesterday and the day before that. The only meal she never skipped was dinner, and that meal she ate alone in her bedroom.

Maria plucked the fork off the tray and squeezed it between Audrianna's fingers, then scooped up a small bite of egg puree. She placed her opposite hand on the side of Audrianna's skull to imprint the lesson and guided her hand toward her mouth. Audrianna did not part her lips.

Ducking her head around to look into Audrianna's eyes, Maria said, "Dearest, it's time to eat."

"Good morning, Master." Hannah came in like a whirlwind and sat down next to Maria's desk, opening her portfolio and pulling out a tablet of paper—this was her morning report. Maria glanced back without further acknowledging her, quickly returning her perplexed attention to Audrianna. Hannah began reading the report out loud. "Last night we experienced a momentary loss of power to the plants in sections F12, B9, M1…"

While she talked, Maria attempted to feed Audrianna again. Again, Audrianna refused. Mildly frustrated, Maria sighed; she shook her head, then put the fork down, gently turning Audrianna's face her way to delve into her eyes. "What is this?" she asked. "A hunger strike?"

Audrianna blinked once for yes and Maria started chuckling. "You're no more unaware than I am," she whispered, kissing her on the forehead. She turned to Kuniko and said, "Very well. Bring me some toast and a dish of prunes, so I may eat alongside my mirror. I have not the strength to fight you both."

"Yes ma'am." Kuniko curtsied, then headed to that task.

"Shall I wait, Master?" Hannah asked.

"No. We needn't make ourselves any later than we'll already be. Continue your report, please. Why do these power outages continue to plague us?"

"The power grid is overtaxed, Master."

"Why?" Maria asked.

"There are defects in the irrigation system. We no sooner repair one leak than another pops up. It almost seems like a contaminant is chewing up the lines, impossible though it may be."

Kuniko came in with a plate for Maria, placing it on Audrianna's tray. She waited for Maria to take a bite of toast before moving on to other chores outside the room.

"The irrigation fluid contains trace amounts of Vril. How much total Vril volume has been lost because of this?" Maria asked.

Consulting her notes, Hannah replied, "Two ounces."

"Well," Maria cocked her head, "with that amount, we can at least be assured that a weapon is not being constructed. Right?" She fed Audrianna a forkful of eggs. This time, Audrianna ate them.

"Yes, Master."

"Still." She flashed Hannah a reassuring smile. "Let us not be complacent with this issue. We'll take next week to walk the lines. Notify the department heads that I'll be in attendance. If we all work together, surely a solution can be identified."

"Yes, Master," Hannah said, putting away her tablet. "Is there anything else before formation?" She started to rise.

"Is there news of Lorna?" Maria asked. "What's being said?" She fed Audrianna another forkful then took another bite of her own food.

Hannah sat back down and adjusted her seat. "Not much. Magda's people are being very secretive and I've only been in the Officer's Club a couple of times since it all happened. I really haven't heard anything." Maria's hand froze halfway to Audrianna's mouth and Hannah quickly stammered, "Of course there are rumors, Master, of course. What I meant to say is, I've heard no credible information regarding Lorna—in fact, I believe there *is* no credible information regarding Lorna." She nodded earnestly.

Maria slowly turned her head, anchoring an unblinking gaze on Hannah. "Darling, I asked you a question. Please don't make me repeat it," she said.

Glancing at Audrianna, Hannah quietly replied, "There's talk of Lorna's involvement in Audrianna's attack, including his direct culpability. Some say they quarreled over a rival lover and Lorna lost his temper. He's chosen a life in hiding over the shame of excommunication or worse. If Baroness von Traugott should die, you would be entitled to collect his biverse energy."

Maria put the fork down and adjusted her glasses. "Surely you can appreciate the absurdity of such a claim," she said indignantly.

"Of course, Master."

"A rival lover!" scoffed Maria. "Lorna has a rotating menu of lovers from whom he siphons energy; it is no secret. Why would they quarrel over such a trivial matter?"

"Forgive me, Master. It is Baroness von Traugott who is rumored to have had another lover, not Lorna. There is some mention of her wearing another woman's clothes the night of the attack. That's what Eva's players are saying, at least."

"That's preposterous," Maria said. "Her dress was tattered and begrimed with blood, I'll admit, but it *was* a part of her wardrobe." She swept her hand across her brow, quickly adding, "Besides which, Audrianna is plighted to me. She would not dishonor that commitment by taking another lover."

Beads of perspiration trickled down Audrianna's face; her respiration accelerated. The idea that Maria would find out about Kendis caused just as much anxiety as believing Lorna had attempted to kill her over it—Maria was the only one who could help her recover from her injuries. Audrianna could not afford to lose her support.

Recognizing her distress, Maria set aside the tray, and retrieved a damp towel from the bathroom to sponge off Audrianna's face. She said, "Hannah, I do hope I can depend upon you to champion my position."

Hannah clutched her satchel to her body, her expression hurt. "Master, I didn't *want* to tell you. I know it's a pile of rubbish; we all do. It's Eva's players stirring the pot."

"Hannah, your locution," Maria snapped. "If you must speak in slang, you must also explain it."

Visibly upset by the reprimand, Hannah began to stutter. "Master, it—it's Eva's team perpetuating the rumors and of course I dispute it, but honestly, *no one* from Magda's camp is talking, so right now all that's certain in this group are the two undeniable facts—Audrianna *has* been shot. Lorna *is* missing. There is no evidence those things aren't connected! How can I effectively defend your position without evidence?" She started to cry.

Maria quickly dropped the rag and went to her, kneeling to her level and pulling her into her arms. She held her until finally Hannah came out of it, wiping her eyes. "I'm sorry for speaking to you that way, Master," she whispered.

"Not at all," Maria said, shaking her head. She rested her hands on Hannah's thighs and said, "If I was harsh with you, I apologize. I *do* understand what a precarious position you're in, my darling, and I certainly wasn't questioning your loyalty—not ever would I do that." She pushed herself up off of Hannah's legs and looked down upon her. "Just do your best with the rumors until we have all the facts in hand. It shan't be long, I'm sure."

Now, let me see you, please." She picked up Hannah's chin and examined her energy loss, then reached into her pocket, pulling a tiny vial of clear liquid. She dispensed a single drop into each of Hannah's eyes. The vial struck a chord in Audrianna's mind, and she remembered.

> *"Take hold of this one please." Maria directed.*
> *Audrianna cinched her fingers around the ampule, tucking it in her palm.*
> *Maria retraced their steps, shutting the doors behind them. "You may open your eyes. Thank you for honoring my request," she said.*
> *Audrianna opened her hand for a look. "What is this?" she asked.*
> *"Now is not the time for explanations," replied Maria. "My astral body is fading. Return to your son and instill two drops in each eye. Quickly."*

Hannah inhaled a short, sharp breath, then shook chill bumps off her arms. She cupped her mouth and breathed, "Oh, my, Master, I really don't deserve to have such an extravagant gift lavished on me." Her eyes were positively luminous.

Audrianna now knew how Maria had refueled so quickly. But, what the hell was in that bottle?

"Certainly you do." Maria tapped her lightly on the nose, smiling. She slipped the vial back into her pocket and clapped her hands once. "Off to assembly with you. Take my elevator." She pointed to the lift in the corner. "I'll be along just as soon as Princess von Hohenlohe arrives."

"Yes, Master," replied Hannah. She then scooted into the elevator and down into the underworld.

Checking the hallway for bystanders, Maria quietly closed the door, then picked up the telephone on the desk. She gave the operator an address. When someone came on the line, she greeted them in German.

"*Guten Morgan*," she said. "My client identification is *Teufelhunden*. I would like to arrange a private meeting with The Needle just as soon as he has available time." There was a pause. "No, that is too far into the future. I am prepared to pay double his standard fee for a timely dispensation of my request." Another pause. "This morning?" She looked at her wristwatch, then propped that hand on her hip, mildly annoyed. "Very well. I'll need to meet him above ground, outside the city—somewhere discreet." She squinted her eyes while she listened to the instructions. "Yes, I am familiar with that area. I'll find my way. Thank you. Goodbye." She hung up the phone and knelt down at her safe, dialing in a code, then transferring several stacks of cash to the top of the desk.

Almost immediately, a single knock sounded on the door and Stephanie paraded inside uninvited. Unpinning her hat, she placed a large brown sack on the floor, then turned around and announced, "Here I am." She spotted the money, but said nothing.

Maria rose and approached her, kissing her hand politely, but without warmth. "Good morning, Leyonelle," she said.

"Good morning, Maria. I apologize for my tardiness. My maid was ill and I underestimated the amount of time required to dress myself. Heavens, what is this?" Stephanie strolled over and peered down at Audrianna's breakfast tray, then looked back at Maria. "Is this what you're feeding her?" she asked. "No wonder she's gotten so thin."

Lifting her chin, Maria replied, "I beg your pardon, Leyonelle, but presently that is all she can handle."

"Oh, hooey." Stephanie waved her off. She marched over to the sack on the floor and brought back a box of designer chocolates, placing them on Audrianna's lap. Opening the lid, she chose a raspberry cream truffle and popped it into Audrianna's open and ready mouth: she'd been feeding her chocolate on the sly from week one. It was the one reprieve Audrianna had from Maria's gourmet mush.

"I appreciate what you're doing, Maria, truly I do, but you've undervalued Audrianna's aptitude," Stephanie said.

That statement struck a nerve. "Of cautious advancement, I may be guilty, madam; of undervaluing my mirror, I am not."

Stephanie lit up a cigarette. "There's no reason to be defensive, Maria," she said. "I'm simply trying to enrich the situation. She needs sumptuous food, music, social culture. If you don't reintroduce her to the things she once enjoyed, you won't have saved her at all."

Maria collected her attaché case from underneath the desk; she began placing the cash inside. "Please don't think I'm displeased with your enthusiasm, Princess. But the time has come, perhaps, to appraise your *enrichments* for what they are and historically have been." She snapped the case shut and turned around. "Bad influences," she finished.

Stephanie snickered out a stream of smoke. "Oh, Maria. How typically priggish of you," she said. Flicking her ash in Audrianna's eggs, she took another leisurely drag and exhaled another insult. "Tell me, how does it feel to be the joke *everyone* gets?"

Audrianna stopped chewing, hurt by the remark and angry with Stephanie for making it. Maria had spent every spare moment the past three weeks selflessly caring for her, feeding her, teaching her to live again. Stephanie should have been ashamed of belittling her.

Though the wound was clearly felt, Maria responded with decorum: "Sometimes a little pain must be endured in order to achieve satisfaction."

Stephanie trampled on her response. "Why must you always pretend to be superior to the rest of us?"

"I do not *pretend* to be anything."

Stephanie snorted. "Don't perjure yourself, Maria. I am Audrianna's closest confidant. No one else in this group may be privy to your arrangement—but I am. Now, what were you saying about pretending?"

Audrianna had no clue what she was getting at but Maria seemed to. Eyes locked on Stephanie, she walked straight up into her face and said, "I don't intend to place myself further in the path of your condescension, madam. Excuse me, but I am late for assembly." She took Audrianna's hand from the bed and brought it to her lips, issuing a grumbling farewell: "*Guten Morgan*, Leyon—" She stopped mid-word—her eyes lifted.

Throwing her entire being into one momentous effort, Audrianna uncurled her fingers and touched Maria's face, purposely meeting her eyes. She could not let her leave feeling unappreciated.

Surprised, Stephanie dropped her cigarette in Maria's prune dish and placed her hand on her heart. She said, "Oh, Maria. How wonderful! She's responding to you. Is this the first time she's done that?"

Maria held Audrianna's palm against her face, closing her eyes and nodding. Audrianna felt her solace—Stephanie tuned into it, too. With a little reluctant eye roll, Steffi dropped her attitude and extended an olive branch to Maria: "To climb steep hills requires a slow pace at first," she said.

"Shakespeare," Maria whispered, opening her eyes.

"Shakespeare, yes." Stephanie cleared her throat. "It is a fairly obscure Shakespeare quote, but I should've anticipated you'd know it. I suppose plagiarism is the worst of all evils, in your mind."

Leading with her inexhaustible grace, Maria replied, "A far greater evil is never quoting Shakespeare." She further displayed her relief by selecting a chocolate from the box to feed Audrianna, kissing her forehead and stroking her underneath the chin. She spoke softly to Stephanie as she left. "Dr. Curtis will be here shortly and I'll be back by midday for leaders' luncheon. If you'd like to stay, I'll have a bottle of Romanée-Conti decanted for you."

"Thank you. I shall," Stephanie responded, then she watched with a keen eye as Maria disappeared behind the closing doors of the elevator that would take her underground. Once gone, Stephanie pulled out a compact and checked her flushed complexion.

"Vexatious woman," she whispered, snapping the compact shut. "If we were in public, she'd never speak to me that way," she complained to Audrianna. She put her compact away and fanned herself. "As it is, she can say *anything* she wants in front of leadership, without fear of reprimand. To others she wouldn't dare oppose me: she *could* be excommunicated." Stephanie walked to the outward wall, unlatched and threw open the window. "God help me, it is hot in here."

It was freezing—the fire had not yet been lit. Hot flashes, mood swings, Audrianna was well-convinced by now—Stephanie was in menopause.

"And that thing about pretending: *Ohhh!*" Stephanie turned around in a tiff, collecting her cigarettes. "I'm sorry, darling, I should not have eluded to my knowledge of your sham relationship, but I really just couldn't let her get away with that." She struck a match and lit her cigarette, talking between draws. "Just think of the pandemonium it would cause if everyone knew the two of you haven't yet bonded. This group would fall apart." She shook the match out. "I never really understood why you let her believe she had a chance. You despised her up until three months ago."

What had happened three months ago that changed Audrianna's mind about Maria? *Had* she changed her mind? Or was it all a smoke screen for something more sinister, as Devon suggested?

Her rant completed, Stephanie took another drag and changed the subject back to herself. "Those snails over at *Contempo* outsold me again last week with their spread on your attack. I'm not sure how they managed it, but they have pictures of Maria peering down at you, looking quite pathetic—although," she blew out her smoke, "they're not very good pictures—reality pictures. They aren't professionally staged. Their entire magazine is filled with similar mediocrities. I really can't understand their rise to popularity. Don't people care about quality anymore?" She shrugged. "Were I not fettered by our friendship, I would publish an account of your suffering the likes of which could not be matched. As it is, I merely acknowledged the attack on page thirteen, between China's ban on jokes and the outcome of Hitler's vigorous potty training."

Audrianna felt she should be grateful for Stephanie's allegiance, but suspected it came with a price.

Coming over to the bed, Stephanie mindlessly stuffed another chocolate in Audrianna's mouth. "Oh, well," she said. "I will counterattack this week—something dynamic, something fresh. I need something readers aren't expecting." She pulled out and opened a small notebook, then sat down next to the bed.

"Darling, you must help me choose. Are you listening? Good. Here are the contenders. Number one: Italian dictator Benito Mussolini wards off the evil eye by touching both of his testicles."

Audrianna started coughing, sputtering chocolate all over her face.

"Oh, dear." Stephanie jumped up and grabbed a napkin off the breakfast tray, covering her mouth. "I do wish Maria would teach you to chew with your mouth closed. Hello there!" she called outside the room to Kuniko. "Are you lurking out there, girl? Come quickly and help me."

Kuniko flitted into the room with a pail of firewood, and dropped it on the floor, mouth agape.

"Don't just stand there," Stephanie snapped. "Bring a glass of water and a drinking straw. Quickly, girl. Quickly!"

Audrianna inhaled a choking, stridorous breath as Kuniko dashed into Maria's bedroom, returning with a heavy crystal water glass and straw. She handed it to Stephanie who encouraged Audrianna to drink. "All right, love," she soothed, holding the straw for Audrianna while she struggled a sip. She patted her back. "All better?" she asked, wiping the remaining chocolate off her face. She put the glass down, then put the lid on the box and set it to the side. Turning to Kuniko she said, "Thank you. You may go."

"I need to lay fire, Princess," Kuniko said. "Maria wouldn't like Baroness von Traugott shivering like she is."

Stephanie did a double take at Audrianna. "Good heavens! You are shivering. Poor darling." She went to the window and pulled it shut, then came back to the bed and watched with a raised eyebrow as Kuniko stacked kindling in the fireplace. "Girl, why does Maria house such expensive glassware in her bedroom? It doesn't correlate with her usual stuffiness."

Audrianna had never thought about it before, but Stephanie was right. It *was* rather odd. Beyond that, no dishes or trays were ever brought to Maria at dinnertime, no bottles of wine were delivered to her room. She simply excused herself for her meal and reappeared an hour or two later with a glass of wine. What kind of world was Maria concealing behind her closed door? A recollection was awakened in Audrianna:

> *"This is my bedroom," Maria said. "Please close your eyes until I've said you may open them."*

In real time, Audrianna closed her eyes, racking her brain for the details.

> *The doors squeaked open and she felt herself being dragged along a smooth, polished path. The climate inside the room was crisp and clean. The entire space was alive with aromas of lavender, eucalyptus and mint.*

How much of this memory was accurate? Audrianna opened her eyes as Kuniko ignited the fire, then got up and brushed her hands together, facing Stephanie with a scowl. "I'm not discuss my mistress' private affairs, ma'am," she said.

Smirking, Stephanie flicked her ash in Audrianna's eggs. "Right. That was terribly forward of me to inquire." She pointed to the tray. "Would you take this please? The sight of it sickens me."

Fire made and tray collected, Kuniko left the room.

Stephanie turned to Audrianna and whispered, "I think I'll have a peek inside the secret boudoir of the Maiden of Gavrilek. That could very well be the headline I'm after." She tiptoed across squeaky floorboards, hand outstretched, slowly twisting the glass doorknob of Maria's bedroom door.

Cuckoo! Cuckoo!

A Black Forest Cuckoo Clock hanging above the doorway announced the top of the hour.

Startled, Stephanie shuffled sideways into a bureau, knocking over and breaking an expensive looking lamp; her cigarette flew out of her hand unchecked, landing on Audrianna's bed. Stephanie's first concern was for the lamp.

She sank to her knees, picking through the pieces of multicolored glass. "Fabergé! No! No! No!" The clock clucked again, inciting her rage.

"You stupid chicken!" she shouted, stumbling up to her feet and extracting a small caliber pistol from her handbag. Releasing the cylinder, she checked it for bullets, then snapped it shut, laughing maniacally. "I'll get you; oh, yes!" She fired in rapid succession at the clock until one shot landed true; the bird shattered into bits.

"Stephanie!"

Stephanie turned to the voice, quickly hiding the gun behind her back. Avoiding eye contact, she fussed with her hair as a perfectly polished Magda Goebbels stood in the doorway staring at her. "Why have you set fire to your friend's bed?" she asked, gesturing to the smoldering linens.

Snapping her head around in horror, Stephanie placed the gun on the bureau and grabbed the glass of water, splashing out the burgeoning flame. Through labored respirations, she kneaded the charred hole in the bedcover.

"This was a mishap," she said over her shoulder.

Magda walked into the room and looked down at the shattered lamp.

"That was also a mishap," Stephanie told her.

Magda's eyes tracked upward to the clock and Stephanie pivoted to face her, hands clasped together at the waist. She answered the unspoken question.

"No, Magda. That was deliberate—very, very deliberate."

Elegantly stoic with a transfixed smile, Magda said, "May I know what infraction prompted you to execute such an exacting punishment?" Her sarcasm was barely noticeable: people of true class had subtlety in their blood.

"It had incorrect timing," Stephanie replied.

Callum and Dr. Curtis rushed around the corner with worried expressions, freezing when they spotted Magda. Rich's concern for Audrianna supplanted protocol. He brushed by her without the customary deference, saying, "Excuse me, Master. I must see to Baroness von Traugott."

"Certainly, you must, Dr. Curtis. Don't let me detain you from your duties." Magda turned and addressed Callum. "I apologize for the disturbance, Callum, but Princess von Hohenlohe has encountered a series of *mishaps* this morning, resulting in the destruction of Maria's property. Please allow me to remunerate the loss." She withdrew a wallet from her Hermès shoulder bag and counted bills into his hand. "This is for the duvet, the lamp and," she minutely shook her head, "the clock. There. All better, now? I'll inform Maria of the damage myself."

"Very good, Master," Callum replied, backing out of the room with a duteous downward gaze.

"Tough morning, Leyonelle?" Rich quietly joked with Stephanie as he ran his crystal over Audrianna's body.

"Something like that. Yes," she replied, pulling the duvet off onto the floor. Immediately she noticed evidence of Audrianna's incontinence and said, "When you're finished, Dr. Curtis, would you send a nurse in to clean Baroness von Traugott? I've frightened the pee out of her."

Audrianna felt the tips of her ears explode with heat. She wondered whether Stephanie would be so quick to humiliate her if she actually believed her conscious.

Rich chuckled. "It likely wasn't anything you did, Princess," he said, putting away his crystal and collecting a reflex hammer; he tested Audrianna's reflexes, one side at a time, turning to Stephanie when he was through. "Maria is working on bowel and bladder control: it just takes time. Excuse me, Leyonelle. I'll send in the nurse when she arrives." He kissed her hand, then spoke to Magda as he left, "Good morning, Master."

"Good morning, Dr. Curtis," she replied.

As soon as he was gone, Stephanie dug a bottle of pills out of her purse and popped one in her mouth, chewing it up. She grabbed the pistol and re-holstered it in her bag as Magda approached from behind, resting her hands on Stephanie's shoulders, lips gently pressed into her hair. Stephanie reached back and touched her hands, silently marinating in their connection before finishing with a tender embrace. Acknowledgement, acceptance and affirmation—that was how watching them felt.

"Why are you here so early?" Stephanie pulled back from her. "Did the bank call you?"

"The bank? No. I've come early to speak with Maria. My investigation of Baroness von Traugott's attack has yielded some intelligence she is sure to find unsettling—I wanted her to know beforehand." Magda glanced around. "Is she here?"

"No, she went to morning assembly. What intelligence?"

"It's nothing to trouble you with," Magda said, starting to move away. Stephanie stopped her with a hand on the arm.

"Magda, what intelligence?" she asked.

"Darling, I'd rather not say before first informing Maria. Also, it's likely to negatively influence your impression of Baroness von Traugott. I don't want to cast a pall."

"You don't want to cast a pall on our garden party." Stephanie laughed, gesturing to Audrianna. "That's kind of you, darling."

Magda sighed. "Stephanie, please don't catch me out. I'm simply saying it isn't news I'm anxious for *anyone* to hear."

"Tell me," said Stephanie, waving off Magda's forewarning. "I want to know."

"If you insist."

"I do. Yes."

With compunction, Magda said, "I'm sorry to tell you this, but Baroness von Traugott has been untrue to Maria."

Stephanie started laughing. "Oh, dear. Is this really about Kendis Lewis? I thought Audrianna had done something truly worthy of such a climax. Honestly, Magda. I've never seen you so upset before."

"Stephanie Julienne. You were privy to this infidelity and you did not see fit to tell me?" Magda asked.

"Don't call me that, please. I detest being addressed by two names."

"I'm expressing my disappointment. We've agreed you'll allow me that."

Stephanie rolled her eyes. "Magda, you and I have a myriad of lovers outside our relationship, as do Eva and Hermann, and no doubt that clown and his mirror. Why should you be so disappointed in Audrianna?" She lit up another cigarette, offering the case to Magda.

"You and I have a different understanding than Maria and her mirror—you slept with me two hours after we met and

cheated on me the same night. I cannot speak for the others."
Magda fumbled with the case, uncharacteristically flustered.
"Baroness von Traugott has dishonored her commitment to
Maria by engaging in relations with another Gavrilekian—a
Master Gavrilekian from another group, at that. Heaven forbid."

"Maria can't find her way around the bedroom with a flash-
light and a compass, Magda. Is it any wonder that Audrianna
sought satisfaction elsewhere? I'd say her relationship with Kendis
was born from necessity rather than treachery. It doesn't speak
to her overall character." Stephanie finished with a long deep
draw on her cigarette.

Pulling a cigarette out, Magda tapped the end on the case
and struck a match. She took a puff and shook out the match.
"I take it you know this woman? This Kendis Lewis?"

"Yes," replied Stephanie. "I've met her only casually, but
yes. I know her. I like her."

"You like her," Magda repeated.

"Yes."

"You speak of her with a warmth I haven't heard in your
voice since Coco. I'm not sure what to make of it."

"Good," Stephanie said. "I'm glad it's so evident. But it's
you she reminds me of, not Coco. She reminds me of you before
you spent all of your lifetime, every lifetime enslaved to the
propaganda of war. Back when I believed in this cause. Back
when I believed in you."

Magda took several draws on her cigarette before quietly
responding, "I'm doing the best I can."

"I'm trying to understand that, Magda. I really am,"
Stephanie told her. "And," she flicked her ash, "I'm still willing
to help you. That's why you're not going to tell anyone else this
news—it dies here."

"Darling, I'm sorry if I haven't been clear," Magda said, "but I intend to apprise the others at our meeting today."

"No, you were perfectly clear. You plan to drop a bombshell on everyone's head and justify the destruction through some deluded sense of duty. Thank God I've intercepted that ambition."

Magda appeared put off. "Stephanie, I really haven't the temperament for this today. What *are* you trying to say?"

"I'm asking you to keep this discovery between us." Stephanie gestured behind her. "And Audrianna, if she's listening."

"I have no mechanism in my contract for deceit," replied Magda.

Undeterred, Stephanie repeated, "I'm asking you to keep this discovery between us. *Please.*"

"Darling, did you hear me? I am obligated to divulge the details of any investigation I undertake on behalf of the group; are you asking me to breach that covenant? If they found out, I would be held accountable, demoted, even. Eva *would* challenge my position."

"Imagine the injury to the generationals in this group if they find out Maria can't keep the only lover she's ever lived for, ever worked for—they would cut open their veins for her. Are you prepared to deal with that sort of emotional upheaval at this critical junction?"

"I would instruct the leadership to keep it quiet."

"Magda, it *will* get out. We both know it."

Magda turned around, hugging her body. She smoked the rest of her cigarette, as Stephanie continued,

"Imagine the injury to Maria. Do you really want her doubting her mirror just as she attempts her resurrection? Forgive me if I'm misquoting your creed, but, 'if one of you can't get home, none of you will.'"

With that one statement, Stephanie proved herself trustworthy—Magda had no idea that Audrianna and Maria were not yet bonding. She had kept Audrianna's secret. More than that, she now sought to protect her from the aftershock of this scandal.

"All right," Magda whispered, turning back around, her tone defeated.

"Do you mean you'll do it?" Stephanie asked.

"I'll try to do it. Yes." Magda walked over and flicked her cigarette butt in the fire. She looked back at Stephanie, saying, "I won't volunteer the information, but if I'm asked directly whether or not Baroness von Traugott had another lover, I cannot lie. Will that do?"

Stephanie came over to the fireplace. "Yes. Thank you, darling," she said.

Magda shook her head. "I don't understand you. Why not invest this energy on the front end and help her avoid the trouble, all together?"

Stephanie tossed her cigarette in the fire; she turned to Magda and replied, "Where's the fun in that?"

Later that morning, tables were brought in and set up for leaders' luncheon. A monthly occurrence, the principal attendees were the four masters and their lead players. The site of the luncheon rotated through each of the masters' domains and this month was Maria's turn. Normally held in her underground boardroom, she chose to host the gathering in her private library so she could help Audrianna with her lunch.

Stephanie sat beside Audrianna's bed with an individual tray, dining on minced lamb kebab and mint yogurt, torturing

Audrianna with the mouth-watering aroma. She swirled a glass of red wine under her nose, speaking to Maria as she fed Audrianna across the way. "This is delicious, Maria. I don't suppose you'd spare me a bottle or two? Magda's cellar has minimal variety. She lacks your oenophile sensibilities."

Listening to the conversation being had by the others, Maria cut her eyes at Stephanie and quietly replied, "Of course, Leyonelle. I'll have it brought up for you." She spooned a portion of pureed carrots into Audrianna's mouth, letting loose of her hand as a test of strength. Unable to hold the position on her own, Audrianna's hand floated down to her lap, but she managed to keep hold of the spoon and Maria applauded that achievement. "That's excellent, dearest," she whispered.

"Maria, may we have your opinion on this matter, please," Magda called from the main table.

Clearing her throat, Maria replied, "I do not think a group wide internment is necessary, no. None of my team is suffering with symptoms of emotional distemper as Eva claims to have witnessed from her people." She glanced at Hannah but Hannah averted her eyes.

"When was the last time you engaged with your team?" Eva asked. "You've been isolated here for a month playing wet-nurse to your leyonelle."

Before Maria could respond, Magda stepped in. "I'm sure Maria knows her own team, Eva, let's not diverge from the issue at hand. Mr. Evans, is there any evidence of emotional distemper amongst your team?"

Hunching over his plate, Hiram stopped gobbling his food and sat up. He wiped his mouth on the back of his hand. "Well, I'm not sure I'd know it if I saw it. What is it, exactly?"

"Emotional distemper is a condition in which the mind becomes deranged with emotion. A hallmark characteristic is unmitigated displays of weeping," Magda said.

"Oh, weeping. Uh—" He looked to his lead player for help—head of German Military Intelligence, Reichsmarine Captain Wilhelm Canaris. Canaris shook his head and Hiram said, "Nope. We haven't seen anyone weeping."

Eva turned aside with a scoff.

"Very well. Thank you all for your observations." Magda looked around. "Let us vote on this measure. What say you, Maria?"

"No restriction."

"Eva?"

"Group wide internment," Eva replied.

"Mr. Evans?"

"Uh—" He looked to Canaris again. Again, Canaris shook his head. Hiram cast his vote."No restriction," he said.

"This is ridiculous," Eva grumbled. "Captain Canaris, on whose behalf are you offering advice? Mr. Evans or your former master, Maria Orsic?"

Maria narrowed her eyes. "You don't have to answer that, Captain Canaris," she said.

Magda agreed. "Eva, that question is a violation of Section 10.9.1, Interrogation of Another Master's Officer Without Just Cause. The standard fine of property is imposed, collectible by Master Hiram Evans."

Eva sat back in her chair with a huff, exchanging angry glances with her lead player, SS-Brigadeführer Reinhard Heydrich.

"I got something from that?" Hiram laughed. He slapped Canaris on the back and said, "Ha! Great job."

Ignoring his juvenile response, Magda returned to the subject. "Although I have witnessed some unusual behavior amongst our people," she acknowledged the look from her lead player—German film director, Leni Riefenstahl, "I am disinclined to support a group-wide internment. I vote no restriction, with this caveat: those group members identified with suspicion of distemper must be quarantined until cleared."

Maria popped her head down in front of Audrianna. "Too much chocolate this morning?" she asked with a smile. Audrianna glanced at the spoon of carrots and opened her mouth, more interested in watching the proceedings than eating.

"Let's move on to the last order of the day," Magda said. "I have completed my preliminary investigation of Baroness von Traugott's attack, and I am prepared to issue my findings." She looked over at Maria. "I recommend you block the sound waves to her ears. This might be distressing for her to hear."

Unsure of what to do, Maria examined Audrianna's rapidly blinking eyes before making a quick decision. "No," she told Magda. "We'll hear the news together and deal with it together." She kissed Audrianna on the top of the head.

Magda got up and opened the door. "Very well, I've invited my hawk, Fulco Gerhard to present the report to the group. Come in, Fulco." She welcomed inside a professional-looking man in his thirties wearing a double breasted suit and tan suede shoes. Upon entering the library, he attempted to make his obeisance to Magda but she pulled her hand away, casually motioning behind her. "Princess von Hohenlohe is present," she directed.

"Ah, Leyonelle." Fulco tapped his forehead in a half apology, half salute. He strode across the room and greeted Stephanie first, reinforcing Audrianna's understanding of the group hierarchy—as Magda's mirror, Stephanie was exalted above all others.

He kissed Audrianna's limp hand second, then gave a genial nod to Maria. "Good afternoon, Master. May I use your blackboard to illustrate the report?"

"Please do," Maria said.

He wheeled the blackboard to the center of the room and picked up a piece of chalk.

"We constructed this timeline using Baroness von Traugott's thought imprints on the day of her attack," he explained. "Using a reverse filtering method, we lifted those imprints from the space-time continuum and deciphered them to produce this report."

He sketched out Audrianna's movements on the night of her attack; occasionally he looked to Magda. "At a quarter past seven, Princess von Hohenlohe and Baroness von Traugott entered the Adlon Hotel. They took a seat at the bar, here," he circled a spot on his drawing, "and were immediately joined by Herr Hitler's adjutant, Fritz Wiedemann. By half past seven, the princess and Herr Wiedemann were gone and Baroness von Traugott was sitting alone at the bar."

Stephanie shifted her seat.

"At five after eight," Fulco continued, "Baroness von Traugott asked to use the house telephone; shortly thereafter, Lorna arrived." He drew a series of arrows. "They exited the hotel together through a side door, like this, and traveled along several obscure alleyways to the Hereditary Health Court building. A security officer spotted them entering Baroness von Traugott's office at half past eight."

Hereditary Health Court? What kind of operation was that? Why had Audrianna kept an office there, she wondered.

Fulco went on. "An hour later, Baroness von Traugott emerged in a bloody state and stumbled across the street into a local club where she was picked up by Princess von Hohenlohe and driven to Master Eva Braun's manor for assistance. This was all recorded in general time scripts from that block."

"How did you know where she was?" Maria looked at Stephanie, eyes probing. Stephanie did not fumble the answer. "I got a phone call from the owner," she said.

Maria accepted that response with a single nod and Fulco carried on with his report. "However clear it may be that Lorna was the perpetrator of the attack," he said, "it is less clear what happened to him in the interim or afterwards. Or, for that matter, his current whereabouts. In that the Hereditary Health Court building is connected by elevator to the underground," he drew a downward arrow, "he might've easily escaped and fled into the countryside, then traveled internationally."

Clearly taken aback by the notion, Maria stopped feeding Audrianna. She stammered out an alternate theory. "Lorna is a prominent player within our group. Is it not possible that he has been abducted, and it is that abductor who's inflicted this injury upon Baroness von Traugott, not Lorna?"

Eva laughed under her breath: "Lorna would never allow himself to be *abducted*."

Nodding, Fulco turned to Maria, sympathy in his tone. "Anything is possible, Master, but, as you know, Lorna is a latent carrier of emotional distemper and many of his decisions are determined by passion, especially where Baroness von Traugott is concerned." He bowed his head. "Forgive me. I do not seek to offend."

Maria petted Audrianna's hair, transmitting dismay through her touch; she replied as if unaffected. "Gallantry is an unwelcome touch of sentimentality, if there's no call for it, Herr Gerhard."

Audrianna could not tell if Maria believed his assessment, or was merely too stunned to argue. For her part, Audrianna readily accepted Lorna had been her attacker, the catalyst being her affair with Kendis.

"What about his code? Haven't you been able to track it?" Eva inquired.

"No, Master. His biverse code is being scrambled and his imprints have been erased."

Maria spoke up again in Lorna's defense. "Scrambling is an extremely delicate process, Sir. The tiniest miscalculation would result in vaporization of his biverse energy. Lorna has neither the expertise nor the strength to accomplish such a feat."

Eva agreed with her, saying, "There are few *masters* who can accomplish such a feat, Herr Gerhard, much less a generational Gavrilekian. Are you suggesting Lorna is receiving help?"

"It *is* my belief he is being sheltered by someone powerful enough to scramble his biverse code. Yes, Master."

"Sheltered by whom?" Maria asked.

Eva chuckled a few times. "Someone more powerful than you, Maria. Lost control of your disciple, did you?"

"Excuse me, Master," Hannah said, clearly terrified at interrupting. "but we've all lost out if Lorna has defected. If one of us can't get home, none of us will."

Fulco nodded his head, taking her lead. To Magda, he concurred, saying, "I agree, Master. There is no one among us willing to go home without Lorna. You cannot un-hero a hero. He's the only one in this community who appears to have survived love."

"That is irrelevant," Captain Canaris stated.

"I agree," Magda said, nodding. "Fulco, let's keep to the subject matter, please."

Fulco looked down at his cards, shuffling them in his hands. His cheeks turned red. "Yes, well, the tangled mosaic of blocks being devised by this protector is something the likes of which

I've never encountered. I would need a dozen pattern theorists at my disposal to penetrate it."

Blocks were high frequency electromagnetic fields, harnessed and deployed in repeating patterns by "blockers" to conceal certain objectives. Audrianna had learned that. If "searchers" or pattern theorists could determine the sequence, the cover could be infiltrated, the objective revealed. Each of the masters had their own team of blockers and searchers to attend to their individual needs.

Wiping her brow, Maria declared, "You shall have pattern theorists from my team to bolster your investigation."

"The only reputable theorist you have is sitting at this table." Eva came out of her chair, pointing at Hannah. "Are you prepared to surrender your lead for this purpose?"

"That's my business, not yours," said Maria.

"I'm sorry, Maria, but this isn't your jurisdiction," Magda told her. "It falls within the scope of military intelligence. Along with recovering Lorna, we must discover what else is being hidden behind this sophisticated screen. Mr. Evans, do you have enough pattern theorists to oversee the remainder of this operation?" Magda asked him.

Hiram checked in with Captain Canaris. "Uh, I think so. Right?"

Canaris nodded, then turned to Fulco and asked, "Might we inquire about Lorna's mirror, Niklas von Traugott? What part, if any, does he play?"

"We've had Baron von Traugott under surveillance since the night of the attack," Fulco answered. "By all outward appearances, he has had no contact with Lorna. The only movement he makes outside of his home, is to the local monastery to attend Mass. Whether or not he and Lorna have spoken telepathically, we cannot know. Perhaps he is privy to Lorna's agenda, but it is more likely he has been abandoned."

Maria tilted her head upward, jaw jutted. "He wouldn't willingly abandon his mirror," she argued.

Magda nodded. "I agree that it is unlikely, Fulco. If there is one thing that can be said about Lorna with any degree of certainty, it is this—he adores himself—that includes his mirror. Please take Baron von Traugott into protective custody. If Lorna has defected, detaining his mirror might flush him out. On the off chance he has been abducted, we must work to ensure Baron von Traugott's safety. Until Lorna's disloyalty can be definitively determined, both he and Baron von Traugott remain a part of this group. We will not be going home without either of them. Are there any amongst you who oppose my order?"

No one protested.

Magda nodded to Fulco, who then bowed to the group and promptly left the room. Magda finished her glass of wine and called an end to leaders' luncheon, thanking Maria for her hospitality. "As always, the feast was delectable."

Maria walked over to converse with her as the others began to rise, exchanging similar pleasantries. Quiet through most of the meeting, Stephanie got up and met them as they bid their farewells, sticking close to Maria, presumably to intercept any mention of Audrianna's affair. Audrianna silently willed the universe to spare Maria further disappointment. It was Maria she felt for.

"Maria," Eva called out, approaching and handing her a parcel. "Here is a dress belonging to your leyonelle. It was left under the bed at my house on the night of her attack. It had a *foreign* smell, so I had it cleaned and pressed."

Maria pulled the string on the parcel, releasing the paper wrap. Kendis' flashy garment fell out in her hands. "You're mistaken." She handed it back. "This is not a part of Audrianna's wardrobe."

Stephanie stepped in and seized the dress. "It's mine," she said.

Eva did not back down. "No, Princess. It isn't. Baroness von Traugott was wearing this *thing* when she arrived at my house. You helped her change behind closed doors. Do you deny it?"

The room turned quiet; Hannah moved closer in support of Maria.

"I have no wish to deny it," Stephanie spat. "So what if I helped her change? It is still *my* garment. I loaned it to her because she likes to sing on stage—we *both* like to sing on stage. There. I hope you're happy! You've provided Maria with irrefutable proof that I am the miscreant she believes me to be."

Audrianna wet herself again. She couldn't carry a tune to save her life; she doubted Stephanie could, either.

"Enough." Magda came and took Stephanie by the arm, directing her to gather her things. "If you'll excuse us, Eva, we're in the middle of filming *Tag der Freiheit*. The entire set awaits our arrival."

Eva turned her chicanery on Magda. "And Princess von Hohenlohe is to perform the musical interlude, is she? I didn't realize your leyonelle was such a songbird, Magda."

"She is a woman of many aspects," replied Magda, finding a way to remain true to Stephanie without compromising herself. "Leni, let's go, please." She motioned her lead player out the door as Eva collected her belongings and headed underground with her lead player, Reinhard Heydrich, grumbling all the way. Stephanie went to say goodbye to Audrianna.

"*Auf Wiedersehen*, darling. I'll see you next week." She kissed her on the forehead, then turned and bumped into Maria, who had followed her to the bed. She pushed her back. "Yes, Maria? What more?" she asked, hands up.

"Was Audrianna in that club because she had a singing engagement that night?" Maria asked, almost timidly. "Have you both been singing there? Is that why the owner knew to call you when Audrianna was found injured?"

"That's right, Maria. We're both showgirls," Stephanie lied.

Magda came over and urged her along, saying, "My darling, I do not know which concerns me more: your determination to overstep the line or your inability to see it. *Auf Wiedersehen*, Maria. I apologize for the destruction of your home and the undue consternation brought down upon your head this day."

Callum entered the room carrying two bottles of wine and Maria called out, "Wait!" Handing the wine to Stephanie, she said, "You've provided me with clarity when Eva was fixed on rendering a more sinister perspective. I thank you for that."

Stephanie's expression changed, and she appeared truly conscience-stricken by Maria's gratitude. It stung Audrianna's heart, knowing her affair with Kendis was the basis for that uncertainty. If not for Audrianna, the lies Stephanie told Maria would have been unnecessary.

"Stephanie, is there some internal crisis of which I am unaware?" Magda asked, her tone impatient.

Stephanie snapped out of it. "All right, Magda! Is everyone's life set to your timer, or is it just mine?" She marched out the door, the sound of her arguing gradually trailing off down the hall.

"Master?"

Maria turned her head as Hannah crept up beside her; everyone else was gone. They made an intimate sort of eye contact for several long moments, ending with an embrace. When

Maria pulled away, she turned around and took off her glasses, pinching her eyelids shut. "Showgirls," she muttered, shaking her head. "If Lorna *has* attacked her, it was likely for *that* reason. He despises anything undignified like that, you know."

"Are you very disappointed in her?" Hannah asked.

Chuckling, Maria replied, "Disappointed? No, I'm … relieved." She put her glasses back on and stared at Audrianna with arms crossed over chest, her expression pensive. "I've done something today I'm not especially proud of, Hannah. May I confess it to you?"

Hannah's lips parted. She stammered, "Yes, Master. Of course."

Maria selected a glass from the table and poured herself some wine—Audrianna had never seen her drink before dinner. She sat in a lounge chair and invited Hannah to join her, taking a moment to herself before speaking. "Following our discussion this morning," Maria started, "I laid out a small fortune for the expedited services of an independent sleuth."

"A sleuth, Master? To what end?" Hannah asked.

"To investigate Audrianna's activities," replied Maria, taking a sip.

A whirlwind of panic tore through Audrianna's body, leaving nausea in its wake. The trouble had not been averted—Maria was going to find out. It was only a matter of time. *God!*

"Whether or not it was apparent to you," Maria went on, "I was distraught by rumors of her affair. I was affected with emotion, that is to say."

"Master, I'm sorry."

"No." Maria held up her hand. "Please don't apologize. It is a very fine lesson on how impacting my lack of practice with emotion can be. I acted on an impulse of jealousy, instantly regretted. Had I felt her echo inside of me, I would not have been so diverted. I do worry about our connection sometimes. Especially now. It's been such a short time since we've ... lived together."

Tenting her hands over her mouth, Hannah quickly shook her head. "We all worry about connections with our mirrors, Master. None of us has an easy time with it." Her hands flitted back to her lap.

"That's helpful," said Maria, flashing her shy vulnerable smile. "Thank you for saying that. Still, I've been proven a fool today. Eva has seen to that."

"But it was Princess von Hohenlohe's dress." Hannah emphatically proclaimed. "Eva was proven the fool, not you! She put gossip into the group and it backfired on her."

Maria considered Hannah's response for a moment. "She may've missed her mark, yes, but the blow was still felt. She was disproven, yes. But, so was I, in my suspicion of Audrianna, my doubt in her fidelity. I spent too much money on an unnecessary investigation and Eva was the deliverer of my shame. She always finds a way to come out on top, doesn't she?"

Audrianna could not swallow her nausea. She spewed carrots and chocolate all down her nightgown and onto the newly replaced duvet. Maria jumped up and rushed over, tilting her head to the side to keep her air passage free.

"What can I do?' Hannah sprinted up behind her.

"Towels, from the bathroom."

"Right."

Experienced now in the art of sickness, Audrianna took a calm solid breath between heaves, catching up with air hunger once she was through. Hannah produced a towel and Maria tilted Audrianna back, wiping her face clean. She looked into her eyes and whispered, "I'm sorry." At the exact same time, Audrianna felt the same towards Maria.

A green prism shot from Maria's eyes, illuminating Audrianna's soul. She found herself in a vision, standing on a stage in a sun-drenched field of cyan blue tulips: stormy sky, white nightgown. A single raindrop fell upon her arm, burning her skin. She looked up—the clouds dripped with black acid and Audrianna came out of the vision screaming: her first successful vocalization.

"Oh! Master!" Hannah caught Maria as she fell backwards to the floor, breaking her fall. She sat up, cradling Maria's body. "Are you okay?" she asked, breathless.

Maria stood with a purpose, glancing back and forth over her shoulder. "Did you hear that, Hannah? She spoke. It's an encouraging sign."

"Master, you two nearly just bonded with your eyes: *that* is the encouraging sign. Celebrate *that*."

Maria fanned her fingers out against her breastbone, staring at Audrianna. Hope was in her visage—hope of the highest order. "Short of the opening of World War Two, I would like to remain undisturbed for the rest of the day," she said, her voice trembling slightly. "Will you see to it?"

Blushing, Hannah backed into the bureau, pushing off with her hand. "Yes, Master. I'll see to it. Thank you. Good day." She went quickly to the door, but Maria stopped her.

"Hannah. My elevator; my office. Today, you are my deputy."

It was the ultimate compliment: Master Gavrilekians rarely granted absolute authority to anyone.

Rushing into the room with buckets of soapy water, Alex and Tyler smacked into Hannah.

"Oh, hello," Hannah lurched away from them.

They jumped to attention in front of her, sloshing water on the floor. "We're ready," they said.

Confused, Hannah glanced at Maria first, then turned back to them. "What work detail are you on?" she asked.

Maria came to the rescue, pointing sternly between Tyler and Alex. "I wish to be understood," she said. "After you've summoned the *appropriate* personnel to wash my leyonelle, you will go away. You will go far, far away, not to return until tomorrow morning. Have I made myself clear?"

"Not really, Master," Tyler answered. "You said she needed to be cleaned, and we're here. What's the problem?"

Hannah's eyes popped out of her head at him. "Hush," she said. "The master clearly meant for you to summon nurses."

"Oh, that reminds me, Master," Alex said, offhandedly. "Your last body died today. Would you like me to commission some more?"

Maria pulled her whip, cracking it on the floor. She meant business when she did that. "Out! Get out. Send back the nurses." She pivoted to Hannah, staying quiet until after they left. "To your station, please," she commanded. Only, Hannah did not move.

"Master, why have you let your line die out?" she whispered, lips quivering. Her unblinking eyes filled with tears as she tried to navigate her confusion. "Are you trying to disappear? Is that what's going on?"

Frustrated in her own right, Maria shook her head and sighed. "Darling, please don't make this bigger than it is."

"I won't live in a world without you!"

"Oh, dear." Maria rubbed her eyes beneath her lenses. "These displays of histrionics are concerning; should you be in quarantine? Are you infected with the distemper? Is the rest of our team and you haven't told me?" She resituated her glasses and waited for an answer.

"No, Master." Hannah wiped her eyes. "I apologize for my lack of discipline."

Maria took her by the shoulders and shook her. "Your discipline is impeccable. It's your spirit I'm talking about. Go to your mirror—you have one week's furlough. Should you require more than that, you will let me know. Do not come back here in this state. Am I understood?"

Tears streaming down her face, Hannah reluctantly nodded. Maria took the vial of mystery liquid from her pocket and put it in her hand, but Hannah pushed it away. "I cannot accept that," she sniffed.

"You will take this," Maria said firmly. "That is an order."

She gently tucked a finger under Hannah's chin, "Because I am completely unprepared to live in a world without you, too."

CHAPTER 5

"What do you know of my heart? What do you know of anything but your own suffering?" Maria read aloud from Jane Austen's *Sense and Sensibility*. "For weeks, Marianne, I've had this pressing on me without being at liberty to speak of it to a single," she put some heat into the hand resting against Audrianna's skull, "creature," she finished.

After a day of playing hardball with her advisors, Maria disappeared into her bedroom and returned in her nightgown, freshly bathed and smelling of lavender; her gorgeous blond tresses hung to her waist. Tucking herself behind Audrianna, she read aloud from a novel whilst using her biverse energy to remap speech to a functional part of Audrianna's brain. It hadn't worked entirely yet, but Audrianna could feel the muscles of her mouth strengthening, her tongue becoming agile. She could whimper and moan if she wanted to. Having never read a single novel before her attack, she now had a passion for them. Equally, she had a passion for this nightly ritual with Maria—reading together.

Maria blotted Audrianna's saliva with a cloth and continued, "It was forced on me by the very person whose—"

"Master?" Alex knocked and rushed inside without permission, averting his eyes when he saw Maria and Audrianna in bed together, both clad in nightdresses.

Maria folded the corner on her book and lifted her gaze. Pushing her glasses up on her nose, she said, "Wait a moment, Alexander, while I make us decent. Oh. You're already here. I beg your pardon."

Audrianna internally giggled.

"Master," Alex panted, "The Needle has come to see you."

The statement caught Maria off-guard. She scooted out from behind Audrianna and placed the book face down on the nightstand, quickly attempting to re-pin her hair. "Have him wait for me in the main library," she said. "Stall him with a glass of Madeira."

"Master, I think we should contact security, or something."

"Why?" One strand of hair came loose, then two.

"Because he's a..."

Maria continued to struggle with her hair. "Yes?"

"He's one of those funny kind of..."

Her entire hairdo unraveled in her fingers. She closed her eyes and issued a solid calm command. "Speak plainly, Alexander."

"He's a creep, Master. I think it would be a good idea to—"

"Bring the Madeira, please," Maria told him, fatigue in her voice.

"Master—"

"I gave you an order, Alexander!" she snapped.

A green-eyed, middle-aged man with greasy hair barged into the room with a limp, interrupting them. His cheeks were rouged, his lips were glossed; he spoke with an androgynous whisper. "Kind of you, but, let's just get on with it," he said. "You're not the only stop I'll make tonight."

Alex lost his cool in the gentlest of ways. "What's wrong with you?" he asked the Needle. "You are before a master of highest distinction. Are you begging for a thrashing or something?"

"From whom?"

"What?" Alex grimaced.

"From whom will I receive the thrashing? Not you, I hope." The Needle sat his knapsack down on Maria's desk and pulled open the straps, watching with one eye as Maria slid into her boots, then slunk across the room to the closet. "Bring me a younger man with considerable girth," he told Alex, "and then I'll consider it."

Inside the closet, Maria donned one of Audrianna's robes. Unsheathing her whip, she cracked it on the ground loud enough to be heard.

"Leave, Alex," she said as she re-entered the room. Swiftly, he obeyed her. Turning to the Needle, Maria admitted, "I'm ill-prepared for this meeting. Thank you for your forbearance."

The Needle stared at her without blinking, slowly raising his hands. "I am unarmed, Master," he whispered. "Truth is my only weapon." Maria put her whip away and the Needle moved on.

"May I sit here?" he asked, pointing at her desk, then he did so before she could respond. From his satchel he withdrew a short stack of papers; a key spun off onto the floor. "Baroness Audrianna von Traugott of Austria—also Dr. Audrianna von Traugott, Hereditary Health Court Medical Officer. Clever woman, in many ways, but not—it seems—in covering her tracks. Incidentally, I made quite a mess in her office just now. I apologize, but I must stage these investigations as burglaries, in order to avoid suspicion."

"Understood," Maria whispered.

Audrianna felt her heart accelerate. Hereditary Health Court? What was that? Covering her tracks? Oh, God. The dreaded day had come. Maria was going to find out about Kendis.

The Needle reached down, plucked up the key and handed it to Maria, mustering a thin-lipped smile. "This is to a bank vault commissioned under the alias Frauline Zoe Biel. I house a copy of every report I create at the City Bank of Berlin so you may access it under guard—the paper belongs to me and may not be removed from the bank. If you attempt to do so, it will dissolve, like this." He flicked the top paper off the pile—it vanished, ink dust flitting in the air. "This copy," he pushed the rest of the stack into Maria's hands, "is to be read here, in front of me now—then burnt. Your allowance is ten minutes. Any time over that will be charged at triple my hourly rate. Are you ready?" He pulled out a stopwatch.

Maria unlatched a secret compartment within the desk and extracted a bottle of scotch. She poured herself a glass and choked back the entire amount, then offered some to the Needle as an afterthought. He declined.

Audrianna had never seen her drink anything in such an uncivilized manner: she was steeling herself to learn bad news. That much was obvious. Helpless to prevent it, Audrianna watched as she began to read, her expressions running the gamut of the emotional spectrum: stunned, confused, sad, bitter. They all dealt Maria discernible blows. When she was through reading, she handed the papers back, and the Needle tossed them in the fire, watching them burn."

"If you wish me to further investigate—"

"No." Maria cut him off, pouring herself another scotch, chugging it back again. She slouched over the desk. "I cannot investigate my partner. It is a violation of our contract."

Her *partner*? Who was she talking about. And how was Audrianna involved? She did not understand.

"The other issues you've exposed will be dealt with by my team," Maria continued. "Baroness von Traugott has fixed her own involvement, as you see."

Without making eye contact, The Needle buckled the straps on his bag and limped out the door. On a whim he turned back and said, "Incidentally, there was a heavy feeling of deliberation in her final moments."

"Deliberation. Yes." Maria nodded with a laugh: she was not amused. Turning, she pierced Audrianna's soul with her dark bloodshot eyes. "I imagine anyone making an attempt on his or her life experiences that sensation—in one way or another. Thank you, Sir."

The Needle had just contradicted Fulco's theory of assault and bolstered Devon's theory of suicide. Audrianna could not pinpoint her sentiments on the matter. On one hand she was relieved that Lorna had not attacked her; on the other she was desperately sad that suicide had once seemed a way out of whatever she'd become entangled in. What had she become entangled in? And, what had become of Lorna?

Maria closed the door behind the Needle and walked back to her desk, snatching up the rotary phone, dialing zero. "Patch me through to the officer in charge of plant security. Thank you." When the officer came online, she said, "*Guten Abend.* This is the Master of Engineering, Maria Orsic. With whom am I speaking?" Pause. "Very good, Major Acker. Please deploy five thousand atomic tracers into the irrigation system at grid markers F12, B9 and M1. I want to know where every molecule of the Vril is going once it passes through those leaks. Thank you." She disconnected and dialed zero again.

Forcing her eyelids shut, Audrianna shuddered at the implication. She must be involved some way or another with leeching the Vril from Maria's irrigation system. But how? Why?

"Patch me through to the Hereditary Health Court Building," said Maria. She held for a moment, then said, "Good evening, Herr Wiese. This is the Master of Engineering, Maria Orsic." She listened, then nodded. "Yes, thank you. I've already been made aware of the break-in. I'm sending two members of my personal guard to secure and investigate Baroness von Traugott's office. Please afford them your utmost cooperation."

After hanging up, Maria sat on the end of Audrianna's bed, holding her forehead, eyelids closed over falling tears. "What more could I have done to win your favor? We share the same consciousness; we are the same spirit. What more could I have done?" she whispered, with a sad shake of the head.

Audrianna tried to speak, but produced only drool, tried to reach out but managed only twitches. Sick with guilt, she whimpered, willing Maria to come to her, touch her, hold her—if she could get her to do that, somehow she could also persuade her that she was innocent of the details. Whatever role she'd played in that report was not the role she played now.

A knock fell on the door and Kuniko came in carrying a basket of laundry. Distractedly she said, "I'm sorry. Late. I'll go turn down bed. Have you chosen clothes for tomorrow?"

"Leave it," Maria croaked, wiping tears away with her fingers. She got up and took *Sense and Sensibility* from the nightstand; she tossed it into the fire and sank into a wingback chair, brooding. Kuniko followed her there.

"I never see you destroy book, before," she said, placing the laundry basket on the floor; she gingerly touched the crown of Maria's downturned head. "Why hide face from me? I don't need to see eyes to know something wrong."

"I won't discuss it with you," Maria whispered.

Kuniko was not dissuaded. "I'm not after discussion; I'm after easing pain." She tilted Maria's chin up for a kiss. Maria dodged it.

Initially elated, Audrianna's celebration faded when instead, Maria pulled Kuniko down into her lap, holding her close. She said, "I've asked you repeatedly not to offer yourself to me in this way. Why do you insist on defying me?" Her words were slurred.

Probably because you're sending mixed signals! Audrianna shouted with her mind. She had no right to be hot about this situation, but she was: her heart burned with a breed of jealousy she had never felt before. Maria was intoxicated, weak and vulnerable. Kuniko was trying to take advantage of that.

Unimpressed with the compulsory scolding, Kuniko leaned against Maria, nuzzling her sideways. "You call defying, I call helping. You speech *precision*," she laughed to overcome her accent, "is more good than mine. We're due over some English lessons, no?"

God, she was good—playing off Maria like that. *English lessons?* Really?

Taking the bait, Maria corrected her with a kiss on the temple. "Overdue," she sniffed. "The word is *overdue*. And, yes—we are overdue for some more lessons. My schedule has been quite hectic, as you know. I apologize for neglecting you."

"I'm here now," Kuniko said, wrenching herself over to straddle Maria; she'd never done that before. Finding Maria's hands, she fixed them around her curvy 20-year-old buttocks. Maria did not resist.

Slinky little vixen. Audrianna could match that. Using just the strength of her fingers, she began pinching and pulling at the sheets, tilting herself sideways in the bed until she toppled over. Snagging the corner of the mattress with her teeth, she yanked herself toward the edge of the bed with successive chomps. She would nosedive to the floor.

Maria glanced around the wing of the chair at Audrianna's squirming but Kuniko pulled her back. "You so infatuated with fantasy you can't see what you put in lap?" she asked, steering Maria's hands up to her breasts. "Why not take it all," she whispered, sneaking a kiss off her lips. "I don't hold you to anything."

Lazy hands drifted from Kuniko's breasts as Maria leaned backwards against the headrest, basking in a soft, sensual smile. She encircled Kuniko's tiny waist, burrowing her fingers in the material of her black and white uniform. She beheld her fondly. "Haven't you a person your own age to behave this way with?" she asked with a chuckle.

Slipping a hand under the hem of Maria's nightgown, Kuniko caressed her thigh and replied, "I don't know. My eyes see only you."

Minx. Audrianna worked faster with her teeth. It was clear Kuniko was going for the kill, nearly there, too.

"What is your intention with this flirtation?" Maria asked. She placed her hand over Kuniko's, but she did not make her stop.

"This not flirtation," Kuniko whispered. "It is *respitude.*"

Maria stroked her hair. "Respite," she corrected softly. "It is *a respite*." Her resistance was gone. Lowered energy and lowered inhibitions simmered in her eyes; she was receptive to what Kuniko wanted to do to her. Kuniko saw it, too. She goaded Maria into a longer kiss, this one uncontested. There was a visible energy exchange between them as Maria inhaled a breath of Kuniko's soul.

Thud. Audrianna finally hit the floor.

Startled out of the kiss, Kuniko spun around at Audrianna, then back. "She jump from bed. I don't know how, but she did."

Maria wiped her mouth and sat up, slowly coming back into herself. "Reckless perseverance," she rasped. "I once found it a charming characteristic, but it's starting to get on my nerves. Up, up." She patted Kuniko on the bottom and Kuniko dismounted, glowering angrily at Audrianna. Maria squeezed her hand as she passed. "Go to your room," she told her. "It's late."

———◦◈◦———

"The Needle." Stephanie read the note out-loud, impressed. "He's the most prestigious sleuth in Europe, if not the world. How very expensive. I wish Maria would extend her patronage to my business." She crumpled the note and tossed it in the fireplace with the others Audrianna had written. Six weeks after the Needle's visit, Audrianna's writing was nearly back to baseline, but her speech was still impaired. Maria had not abandoned her retraining as Audrianna feared she might, but their relationship had certainly changed. Maria no longer read novels to her at night; she never slept in Audrianna's bed, and she did not dance in front of her anymore.

"So she found out about Kendis, did she?" Stephanie shrugged with one shoulder. "Well, I did my best, Audri. I don't know what else to say. You weren't exactly discreet all those years; it's no wonder Lorna came unglued and bashed you in the head— or shot you, or whatever he's supposed to have done—especially after all that mess between the two of you in Switzerland, his going blind to protect you, being relegated to slavery, so on. For Maria, he swallowed your leaving Niklas, but did you honestly think he would acquiesce to anyone else?"

Audrianna handed Stephanie another note: *Zoe Biel. City Bank of Berlin. Read report there.*

"Your faith in me is heartwarming," Stephanie said. "How do you expect me to get this? There's only so much a blow job will do." She tossed the note in the fire. "Anyway, we know what the report contains. It's done now, Audri."

It wasn't anywhere near done, but Stephanie seemed not to know that. She apparently knew nothing about Audrianna stealing the Vril from Maria or conspiring with one of Maria's partners behind her back. If she had, she would have said something by now. Stephanie still believed Lorna was her attacker and Audrianna did not correct that notion, either. It was simply too much to try and communicate without a voice. She must find out what else was in that report before she could ever explain it or really make amends. She thought quickly how to motivate Stephanie's compliance and scribbled another note:

Something about you in it.

Stephanie's hand instinctively flew to her throat, then she quickly tried to disguise her concern. "Oh, hooey. Maria's told you that to get a rise out of you. That's all. She has no information on me." Her skin remained flushed, her eyes overly bright. The wheels had been set in motion: Audrianna could see it in her face. Stephanie would use whatever means necessary to get that report.

Audrianna handed her another note: *Sense and Sensibility.* Fanning herself, Stephanie replied, "Yes. You've expressed an interest in that before. Unfortunately, I haven't located any for you, yet."

Audrianna looked up, her expression snippy. "It—is—a—book."

"Oh, darling. I detest a bookstore," Stephanie whined. "Surely Maria has a copy."

"P…p…please." Audrianna spat it out.

"Fine," Stephanie agreed, waving her hand.

Kuniko entered with a rolling cart, cutting her steely eyes at Audrianna. "Beg pardon ma'am. Callum sent me with Princess' snack." It was Stephanie's typical mid-morning order: brie, apple strudel and champagne. There was a dish of chocolate ice cream on the side for Audrianna.

Stephanie clasped her hands gleefully under her chin. "How wonderful, Audrianna! Is that Château d'Yquem? Generous of Maria. Please pass along my compliments."

Stephanie had dictated the order to Audrianna an hour ago—she knew it was Château d'Yquem. Drinking Maria's prized bottles of wine was one of her favorite provocations, one Audrianna felt she must indulge, or risk losing her alliance. She forced a smile and nodded at Stephanie, playing along with the feint.

"Will you be needing other things, ma'am?" Kuniko asked Audrianna.

Audrianna shook her head. She took the ice cream off the tray and instantly dug in, slowing her enthusiasm when she noticed Kuniko still staring at her. She wiped her mouth with a napkin and shrugged at her. *What?*

Stephanie noticed their interaction; to Kuniko she said, "Is there a problem, dear?"

Kuniko snapped out of it; her expression turned innocent. "I'm sorry, ma'am. Maria say Baroness von Traugott get fat."

"Oh, get along, you nasty little creature." Stephanie came around the bed at her. "You'll be this age, too, one day, and besides, it's not fat, it's insurance in case of famine. You tell Maria that!" She yelled after her, as Kuniko went out the door.

Audrianna closed her eyes. Had Maria really said that? *Was* she getting fat? It was difficult to tell because she always wore a nightgown. But, two months of inactivity and all the chocolate Stephanie could sneak to her was a recipe for obesity. Placing the bowl back on the tray, Audrianna sank into the bed, covering her face with her hands. Stephanie attempted to salve the hurt.

"You shouldn't let her keep you from your treats, darling. She's a child and she's jealous. I haven't noticed any significant weight gain." She poured herself a glass of champagne and changed the subject to Audrianna and Maria's birthday—it was the standard practice in the Gavrilekian community to adopt the birthday of one's mirror. "Anyway, what are you planning on doing for her? She has a smashing surprise for you. Count on it."

Audrianna doubted it was true, not now. Still, she was curious. She uncovered her face and asked, "How—do—you—"

"Because I know Maria," interrupted Stephanie. "She always has some kind of elegant gala sorted out in honor of your birthday—well, maybe not after the Havel debacle." She took a sip of her champagne and a pinch off the Brie wheel. Popping the cheese in her mouth, she chewed and swallowed. "I think she gives you only medical equipment or jewelry, now. You generally pawn the jewelry."

Audrianna flogged herself mentally. She pawned Maria's gifts. Really? And, what was the Havel debacle? She tried to ask. "Havel—river?"

Stephanie chuckled. "Havel, the river, yes. Ten years ago Maria commissioned a river yacht for your birthday celebration. You jumped off the side of the boat, drunk, and disappeared in the water: you and Tru. He was only eight years old at the time."

Great. Audrianna rolled her eyes at herself.

"Naturally, Maria deployed her entire team to look for you, but because your thoughts were mostly protected by your necklace, she had a very difficult time."

Audrianna reached up and fondled her necklace.

"Turns out," Stephanie continued, "a water nymph rescued you and Tru from drowning and carried you to a nearby house. Can you imagine whose house that was?"

"Ken—dis."

Stephanie nodded. "That's right. Kendis. You do remember. You went there with your son: you went to her island: *Tybee Island.* She calls it that as tribute to her childhood homeland, I believe, somewhere in the southern United States."

Potent imprints of her imagined life with Kendis flashed in her mind; her memories were only partially correct. She and Devon *had* been rescued from drowning by one of Kendis' kinsmen, but not from the Atlantic Ocean as her subconscious would have had her believe.

Stephanie took another pinch off the cheese and bobbed it at her. "You should paint Maria a picture." She popped the morsel into her mouth, then brushed her hands together. "I'll come next Thursday after breakfast with the supplies. By then you'll have an idea of what you'd like to create, right?"

Audrianna nodded. It was worth a try. She'd try anything to get Maria's attention. Yes. She would paint the Gavrilekian ruin depicting their mutual psalm: The Wind Is My Master.

Noise from the elevator brought a moment of pause. The lift door opened and Maria walked in with a young, unknown man, hair spiked with pomade, glasses thick. He read notes off a small notepad at the point of a pen, terror in his expression.

"Master, the Vril molecules are migrating up through the soil and entering through various places along the Havel. They seem to be headed in the general vicinity of Pfaueninsel Island—all of them."

"Pfaueninsel Island is deserted," said Maria, casually.

"Right. Well—could be next door."

"Next door sounds like a figure of speech, Zaldy. You've been briefed on my communication preferences, no?"

"Oh—" His eyes turned to saucers. "I'm sorry, master, I—"

"Thank you, Zaldy," she interjected. "Tell Major Acker I'll meet him in my office after lunch and I need to see Captain Canaris here by the end of the day. If he is elsewhere in the world, send *Die Glocke* to collect him. Please obtain Mr. Evans' consent prior to doing so."

"Yes, Master."

Maria approached and kissed Stephanie's hand, then Audrianna's. Her eyes lingered a moment on the melting ice-cream. She turned to Zaldy and said, "You are dismissed."

"Thank you, Master. I won't let you down. I promise." He tread backwards on the exotic hardwood floor, still writing in his book.

"Zaldy," Maria called.

He stopped and looked up, pen still in place.

"Manners, please," she said.

Eyes skipping first to Stephanie, then to Audrianna, Zaldy snapped his book shut, balancing his pen behind his ear. He shuffled with quick, short strides around the bed, awkwardly kissing Stephanie's hand. "Please forgive my discourtesy, Leyonelle. I'm not used to being around important people." He kissed Audrianna's hand, then nodded between them as he backed out the door.

"He's adorable, Maria," Stephanie said. "I do hope your regular hawks haven't taken ill with distemper."

Maria walked over to her desk and sorted through some geographical blueprints. Inattentively, she replied, "Zaldy is my scribe. He's also working on a special project for me." Unrolling one of the maps, she nodded to herself, then took it with her to the door, turning back. "I'll be in the main library, if you need me." She never spoke to Audrianna directly and she never gave her more than a glance.

"Oh, dear. She is taking this badly. Isn't she?" Stephanie said when she was gone. "She barely noticed the champagne."

"Princess von Hohenlohe?" Callum came into the room. "There's a telephone call for you from Berenberg Bank. Would you like to take it in here?"

Stephanie glanced at Audrianna and said, "No. I better not. Tell them I'll return their phone call in half an hour from my home. I'm headed there right now." She corked the champagne. "You don't mind if I take this with me, do you? I'll get your book while I'm out."

As much as Audrianna did not understand the reason for Stephanie's abrupt departure, she kept quiet. She wanted that book. It was instrumental in her apology. She scribbled out one more, quick note, desperate for more puzzle pieces: *What Is Hereditary Health Court?*

"That's your profession, darling. You conscript children with disabilities from their homes and impose various racial hygiene sentences: sterilization, euthanasia, so on. You work very closely with Eva and her team: supplying *participants* for her experiments, though why you do, I'm sure I don't know. You despise the woman more than anyone else on the planet, or so you adamantly profess. Why you've chosen to work with her in this garish manner is anyone's guess." Stephanie looked at her wristwatch. "Oh, I really must get on," she said, waving goodbye overhead. "Toodle-oo!"

Audrianna's mind reeled from the trauma of yet another horrific revelation. Had she fallen down the rabbit hole? There was no way she would have freely sentenced helpless children to Eva Braun's masochistic pursuits. If she was indeed guilty of such an atrocity, Eva had dragooned her into it, somehow. What means of extortion had she used? What could be so important to compel Audrianna to abandon her Hippocratic Oath? Was *this* the secret conspiracy the Needle had uncovered?

"Mutti? Are you alone?" Devon whispered outside the door.

"Yes," Audrianna replied.

Abruptly, he and Kiah charged into the room with Rodney. Looking around, Devon perched at the door as a lookout, Rodney tucked under his arm. Kiah went to see Audrianna. He bent down and kissed Audrianna on the cheek. "Don't worry about Harrison Steede," he whispered. "We'll take care of him. Get some rest, Mutti. God knows you deserve it."

Audrianna's heart sank. Harrison Steede was Devon's bootlegging alias in her tangled memories of the past. Kiah had just reawakened that plot—*wait!* Audrianna shifted her gaze laterally. What did that mean? *God knows you deserve it.*

Standing, Kiah slipped a shell into her palm, then tapped it twice with his forefinger, saying, "Play message in forty seconds, thirty-nine, thirty-eight, thirty-seven…" When he walked away, Kendis' voice took over in Audrianna's head.

"Thirty-six, thirty-five…" Her heart began to pound. It was the first time she'd heard Kendis' voice since the night of her accident.

"Let's go, hurry." Devon gestured Kiah out the door, but it was far too late for that. Maria was aware of his presence and now she was at the door to stop them. Kendis continued to count backward in Audrianna's mind.

"Twenty-five, twenty-four…"

"Good afternoon, gentlemen," Maria purred, oh-so-certain of herself. "Have I interrupted your visit?"

Rodney started barking.

"Master, this is my friend, Kiah from the church choir," Devon spoke over the barking. He leaned over and pressed a finger to his lips: "Shhh…" he told the dog, but he continued to bark.

"Choir friends. How nice," Maria said, her tone clearly skeptical. She offered her hand to be kissed but Kiah did not oblige. Devon quickly stepped in and kissed it instead, then slipped by her.

"Master, if you'll excuse us, we'll get outta your way," he said.

Maria stopped him with her voice. "*Outta* my way?" she said, eyes narrowed. "I am unfamiliar with that word. What does it mean?"

"Ten, nine, eight…" Kendis' countdown broke through. Audrianna internally whimpered, deciding to which conversation she should listen.

Bark, bark, bark …

"Out—of," Devon corrected himself, laughing. He scratched his head and continued to creep. "I guess I'm impressionable to accents," he said. "Come on, Rodney." He snapped his fingers.

"You are not dismissed," Maria told him. "Get back inside." She turned immediately to Kiah. "Weren't you at all afraid to come here?"

"Yes."

Devon swatted him in the gut.

"Um—no, I mean."

"Tell your master, this one-time breach of boundary shall be excused. Have I made myself clear?"

Bark, bark, bark …

"Yes, Master." Kiah bowed his head a little, glancing at Devon. He backed out slowly, hat in hand. When Maria closed the door, Kendis' voice jabbed in.

"Audri, I found the papers you left behind—your agreement with—"

"You're taking advantage of your position, Devon." Maria's voice knocked Kendis out. "Quiet!" She snapped Rodney silent. Devon bent down and picked him up.

"I'm sorry, Master," he said. "I brought my friend here to see my mother. My lifesaver has nothing to do with it."

A recollection pushed into Audrianna's head:

> *"You need to get Devon a dog," Kendis said. "That will keep ya from havin' to isolate him from others so much."*
> *"Why is that?" Audrianna asked.*
> *"Oh, because companion animals share their souls with their owners," Kendis said. "Lifesavers—that's what we call 'um."*

Damn! Audrianna cursed in her head. Momentarily she refocused, trying to listen to Kendis' voice.

"Honey, don't do this: trust me. I know you miss your mother, but ya simply can't do this!"

"Don't interrupt me, Tru!" Maria shouted in an uncustomary show of anger, displacing Kendis' voice again. "I may not be your equal in the biverse, but here, in *this* dimension, I am your superior. You will afford me that respect, please."

"Of course, Master," Devon replied. "I wasn't being purposely—

"Audrianna, I've dropped my wallet somewhere." Stephanie pushed in at that moment, drawing up at the scene. "Heavens. What have I interrupted?" she asked, glancing around. "If there's one thing I love, it's an atmosphere. And that's what we've got here: an atmosphere."

Audrianna listened again for Kendis, but her voice was silent. She had missed her message.

———◦◦◦———

"Captain Canaris, I hear you've come from the South Pole. I apologize if my summons has inconvenienced you. Sit, please." Maria directed him into a chair by the fire.

"Thank you." Canaris sat down. "It's always a pleasure to be in your company, Master. Even if one must travel from the South Pole, yes," he said with a smile.

"May I know the nature of your work, or is that privileged?" Maria asked, still standing.

"It is privileged, yes. I could petition Mr. Evans to include you in the work, if you wish."

Maria shook her head and laughed. "No, thank you. There is no one less informed on Antarctica than me. I would hinder your investigation, I fear."

Canaris chuckled.

"But," she flashed him her shy little smile, "I do want a favor from you, Wilhelm. I wish to be perfectly candid about that."

"You need only declare it, ma'am," replied Canaris. "Though I guide another vessel, my keel is fashioned to your course." He bowed his head.

These types of interactions happened nearly every day. Humans and Gavrilekians alike—they all worshiped Maria. Rightfully so. She was the most exquisite being Audrianna had ever beheld: beautiful, yet wise; gentle, yet strong; confident, yet humble. How was it that between them, *Maria* was considered the mistake?

Retrieving an onyx pillbox from her desk, Maria brought it to Canaris and said, "What do you make of this?"

Eyes down, Canaris sprung the lid and focused on the contents; he looked back up. "Some species of beetle, I'd say."

Maria poured a glass of water from a crystal pitcher and lowered it in front of him. "It isn't a beetle. Drop it here."

Canaris tipped the bug overboard and it immediately dove to the bottom of the glass, swimming so hard it created ripples in the water. "What the devil is it?" He asked Maria, equal parts disgusted and amazed.

"It's a mechanical contraption—a robot of sorts."

Audrianna inhaled sharply, drawing a cool look from Maria. "Here's another given to me earlier by Major Acker," she continued, placing the glass upon her desk and extracting a second bug from another box with a set of tweezers. She held it up to eye level. "The motor's burned out on this one. Come look. Do you see what it's carrying in its belly?"

Canaris stood and examined the bug. His expression turned grave. "It's carrying the Vril," he said.

Maria nodded. "Yes. This pestilence has been leeching tiny amounts of Vril from my irrigation system and carrying it out into the Havel." She put the bug back into the box and snapped the lid shut, gesturing for Canaris to sit. She then joined him. "Although nothing of consequence can be gained from such an infinitesimal amount of Vril," she said, "I do wonder about the intention of the heist."

"Naturally."

Maria adjusted her glasses: her hallmark nervous gesture. "Let me be direct," she said. "The security of my operation has been compromised from *within*."

"That is most distressing news, Master."

"Indeed," Maria replied. She waited for him to say something else and eventually he caught on.

"Of course I'll help you in any way I can," he stammered.

Maria fluttered her eyelashes down, keeping her gaze lowered. "I've identified the culprit within our group, but I know very little about the conspirators, other than that they're a small group of water nymphs based here and in England. For reasons I'll not go into, I cannot involve my team in the investigation." She looked up with a watery gaze. "I realize this puts you in a difficult position, Wilhelm, but I must require absolute discretion. If you cannot promise discretion, please don't pledge me your assistance."

A knife twisted in Audrianna's gut as she witnessed Maria's humiliation—all of it because of her.

"You may be assured of my silence," said Canaris. "I'll launch this initiative immediately, Master, and update you with my progress by next week."

Maria's glossy eyes became tinged with gratitude. "Thank you," she whispered, then rocked herself up and smiled. "You must be quite famished. May I give you some dinner before you return south? I have prepared roasted duck and Pommes de Terre Lorette, with delectable Bordeaux alongside. You have a fondness for Bordeaux, do you not?"

Canaris came up next to her with a kiss on the hand. "I do have a fondness for Bordeaux, Master, but the only way I can be tempted into your offer is if you'll consent to be my dinner partner. Otherwise, I have a very fine ham and dill pickle sandwich awaiting me, alongside stale beer."

Maria burst into laughter, the sound of it filling Audrianna's heart with an exuberant, albeit short-lived high. It was the first time she'd seen her cast a genuine smile in more than a week.

Patting Canaris on the shoulder, Maria then went over and opened her bedroom door. "Come inside," she said. "You are most welcome at my table."

Her table? Audrianna suddenly realized the door that separated them at night must hide an entire living space, not just another room. It was clear now why nothing was ever brought to Maria when she was in there: she must be cooking her own food, serving herself. She had a full-time cook and a house full of servants, yet she chose to be self-sufficient.

Watching them go inside, Audrianna felt excluded. When they reemerged two hours later, she felt invisible. After Maria took a book from a shelf and bade her an aloof good night, she felt forlorn. When the emptiness sucked her dry, she worried about something different.

What had happened to Lorna?

One week later Audrianna was well enough to sit up in a wheelchair. She now fed and bathed herself. For the first time in two months, she wore real clothes. Parked alongside Maria's desk, she read the newspaper out loud—this was their morning speech exercise. Maria sat with her own work, engaging herself only when Audrianna struggled with a word.

The telephone rang and Maria answered it without looking up. "*Guten Morgan:* Maria Orsic," she said.

Audrianna stopped reading, her attention piqued—this was now her only way to obtain clues. Maria no longer held important meetings in front of her.

Adjusting her glasses, Maria glanced at Audrianna as she listened to the caller. Her response she kept low. "I appreciate your, diligence, Captain Canaris. When can you show me this place?"

What place? *Oh, God.*

Maria reached for a scratch piece of paper. "Yes. I am able to come now. Please give me the directions." She dipped her fountain pen in ink and scribbled out the address, then hung up the handset. She rose and rang the servants' bell. Callum answered her call.

"Yes, Master?"

"Please have my motorcycle gassed and brought up to the house," she told him. "I need to go out by myself for a short while."

Her motorcycle?

"It's very cold outside to be riding a motorcycle, Master," Callum advised her.

Maria missed his point. "Thank you. I shall clothe myself accordingly. Send Kuniko to me, please. Quickly, I have but a small budget of time."

Warily, Callum obeyed her.

When Kuniko arrived, Maria unbuttoned her blazer, slipping it off into Kuniko's hands. "Come help me dress," she said, heading toward her door. She returned within minutes, wearing pants and boots, a headscarf and a thick overcoat. Kuniko wore a smirk. Audrianna was not sure which was more infuriating: Kuniko helping Maria out of her clothes, or Maria allowing her that privilege. Both were torturous to endure.

"I shan't be long. An hour, two at most." Maria said, pulling on a set of riding gloves. She guided Kuniko into her desk chair, handing her a tablet and a pencil. "Be a doll and help Baroness von Traugott with her speech lesson. Listen as she reads and make note of words she can't pronounce, so I may review them with her later."

Here was an *opportunity*, Audrianna thought. She would send Maria a message through her smug little sweetheart. Two could play at this game. After she left, Kuniko made a puckered face at Audrianna and said, "Okay, Baroness, start reading."

Audrianna set aside the newspaper and pulled *Sense and Sensibility* from the pocket of her wheelchair. She tried numerous times to give it to Maria, but Maria continued to brush her off. Let's see her snub this attempt. She flipped open to the bookmarked page and read. "What do you know of my heart? What do you know of anything but your own suffering?" She mispronounced every word.

"That's really bad." Kuniko shook her head. "I don't know how come Maria calls this *process*."

Progress. Audrianna corrected her with her mind, giggling internally because she finally *felt* as clever as Maria. She read the sentence again, this time backwards, laying the bait for Kuniko.

"I don't understand you," Kuniko said, standing up in a huff. "Show me where you reading."

Audrianna ran her forefinger across the page and Kuniko scribbled down the words. *Snap.* The trap door shut, ensnaring its clueless prey. An hour later, when Maria returned, she had copied down three entire pages of *Sense and Sensibility.*

Taking off her headscarf, Maria came in and tossed her gloves on the bureau, then went to warm herself by the dwindling fire. She fumbled with the buttons of her coat, her fingers absent their usual dexterity. Looking over her shoulder, she called to Kuniko for assistance—her voice was tremulous.

For once, Audrianna was concerned rather than jealous. She took the writing tablet away from Kuniko and gave her a little push. "Help—her," she said.

"You couldn't say that a minute ago."

"Help—her!" Audrianna snapped, pointing to Maria.

Kuniko stumbled over to Maria and helped her off with her coat. "Why is this all wet?" she asked, dropping it on the floor. She ran her hands across Maria's body in a panic. "Why you all wet!?" she shrieked. "Out in snow, all wet like this!" She glanced at Audrianna and Audrianna wheeled closer, on impulse.

It was the middle of January, only 25 degrees Fahrenheit outside. Hypothermia was a real consideration, especially if Maria was waterlogged. "More—fire," Audrianna told Kuniko. Oddly, Kuniko obeyed her. She collected the firewood bucket and ran out the door as Maria continued to bungle with her buttons.

"Let—me," Audrianna whispered, inching out her hands.

Maria pulled away, teeth a-chatter. "I don't need your help, madam. Do not insult the hopes I once cherished by trying to resurrect what you so thoroughly laid to waste!"

Audrianna absorbed the blow. Whatever Maria found out on her trip had aggravated her bitterness. She tried again: a different approach. "Frozen—heart—beats—bad."

Maria laughed at her, a mean laugh. "If there is *anything* you are indifferent to, surely it must be the condition of my heart."

Browbeaten, Audrianna stayed down. Maria was a word shark—she'd proven it time and time over. Gestures—that perhaps was a better strategy. Ducking her head a little, half in pain, half in remorse, Audrianna played on Maria's Achilles heel: her kindness. It worked. Maria allowed her to unbutton her pants, although at a price.

"Do you know where I've been?" she hissed.

Refusing to bandy, Audrianna minutely shook her head. She tapped her on the leg and Maria lifted it up, wobbling on the other. Hope flickered in Audrianna's heart—if Maria had decided against her entirely, she would not cooperate with this effort. She would be completely indignant. That much Audrianna had learned about Maria Orsic.

Kuniko came in with the firewood, dumping the entire pail into the hearth. "I'll draw bath for you," she told Maria, steadying her while Audrianna pulled her pants down to her ankles. Maria sat with a bare bottom on the sofa, fire now blazing. Kuniko reached for her shirt, but Maria resisted.

"Start the bath," she whispered, and Kuniko hurried into the bathroom. The faucet squeaked on. Water began to pour.

Over the waterfall, Maria looked at Audrianna and said, "I've been out on the Wannsee in a sloop: down the Havel close to Pfaueninsel Island. What say you to that?"

Audrianna unlaced and pulled off her boots, then her pants. She massaged her frozen feet, one at a time. Again, Maria allowed it, but she did not abandon the subject. "Nothing to say?" she prodded.

The Wanssee was Berlin's largest lake, run through by the river Havel. Audrianna had no idea what a sloop was. Seeking to appease Maria with *some* conversation, she asked, "What—is—a—*slip*?" She mispronounced the word because she hadn't yet been taught it.

"A *sloop* is a small sailing vessel," whispered Maria, leaning against the backrest, shivering. "There is no protection from the elements. Thus, I am wet."

Kuniko came back into the room with a plush robe. "Come," she said, helping Maria up, pulling her wet blouse over her head. Shamelessly, Audrianna surveyed Maria's body, flushing with various hues of craving. Only half those desires were wholesome.

Kuniko wrapped Maria in the robe and put her down on the couch, covering her with a soft woolen throw. She went back into the bathroom and splashed around in the water. The fragrance of bath oils filled the air.

Audrianna nudged her wheelchair forward and said, "Can—you—feel your fingers?" There was a three-word burst. Talking *was* getting easier.

"They're throbbing," replied Maria.

"Let me—see."

"I can call Dr. Curtis."

"Or," Audrianna shrugged, "you can let—me see." She reached under the blanket and took Maria's ice-pop fingers out for inspection. Maria resumed her punishment.

"Miss Lewis' team must have frequent cold weather injuries, living out on Tybee Island. That's what she calls it, right? After her birthplace in America? Had you not insisted we sleep separately, I would've noticed your overnight house calls to her compound. What a dedicated physician you are, my dearest."

Eyes downcast, Audrianna rubbed Maria's fingers without responding. At least she was discussing it with her. It was better than the silent treatment she'd been dishing out.

"Master, here are the photographs sent by Captain Canaris." Alex came in and waved a folder at her. He seemed to be in a hurry.

"Perfect timing; put them here." Maria nodded beside her. Alex dropped them on the couch and quickly left the room; one picture slipped out on the floor. It was a photograph of Kendis' distillery.

Audrianna held onto Maria's retreating hands. "Sorry, *Glinda*," she whispered, no idea why she'd called Maria that.

"Glinda?" Maria laughed. "Is that another one of your paramours? One I haven't discovered yet?"

"No, I—I don't—"

"Why is it always so hellish in here?" Stephanie stepped into the room, dropping her bags. She glanced between Audrianna and Maria, immediately recognizing the tension. "Have I interrupted something?" she asked.

"Yes," said Audrianna.

"No," said Maria.

Kuniko stuck her head around the corner and announced, "Your bath, ma'am."

Pulling out of Audrianna's clutch, Maria picked the picture up off the floor and stuffed it in the folder, then got up and locked the folder inside her desk. She coldly kissed Stephanie's hand. "Good morning, Leyonelle."

"Maria, you're not still angry with me about the showgirls, are you? What was I supposed to say?"

Maria did not reply. She went into the bathroom and shut the door. Stephanie changed the subject. "Well, let's take the air together. Shall we, Audri? For the life of me, I don't know how you live in this heat."

Audrianna rolled her eyes. She wanted to be in there with Maria, not outside freezing in the snow. But it didn't matter—she had become the second casualty of Stephanie's menopause.

"Here, lean forward," Stephanie commanded, wrapping blankets around her. "Where are your scarf and earmuffs?" She walked over and rapped on the bathroom door. "Maria? I'm taking Audrianna out for a walk. Where might I find her winter headwear?"

The door cracked open and Stephanie leaned in, listening to something Audrianna could not hear. "All right. We'll just wait out here, then," she said. She walked back to the couch and sat down, pulling out a cigarette. "That child appears to be lovestruck. Have you noticed?"

Audrianna twisted around and looked at the bathroom door. What had Stephanie just seen?

"Of course," Stephanie flicked her lighter, "she isn't the first person to fall under Maria's spell. Won't be the last, either. That's the reason you and I get on so well together, Audri. We've both missed the enchantments of Maria Orsic."

Audrianna hadn't missed anything: the enchantments had been poorly timed, much like the rest of her life. She pointed at the bathroom. "What—did she—say?"

"Oh," Stephanie gestured behind her, "the girl? She's getting you something of Maria's to wear. All your winter things are still at Niklas' house. I suppose you hadn't gotten around to moving them, yet."

That was one way to look at it. Another was, she had no intention of moving them—she had no intention of being in Maria's house that winter. Audrianna must consider she'd been planning suicide from day one. She'd moved in with Maria as a ruse. But why?

"Mmm ... yummy." Stephanie's eyes lit up as Kuniko emerged with a cashmere shawl, hat and matching gloves. "Is that Schiaparelli? How lovely."

"I don't know what *Shees-a-prelli* is," muttered Kuniko, plopping the hat on Audrianna's head, pulling it down to her brow line and over her ears. She wrapped the scarf crudely around her neck, then handed her the gloves. Audrianna put them on.

"Schiaparelli is an Italian fashion designer, dear. It's hardly surprising you've never heard of her, but" she stubbed out her cigarette, "I'm tickled to learn Maria's isn't completely in thrall to that *whore*, Coco Chanel."

"Stephanie!"

"Right. Let's be off." Stephanie stood up, wheeling Audrianna out the door, out the house and down to the lake. Moving along the frosty path, she brought up the Needle. "It's going to take a little longer than I anticipated to get that report," she said.

The wheelchair became sluggish. Audrianna looked over the side. "Steffi—blanket's caught—wheel."

Stephanie ignored her, applying more force to the handles. "I'm well known at the City Bank of Berlin, so I'll have to wear a disguise."

"Wheel—blanket—caught."

"Where is that wig you wore to the *Moulin Rouge* two years ago? Is it still at Niklas' house?"

"Wheel! Caught!"

It was too late. The wheelchair tipped forward. Audrianna went with it. She protected her face from the ground, scraping up her elbows instead.

"Audrianna! What did you do?!" Stephanie shouted, taking hold of the wheelchair, flipping it upright. By the arms, she dragged Audrianna backwards to a nearby tree and propped her up, ranting out loud. "Of course, *none* of this would be possible if Maria would just teach you to walk!" Classic Stephanie: she was never more righteous than when she was in the wrong.

Panting, she looked up at the house and said, "I'll have to go back for help, Audri. It won't take me long—I'll walk quickly." She bundled Audrianna in blankets, then retrieved her purse from the ground. Into the sky she screamed, "Towards thee I roll, thou all-destroying but unconquering snow." It was a quote from *Moby Dick*. Only Stephanie had substituted the original word *whale* for *snow*.

Bang, Bang, Bang.

She pulled her pistol out and shot up the tree. Menopause was Audrianna's horizon, too. Perhaps that was why she'd charted suicide in advance.

Down fell branches, leaves and pine cones, victims of the gunshots. Stephanie gathered them in her scarf and deposited them in front of Audrianna, setting the pile ablaze with fuel from her flask. Over the fire she stood, cigarette in hand, smoking the entire thing without speaking. Then, she reloaded and handed Audrianna the pistol, saying, "Shoot the wild boars: the foxes and weasels won't hurt you."

"Wild—*boars*. That's great—Steffi." Audrianna dropped her head against the tree, closing her eyes.

"And don't go to sleep." Stephanie shook her shoulder. "That's the worst thing you can do in the cold."

Audrianna sat up in anger. "I know—Stephanie," she shouted, poking herself in the chest. "I'm a d..d..doctor."

"You're a washed out obstetrician, dear. It isn't quite the same thing. Stay warm. I'll be back in a jiffy." She blew her a kiss, then left.

After a small period of time, Audrianna heard a motorcar behind her, then footsteps. Expecting Stephanie, she tinkled on herself when Eva Braun squatted in front of her and said, "Hello, Baroness. I was on my way to have an argument with Maria when I became distracted by the smoke."

Audrianna's heartbeat accelerated. She shrunk under the blankets, palming the revolver with sweaty fingers.

"But, how fortunate, my encountering you like this," she continued. "I've been most curious to know how our arrangement goes—your part, that is. Even I can see it isn't as you planned."

There it was. Eva Braun revealed herself as Audrianna's conspirator in a plot yet to be uncovered. If there were lingering doubts, they were no longer.

"Do I scare you?" she asked.

Yes, Audrianna was terrified, but she'd die before admitting it. "Cold," she whispered. That was true, too. She fingered the trigger, resisting the urge to let loose with gunfire. Whatever *arrangement* she'd entered into with Eva could stay buried forever that way. Maria would never have to know.

Eva spotted the wheelchair and rose to retrieve it. She wheeled over to Audrianna and said, "You should abstain from snow bathing if you're sensitive to cold." She snapped her fingers, scooping Audrianna up from the ground.

Audrianna slapped her repeatedly across the face and Eva tossed her into the wheelchair, knocking it backwards. Audrianna lost hold of the gun. "Damn!" she hissed.

Blood dripped from Eva's nostrils. She eyed the gun on the ground. "That would've been most inconvenient for me, Baroness von Traugott." She unfolded a handkerchief and pressed it to her nose, caution in her glare. "Inconvenient for both of us, since we each have something the other wants. Do not forget that."

Concentrate. Audrianna coached herself. These details were priceless—the only person who could make sense of this part of the puzzle was Eva Braun. Maria made it clear she would not investigate their affiliation.

A slow smile spread across Eva's features as she considered the situation. She called the gun to hand and it levitated into her grip. "I'll tell you what," she laughed, releasing the cylinder and extracting the bullets. "If you can load this, you can shoot me." She slapped the cylinder in place and handed the gun back, then the bullets. "You have as long as it takes for me to finish our discussion. Go."

Audrianna bobbled the bullets, dropping all but two. She tried various ways of pushing the cylinder open: none of them worked. What did she have that Eva wanted so badly? As a Hereditary Health Court Medical Officer she had access to victims for Eva's experiments. Was that it? Her supply of bodies was depleted and she needed more? What was she giving Audrianna in return? What could possibly be so important that Audrianna would agree to such an atrocity?

"I'm holding your beloved prize, in good faith, under guard, as promised." Eva blotted her nose, unconcerned with Audrianna's attempt to load the weapon. "Should you be unable to fulfill the terms of our agreement you will not only forfeit said *prize,* but you will also ensure its wasting. Do not try me, Baroness von Traugott. I am unforgiving when someone breaks a contract with me."

Audrianna's heart dropped. What prize? What contract? She banged the cylinder on the armrest.

"The residents of Tybee Island," Eva continued, "will all be destroyed. I am neither ignorant, nor indifferent to that enterprise, madam. I've turned a blind eye as a courtesy to you. There will be no cause for such generosity should our alliance be aborted."

Eva knew about the distillery—of course she did. She'd traced Kendis' dress there. Audrianna found the release lever, and the barrel opened. Hands shaking, she slipped the bullets in the holes and raised the gun, just as Eva's similitude sunk in: *beloved* prize. She was talking about *Lorna.* She had to be. She'd been hiding him all along. He would remain hidden until Eva saw fit to release him. Of this, Audrianna was sure.

"Aren't you going to shoot me?" Eva asked with a smirk.

Audrianna lowered the pistol.

"I thought not," said Eva. She gave her the once over. "If your illness is playing havoc with your memory and you cannot remember our arrangement, so much the better. An attack of the conscience would be most unfortunate at this late stage." She reached inside her inner pocket and handed Audrianna an elaborately decorated dance card. The embossed cover read: *Unmasking 1909.*

"What—is this?" Audrianna snatched it, reading inside. Of ten dance spaces, eight were filled. She recognized only one name: Wilhelm Canaris.

"Your mother's last dance card," Eva told her. "I thought you'd like to have it."

A sour taste emerged in Audrianna's mouth; her throat tightened. "I don't understand," she rasped.

"I think you do," said Eva, smiling. She turned and walked away, calling behind her, "Stay the course, Baroness von Traugott: let the natural progression of things prevail."

CHAPTER 6

Maria sat down opposite Audrianna with a novel she intended to read alone—passive ostracism: week seven. Shortly after Eva's departure that morning, she had zipped down to rescue Audrianna on a green whiplash, slipping in the snow. She had collided with a tree. Her glasses suffered multiple fractures, and she did not have a spare pair. Sipping her after-dinner wine, Maria read quietly by firelight while Audrianna watched. After ten minutes of silence she finally said, "You were charged by rabid boars. That's what Stephanie told me. Did you know beforehand she meant to raise such an alarm?" Her soft, temperate voice bellied her body language: she was heated. Audrianna could tell. "Was my humiliation pleasing to watch?"

"No, *Glinda*." Audrianna shook the word off. She tried again. "No, *Glinda*—damn!" Why couldn't she say Maria's name?

The cords in Maria's neck tensed. She made eye contact over her book and said, "I have a sickly intolerance for crassness, Audrianna. My discomfort means little to you, I know, so I'll add that vulgar language only weakens your rejoinder."

Audrianna had no idea what rejoinder meant. She'd been studying *Roget's Thesaurus*, trying to keep up with Maria's vocabulary, but had only made it to letter *H*.

"Master?" Alex came into the room with a sealed letter and metal file box. "From Captain Canaris," he said, handing them to her. Maria opened the letter and read whilst Alex greeted Audrianna. "*Hallo*, Leyonelle," he said.

Sulking, Audrianna replied, "Hello, *Mad Hatter*—no!" That's not what she meant to say.

Maria looked up from the letter, one eyebrow cocked. After a moment, she turned to Alex and said, "I apologize, Alexander. Baroness von Traugott is still in shock from her encounter with the sounder."

Alex shifted his weight, nervously. "Her what?"

"Her encounter with the sounder: the group of wild pigs." Maria put the box on the floor; her tone turned subtly facetious. "Baroness von Traugott was charged in her wheelchair this morning whilst ice fishing along the lake."

Ice fishing? No. Audrianna started to explain, but Maria spoke over her. "Fortunately, minimal harm befell her because Princess von Hohenlohe spritzed her with swine repellant prior to their outing—or so she said. Wasn't that ingenious of her, Alex?" She forced a smile.

Swine repellant? Audrianna dropped her forehead into her hand. Was Stephanie trying to make things more difficult for her?

Callum walked in with chilled grapefruit juice for Audrianna. She refused it with a wave of the hand. "Our deepest apologies for your ordeal, Leyonelle," he said. "The gardener cannot account for how the wretched beasts got in. I've dismissed him without a reference."

Audrianna ground the heels of her hands into her eyes. This was unbelievable. Maria was letting this continue just to belabor her point. Fanning herself first, Audrianna pointed over the side of the wheelchair and said, "It was blanket in—wheel. Then..." She clapped her hands and nodded.

Callum looked to Maria for interpretation.

Lost in her letter, Maria distractedly replied, "She lured the gullible creatures into her blanket and snapped their unsuspecting necks in the spokes of her wheel. I see no need to dismiss the gardener, however. The blame lies with the swine and the swine have certainly paid the price." She finished reading and took her broken glasses off, pinching her eyelids closed. Her change of countenance carried a chill—she'd read something unsettling in that letter. It was obvious.

Bracing for further reproach, Audrianna turned to Callum and said, "Thank you, *King Brian*—No!" She slapped the armrests, angry with herself. Why couldn't she say anyone's name?

Maria opened her eyes and regarded Audrianna with a tincture of affection. It was first time she'd looked at her without scowling in almost two months. "King Brian. That's most amusing, dearest," she said.

Audrianna's lips parted. Warmth bled into her chest as she soaked up Maria's gilded stare.

"I'm unfamiliar with the pun," Callum said, checking with Alex. Alex shook his head.

Up with a bounce, Maria tossed the letter on her desk and plucked up a pen and stationary. She talked whilst jotting a note. "It isn't a pun. She is using characters from novels we've read as identifiers. King Brian from *Darby O'Gill*—that's you. Mad Hatter from *Alice in Wonderland*—that's Alex." She folded the note and sealed it with wax, impressing her signet. "She's been calling me *Glinda*."

Glinda the Good Witch from *The Wonderful Wizard of Oz*. The moniker fit like a glove. The others did, too.

"Why is she doing that?" Callum asked.

"That's for me to understand," replied Maria. "Callum, you are dismissed. Alex," she turned to him, "please dispatch this immediately under terms of parley." She handed him the letter.

"Parley?"

"That's what I said. Yes."

When neither he nor Callum budged, Maria's tone sharpened. "I have issued orders, yet you both still stand before me. Why is that?"

Callum pulled out a handkerchief and blotted his head. "Beg pardon, Master. Come along, Alexander." He backed away, splashing grapefruit juice all over his tray. Maria seemed especially mindful of the spillage, wary even. "*Gute Nacht*, Baroness. I'm thankful you're unharmed," he said.

Click. The door shut behind them and Audrianna snapped back into focus. Her eyes snagged on Maria's silhouette as she leaned against the desk with her wine. "Aren't you well, dearest?" Maria asked.

Audrianna swallowed and said, "I'm okay. Why?" She looked down to make sure she hadn't had an accident on herself.

"You refused the grapefruit juice."

Audrianna looked back up. "Sorry. I don't—like it."

"You don't like it now?" Maria appeared surprised.

As far as Audrianna remembered she had never liked grape-fruit juice. Maria suggested otherwise, but Audrianna decided to answer truthfully: "Never liked it."

Smirking, Maria poured a little wine into a separate glass, then walked over and handed it to Audrianna. She'd never offered her wine before. "Will you enjoy a taste of Burgundy, then?" She stroked Audrianna's hair; her acerbity was hushed. Something had softened her, though what, Audrianna could not say. It really didn't matter. This was her chance.

She captured Maria's hand and held it against her cheek, whispering, "Glinda—Good Witch."

"Glinda the Good Witch. Yes. I finally guessed that," Maria replied with a chuckle. "I've omitted certain names from your reprogramming, I see, mine included." She stroked Audrianna's hair again, then pulled away, pointing at the wine glass as she walked back to her chair. "Drink. Please. I have a surprise for you here." She collected the box sent by Canaris and brought it back, taking the glass when Audrianna finished. She set the box on the table next to her.

Taken over by a sudden scourge of jitters, Audrianna said, "I don't—startle well."

Maria adjusted her glasses. "That sounds quite ominous. Should I be on my guard?"

Audrianna laughed at her. "How—should I know? You gave—me."

Maria's expression remained serious and Audrianna stopped laughing. They held unblinking eye contact until Maria eventually asked, "Have you really no recollection of this box?"

Butterflies swatted Audrianna's insides; she tried to look away, but Maria held her chin in place. "Please don't avoid my eyes," she whispered, her tone gentle but stern. "Tell me the truth, Audrianna. If we have honesty between us, we have a real chance of moving forward from this."

Audrianna frantically scanned her impotent memories for clues. "No, Glinda. I..." she shook her head, "don't—know. Should I?"

"It's an important part of your past. Yes, I think you should know it."

Tears quickly welled, then spilled over from the corners of Audrianna's eyes; her breath accelerated. "Suddenly—feels less like a surprise and more—punishment. Is that—you intended?" she asked.

"No."

Audrianna rejected her answer. "Could've spared yourself—chore of being nice to me. I can swallow—medicine without sugar."

Maria narrowed her eyes. "My dearest, I do not understand that musical, yet incomprehensible statement. Are you insulting me, or merely questioning the integrity of my word?"

"What?" Audrianna balked. "No, I'm—saying—"

Kuniko entered without knocking and began her nightly chores, caterwauling in her native tongue. Momentarily fazed, Audrianna took a deep breath and bickered to Maria, "Does she have—do that right now?"

"Lower your voice, please."

"Right." Audrianna rolled her eyes. "Come hell or—water, no chinks—in our armor."

Maria snatched her glasses off her face and propped her hand on her hip, annoyed. "Audrianna, do you enjoy toying with me by speaking in idioms? Does my frustration amuse you in some way?"

Kuniko snickered under her breath. Incensed by her mockery, Audrianna made a hasty decision. She yanked on her necklace, once, twice, three times until it broke. Tossing it aside, she spoke to Maria telepathically, her language now open and free of impediment. "I'm not doing it on purpose, Maria; it's a habit. I would never deliberately provoke you like that."

Maria joined her in telepathic conversation. "Since when?"

The question was clearly rhetorical but Audrianna was determined to answer it. "Since I've grown to care for you, I guess." She pulled a tissue from her pocket and dabbed at her tears, allowing Maria time to respond. When she did not, Audrianna nudged her for an answer. "Aren't you glad to hear I feel that way?"

"I'm not sure yet."

A wave of heaviness crept into Audrianna's stomach as she processed Maria's ambivalent response. Regrouping, she channeled her hurt feelings into a soft, sincere redress. "Listen, Maria. I know how badly I've behaved toward you. Believe me. Stephanie takes every possible opportunity to reacquaint me with my alter ego."

Maria nodded a couple times. "You've been reacquainted with your alter ego, have you? Thankfully I have not."

Right on cue, Kuniko came over and inserted herself. "Baroness von Traugott, I lay out new incontinence pads for you."

"Go—away!" Audrianna turned and shouted, pointing out the door, teeth bared.

Maria grabbed her arm and held it. She spoke to her telepathically. "Please don't be so indelicate with my staff. She's only trying to help you."

Audrianna responded in thought, laughing at Maria's naiveté. "She's not trying to help me, Maria. She's trying to embarrass me. This is the first time you've had your eyes on me in months and she doesn't like it. She's trying to commandeer your attention."

"Do not project *your* deceptive nature onto her, Audrianna," Maria snapped. Out loud to Kuniko she said, "Thank you, darling. I'll help Baroness von Traugott to bed tonight."

"Baroness von Traugott hates me!" wailed Kuniko.

Audrianna slumped forward, holding her forehead. Yes, Baroness von Traugott *does* hate you, she thought, quickly remembering Maria could hear her. *Damn!* She looked up, eyes wide. *Damn!* She'd just cursed, too. She slapped her hands on the armrests and growled, frustrated.

Maria walked over and squeezed Kuniko into her side, kissing her on the temple. "Baroness von Traugott is having a fit, as you see—if you'll leave us, please." She patted Kuniko on the bottom and she trotted obediently out the door, blotting her eyes with her apron. Once gone, Maria pivoted to Audrianna and said, "I have a headache. I'll rest in my room awhile and come back to help you to bed."

Audrianna's mind erupted. "Wait, wait. Maria, wait. Please don't leave before I finish telling you this. Please."

Maria came back and stood above her, looking down. "What is it?" she asked.

"I want to tell you that I'm so desperately sorry any part of me—past or present—could ever be so cruel and inconsiderate to you. I want to make it up to you, if you'll let me—try to make it up to you, that is. I know I have no right to ask it."

"What are you asking me for, precisely?" said Maria.

"Another chance."

"Another chance?" Maria laughed. "You have a great sense of self-importance. Do you imagine anyone else in my realm betraying me like you have, then being granted *another chance*? You assume too much, madam."

Audrianna tilted her face down. "Maria, I don't know what I've promised you in the past—"

"No?" Maria queried.

"And I don't know why you should believe me now when I tell you, ahem, most likely the same thing, but—"

"Yes? Why should I believe you?" Maria snapped.

Audrianna gently called her bluff. "Because I think you *want* to believe me, Maria. I think you've had some information tonight, which has mitigated at least some of my offenses and you *want* to believe I am still worth your time. Isn't that so?"

"Hardly," Maria snorted. "You've lied to me, stolen from me. You've mocked my devotion with your promiscuity."

"*Promiscuity*? I slept with one person, Maria. One." That's all Audrianna remembered, at any rate.

"Those offenses have not been mitigated," Maria insisted. "The information I received tonight speaks to your motivation. Nothing more."

Audrianna grabbed the sides of her head, laughing: three sips of alcohol and now she was free. "Motivation? My God, Maria. Look at me." She pulled her forward by the wrist and bored into her eyes: "Look *inside* of me for just—one—second and *see*. Whoever that was, doesn't live here anymore."

Maria tapped the file box next to her and said, "Let's see. Open this."

Audrianna let go of her wrist. "God, Maria, whatever you're trying to prove with this, fine." She ran her hands through her hair, then moved the box to her lap. She lifted the lid and fumbled through a hundred or more black and white snapshots, all children, all with various physical disfigurations. She flipped one of the pictures over and read the notation: Adelaide Lange.

Date of Birth: 21 July, 1929. Primary Disability: Cerebral Palsy. Disposition of Patient: Euthanasia By Order of Dr. Audrianna von Traugott on 13 April, 1933. These were the victims Audrianna had handed over to Eva for her experiments. When Maria chose, she knew how to give a lesson.

"I beg your pardon, but you've confused me with your teacher," Maria responded to that thought, annoyed. Replacing the lid, she took the box away from Audrianna and slid it onto her desk, turning around. "I thought sharing this with you would allow for some peace of mind in your otherwise tempestuous life. Obviously, I was mistaken."

Audrianna clutched her chest, crying telepathically, "You thought bringing me a catalogue of children I've sentenced to death would bring me peace of mind!? Are you crazy?" She pressed the soggy tissue to her nose; it fell apart in her hands. Secretions dripped onto her blouse, precipitating a flood of tears.

Moved by Audrianna's evident distress, Maria fetched her a scented handkerchief, then remained beside her while she cried. "Those children have not been put to death, dearest," she said gently. "Is that what you honestly thought?"

A swell of euphoria suspended Audrianna's tears. She looked up from the handkerchief and sniffed. "What?"

Maria studied her expression for several long moments before replying, "They are ensconced in an orphanage on Tybee Island with your lover, Miss Lewis. You put them there after signing their death certificates, saving them, in effect, from Eva's racial hygiene program. I've always wondered why you pushed me so hard to secure you that appointment to the Hereditary Health Court. Now, I understand. I also see now that you truly have no memory of this, nor do I believe the person who conspired against me is the same person with whom I'm now speaking."

She twirled one of Audrianna's fallen curls around her finger, scrutinizing her so deeply it hurt.

"So, tell me. Who are *you*?" she asked. "And what do you want with another chance?"

Audrianna whimpered as she felt a surge of warring emotions. She reached for Maria, then retracted, wanting to hold her, but uncertain of Maria's mien.

"Master?" Alex's voice called outside the door. He knocked a couple of times, but Maria ignored him, focusing instead on Audrianna.

"What do you want with another chance?" she repeated.

Audrianna did not hesitate with her reply, speaking out loud with a new and undeniable sense of conviction. "I want—help—you get home."

"You haven't the talent for certainty, even when it presents itself as the truth," replied Maria. She exhaled a tired sigh. "Audrianna, what have you been doing in secret with Eva Braun? I cannot investigate the matter, as you know."

"Master?" Alex called again. "I have a situation here."

Audrianna snapped a look at the door. She forgot the question. "I'm sorry?"

"Do you have any recollection of your dealings with Eva Braun?" Maria asked again, softly.

Audrianna shook her head. "No, Glinda, I—*grrrr.*" She slapped the armrests, angered by her disability.

"Shh, shh, shh." Maria captured her skull, holding it against her pelvis. She kissed the top of her head and whispered, "Tell me with your mind. Tell me the truth. We'll go from there."

Audrianna complied, relieved to have the ease of telepathy. "I think she has Lorna hidden somewhere. I thought I might've exchanged children from my office for his freedom. Though

I realize that's less likely now, given what you've just told me about the orphanage. I don't know what I've promised her in return."

Maria swayed.

A lover and a mother of a Gavrilekian for most of her adult life, Audrianna recognized the presentation of emotional distress. Panicking, she pushed back and said, "Maria, look at me, please. Let me see your eyes."

Knock, knock, knock. "Master, I must see you!"

Maria flashed her faded eyes with a little head shake. She collected Audrianna's worried face between clammy palms and said, "I am unfamiliar with this kind of intercourse. I cannot tolerate the deluge of emotion with ease."

"I know. I know. I'm sorry," Audrianna said. Eyes upward, lips parted, she rested her chin on Maria's slim figure, steeling her courage to offer a kiss. A kiss was an open channel to her soul—fuel for Maria, if she wanted it. It was clear Maria had never received such an offering from Audrianna before.

Stroking Audrianna's cheek, she said, "A scene of natural beauty is a storm written over time, day after day, each sheet of lightning leaving its indelible mark. Without turbulent times, a person would not possess his or her unique character."

Audrianna took Maria's hand and kissed it, holding it against her lips, savoring the poetry of her words. How spellbinding it was.

"Maria, I can't promise that you've seen the last of my mistakes—in fact, I'm pretty sure you haven't, but I can promise you that from this day forward, you'll never have to worry about my fidelity, my loyalty or my devotion to you." Her voice cracked with emotion as she adapted the tale of the leyonelle. "If you're sick or wounded or need shelter from the elements, I will close my petals around you and keep you safe until you can fly again. I will help you get home. Give me the chance to show you I'm still worthy of your trust."

"Master?" The door opened and Kendis pushed into the room, Alex close on her heels. Both were breathing hard. "Master, here is Miss Kendis Lewis. I could not stop her without using force."

Maria looked down at Audrianna and spoke.

"Here's your chance."

———•———

"Why have you blockaded my island, Miss Orsic?" Kendis asked.

Maria took Audrianna's necklace off the table and retied it around her neck, stroking the back of her hair. Audrianna's thoughts were once again obscured.

"Good evening, Miss Lewis. I apologize for the miscommunication. I had no idea of you coming here at this time of night."

"You asked me to come at the earliest opportunity. This is the earliest opportunity," Kendis replied.

"Indeed," Maria said, forcing a smile. "Won't you be seated?" She gestured to the chair closest to the fire, opposite of Audrianna. "A drink, perhaps." She came around, hands clasped in front of her. "What would you like? Thank you, Alex," she nodded at him, "you may go. I'll call you when Miss Lewis is ready to leave. Miss Lewis, what would you like? Wine? Scotch?"

Kendis looked at Audrianna but Audrianna averted her gaze, concentrating on not losing her bladder. Her momentary state of tranquility was gone.

"Scotch," Kendis said.

"Yes. I guessed that," Maria remarked, pulling her hidden bottle from the desk compartment and pouring a jigger.

She brought it to Kendis who tossed it back in one gulp, then promptly returned the glass to Maria.

"Very well. Sit please," Maria said. "And if we may," she glanced at Audrianna, "let us openly acknowledge that past romantic interests are not germane to this exchange. It is counterproductive to behave coyly with one another, particularly when we are facing a crisis—the theft of the Vril. Can we all agree on that?"

Audrianna locked eyes with Kendis who gave her a little encouraging nod, and Audrianna nodded in turn.

"Good," Maria said, opening her attaché case and fishing out a stack of papers. She sat down in the last open chair. "Now, I am presented with a difficult problem, Miss Lewis, in that you and your partner Mr. Turing, have knowingly and willingly designed and employed devices meant to rob me of precious resources. In doing so, you have breached the protected boundaries of my group and that, madam, is an act of war, for which I must demand satisfaction."

Audrianna stood a better chance of surviving Maria's reprisal. True or not, she took the blame. Swallowing the lump in her throat, she turned to Maria and whispered, "My fault."

"No, Audri. Lemme handle this, okay?" Kendis warned.

Maria tilted her head, watching their interaction with curiosity. Momentarily distracted, she said, "When you took my mirror for your project ten years ago, what concept did you intend to teach her?"

"Trust," Kendis replied.

Maria chuckled. "And your behavior is generally worthy of trust? You are the example of trustworthiness. Is that right?"

"Yeah, as much as any teacher can be the example. I also have lesson plans as a guide."

Lesson plans? Audrianna rolled her eyes.

"What circumstance in your plan allows for the premeditated deception of one's own consciousness, Miss Lewis?" Maria asked.

"It was never our intention you'd be hurt."

"Yes, but what circumstance?" Maria repeated.

Audrianna shuddered. Kendis was clever in her own right, but she would not win a war of wits against Maria. It did not stop her from trying.

"The circumstance in which one's consciousness must be deceived in order to see a larger picture," she explained.

"A larger picture as you see it."

"As I see it, yeah," Kendis whispered. "What I see is all I have to contribute."

Maria smirked. "Hardly persuasive given your ineptitude of certain simple concepts."

"Such as?

"Such as self-restraint, Miss Lewis. Or do your lessons routinely allow for physical intimacy between teacher and pupil?"

"From time to time," Kendis replied. "Audrianna was mistrustful in general because of what happened with Lorna. I had tuh' open that channel with love."

Audrianna slammed her hands down, screaming. "I am sitting right—here!"

Maria got up and poured herself a second glass of wine, ignoring the outburst. "You had to open a channel of trust with love. What a fanciful abstraction." She looked over her shoulder. "Another scotch?" she asked Kendis.

"No thanks."

"Dearest, would you care for a cool glass of water?" Maria glanced at her.

Yes, a great big one that I can drown myself in, Audrianna thought, flashing her fiery eyes at Maria.

"I do not understand that facial expression," Maria said. "Please vocalize your thoughts."

"No," Audrianna grumbled.

"Very well." Maria went back to her seat and sat down. "Miss Lewis, as much as I would relish hearing more of your far-fetched philosophies, especially as they've affected my mirror, let us please return to the topic of your theft on my property." She reexamined her documents. "Yes, here it is. From early 1933 until now, a total of 2.87 ounces of Vril has been leached from my irrigation system via your robotic pestilence—although, compliments to you, Miss Lewis. It was an artful heist. However, with such an ineffectual amount, I can't help but wonder why—"

"It's only an ineffectual amount if I was usin' it for makin' weapons," Kendis interrupted, looking around, uncertain.

Maria narrowed her eyes. "Quite. Which is why I wonder about your motivation. Why would you go to such lengths, and at great risk to your group, to possess such a small amount? Before you answer—if you intend to answer—let me remind you that Valkyrie Bylaws allow the outcome to be determined through space skirmish. Miss Lewis, a space skirmish between our groups is highly inadvisable. Mr. Turing's league of musical robots may be a match for The Gershwin Brothers or Puccini, but the Incubus clan is quite another matter. My partners will make a savage example of you—I will not oppose them."

Musical robots? Audrianna tried to ask but Kendis spoke above her.

"Miss Orsic, we're a non-violent group, peripheral figures in the Nazis' grand plan. How can we be in your way?"

"Please." Maria held up her hand with a little scoff. "Abandon the misconception that I can be coerced. If I proffer mercy, it will be because your argument has merit, not because I am easily led." She took an exhausted breath and sifted through her papers, shaking her head. "Either way, I cannot act in contravention of my group's contract. Let us hope you two have not done something I cannot save your orphans from."

"The children are blameless," Kendis said.

"Most people are blameless in war, Miss Lewis. "Youth is not an exemption."

Kendis tugged her hands through her hair, frustrated. "What do you want, Miss Orsic. I'm here to cooperate. We don't hafta play these games."

Maria turned directly to her. "What *are* you doing with the Vril, Miss Lewis? Let's start there."

"I'm usin' it to power my island, feed everyone, heat water, that sorta thing. That much traditional electricity is unaffordable. See? There is no treachery here."

"You mean beyond the theft itself."

"Right. Beyond the theft itself," Kendis whispered.

Maria took a sip of wine, contemplating. "Naturally, I'm curious about your robots, especially the musical ones." She flipped to the last page in her stack, running her finger across the paper. "There is no evidence of armaments, I see. So, you're obviously not building an army. It says here that none of Mr. Turing's robots have bodies: they're all just singing heads. Is that true?" she asked with a laugh.

Hunching over, Audrianna held her head in her hand. This was unreal. Just when she thought the weirdness had leveled, singing robot heads were revealed. What's more, she had obviously been a part of it. Devon was *still* a part of it: he'd said so that day with Jörð.

"Metal is expensive. Arms and legs are unnecessary," Kendis said.

"Unnecessary for what objective?" Maria asked, looking up. "Singin'."

"I meant to inquire about your goal for this round of play, Miss Lewis. Which objective are you and Mr. Turing playing for?"

Kendis glanced at Audrianna and Audrianna knew by her look, one part of her memory was indeed accurate: she was playing to win. Kendis confirmed it.

"You're playing to win." Maria adjusted her glasses.

"Yes."

"With musical robots."

"Yes."

"Oh dear, Miss Lewis. I fear your judgment is—" Maria stopped and scratched her forehead, a pained look upon her face. She consulted her papers again. "You have a team of mentally challenged musicians; Mr. Turing has a team of clock makers and scientists—the one notable exception being Aiden Bryant, who does seem a capable warrior, yes, but he is the only one. Neither you, nor Mr. Turing have experienced combat. How do you intend to win this contest with such a roster?"

Kendis did not answer.

"I don't mean to sound impertinent, Miss Lewis," Maria went on, "I've just never encountered something quite this fanciful before. Not from a master, at least." She set the papers on the side table and finished her wine in thought. Eventually, she rose and deposited her glass on her desk. Turning around, she propped herself on the desk's edge and said, "Miss Lewis, one of my players, with whom you seem to be acquainted—Lorna— vanished the night Baroness von Traugott made an attempt on her own life. Did you know she'd discharged a bullet into her head, when last you saw her?"

Kendis' eyes widened. She looked at Audrianna and whispered, "Is that what happened to ya, Audri?"

"I take it you didn't know." Maria said.

"I read she was attacked. Audri, did ya try to kill yourself, honey?" Kendis got up and knelt at Audrianna's feet. She reached for her hands but Audrianna drew back.

"I think so," she whispered.

"Wha'do'ya mean, you think so?" Kendis pressed.

"I can't remember—if I did or didn't."

Maria brushed past Kendis to stand behind Audrianna, hands protectively on her shoulders. "Brain damage, Miss Lewis. We're working to restore her speech and motor skills. However, I fear her memories shall always be marred."

Kendis sat back on her haunches and stared at them, incredulous. "Then how do ya know she did it?"

"The same way I know about you, Miss Lewis. I commissioned a sleuth to investigate her imprints. Her connection with you was easily rendered, much more so than her other connections."

Kendis swallowed. "What other connections?"

Maria answered with a question. "Do you know where Lorna is, Miss Lewis?"

"No."

"But you know he is missing."

Kendis shrugged. "Yeah, anyone who reads *Contempo* or *GSpot* knows he's missin'."

Maria forced a smile. "Miss Lewis, I'd be most obliged if you can tell us anything you can about Baroness von Traugott's mindset prior to this event. It would be helpful to know what made her so unhappy."

"I wanna talk to her alone," said Kendis.

"You are not in a position to make demands."

Audrianna tried to interject, but Kendis talked over her. "I figure we're in equally crappy positions, Miss Orsic."

"I think not."

Kendis laughed. "Really? Chasing the mirror? How's that goin' for ya?

Audrianna snatched her necklace off again and threw it into the fire; she went off in her head, telepathy fluent. "Stop it, Kendis! She doesn't deserve that. It isn't her fault that I misled her, that I'm a liar and a cheat. She's living through the hell I created for her, graciously doing it, though I've brought much unnecessary suffering to her life. So, if you know what happened to Lorna or why I wanted to kill myself or anything about my involvement with Eva Braun—please come out with it! You don't have to talk to me alone. I need Maria now. I want her now. I'm sorry if that is hurtful for you."

In silence, Kendis examined her.

"What, Kendis?" Audrianna pitched, "Don't recognize who you see? Join the queue."

"There's no call for rudeness, dearest." Maria's gentle reprimand filled her head.

Audrianna laughed at her. "If not now, when, Maria? It seems perfectly appropriate to me right now."

"I do apologize, Miss Lewis. She had some wine earlier," Maria spoke out loud.

"I dunno why you tried to kill yourself, honey," Kendis shook her head in earnest. "I dunno what happened to Lorna. I do know that a few months before ya moved in here with Miss Orsic, you regularly met with Eva Braun. Anytime I'd ask ya about it, you'd say it concerned the health court. Except once you told me it was about gettin' vengeance."

Audrianna squinted. "Vengeance?"

Kendis flashed her eyes at Maria before replying. "Vengeance for your mother."

Pain filled the back of her throat. Audrianna thought of the dance card she'd received earlier from Eva. She reached around for Maria.

"All right." Maria gave her a reassuring squeeze. "Is that all you know, Miss Lewis?" she asked. "Does Eva know anything about you?"

"I don't think so," Kendis replied.

"She knows, Kendis," Audrianna said, settling back against her chair. "She knows about you, about the island, the inhabitants. She knows. She made threats against you all today."

"Today?" Maria came down by her ear. "Why did you not say you'd seen her today?"

"I was getting to it, Maria, before all this happened," Audrianna gestured to Kendis.

Maria stepped around the wheelchair with some urgency. Back to her desk, she searched through a basket of maps, speaking with her back still turned. "Let me be direct, Miss Lewis. I do not see your group as a legitimate threat, but I must impose some form of penalty for the theft of the Vril—that is mandated by a clause in my contract."

Audrianna turned her head and stared into the fire, oddly at ease with that verdict. Kendis would pay a price, but not enough to break her. Of this, Audrianna was sure. It was more than understanding Maria's enduring kindness, but feeling a part of it. In that moment, their coherence was tangible.

Maria unrolled one of the maps, placing a paperweight on each end. "Tybee Island will be annexed into the German Third Reich. You may keep your nightclub in Berlin," she said.

"My distillery is the financial backbone of our operation, Miss Orsic. I can't lose it."

"Even if that were my problem, Miss Lewis, I cannot impose a penalty less than that for something as egregious as your theft. Would you prefer I leave you to Eva Braun's savage justice?"

"No."

"No is an excellent choice, Miss Lewis. There. We're getting on so well now. Come join me, please."

Kendis got up and met her at the desk, looking down. "What are you showin' me?" she asked.

"This is a hundred-acre lot along the Elbe in Saxony: an old horse farm called Exeter. I intended to repurpose it into a winery one day. It is an excellent agricultural area for grapes, also wheat, barley, corn and potatoes: everything needed for a sustainable community. Along the property here," she dragged her finger across the map, "are barns, which can be inexpensively remodeled into barracks for your orphans."

Kendis looked up, with a slow disbelieving shake of the head. "I don't understand. You wanna gimme your land?"

"Slowly, Miss Lewis. Please," Maria lifted her hand, shutting her down. "Baroness von Traugott is entitled to half of everything I possess. In that the orphanage is a joint effort between you two, I feel obliged to offer you sanctuary on her behalf. If she'd like to use the property for that purpose, that is." She turned and looked at Audrianna.

Audrianna nodded, tears of gratitude shining in her eyes.

"Very well," Maria said. "The vessels currently surrounding your island will commence to move you up the Elbe. I have engineers aboard who are competent to disassemble and move your distillery, in addition to anything else you'd care to bring along. They'll help you with living quarters once you've arrived. Under contractual provisions governing treatment of our leyonelles and their property, no Gavrilekian in the Incubus clan will molest you while you are on Baroness von Traugott's land. Movements outside the property will be afforded no such protection."

Kendis paced the floor, knuckling her forehead. "You're signing my death warrant by forcing me from my spring."

"Ah, finally—we get to the quick of it." Maria fingered the map with a laugh. She considered a moment longer, then said, "Provided you make no further encroachments upon my group, I will personally ensure the protection of your spring, Miss Lewis. Are we agreed? The moment your singing robots turn commando, I shall fill your watery home with concrete, relegating you to that human casing you're in now. That is, unless you'd prefer to settle this in space, right now. You still have that option."

Audrianna tucked her face under her hand. There it was. Effortless as usual, Maria showcased her tactical skill. As far as Audrianna knew, Kendis did not have a spaceship—Maria likely knew it, too. Even if a spaceship were available, a dogfight in space against a war-hardened team like the Incubus was no choice at all. Kendis must consign her spring to Maria's safeguard. It was her only option. Expertly and without violence, Maria had taken Kendis hostage.

"Miss Lewis, if these terms are agreeable to you, I shall draw up a treaty," Maria said.

Reluctantly, Kendis nodded.

"Very well. Please excuse me. I must petition the Incubus seal from my office and arouse my scribe from his slumber."

Maria walked by Audrianna, gently capturing her chin between thumb and forefinger. Telepathically she said, "I have set in motion a plan to save your lover and your orphans. It will not be easy to work through: I will be overruled. You have power beyond my influence. I will set it up for you, but you must assert that authority."

Audrianna's core collapsed. "Oh, no, Maria. I don't—" She reached for Maria as she walked away. "Maria, wait!" she called frantically with her mind: Maria did not stop.

Kendis returned and knelt at Audrianna's feet, hands resting on her thighs. She said, "I've put a block around us, so we can talk freely."

Audrianna shook her head and shrugged. "There's nothing more to say."

"Then, just listen to me for a minute, Audri. You don't hafta stay here. You can come and live with us on that land in Saxony and no one can hurt either of us. That's what she just said."

"No. I won't leave—her." Audrianna rasped, quickly reverting to telepathy. "She saved me, Kendis, even after she found out about you. I made a fool of her with you. I hurt her the worst with you!"

Kendis looked around. "Nah, honey. She's gonna be most hurt by whatever method you have devised to deliver her biverse energy to Eva Braun. She just dudn' know it, yet."

"What!?"

"My message?" Kendis asked with a shake of the head. "Didn't ya get my message."

Audrianna pressed her skull between her palms, trapping a recollection inside:

"Audri, I found the papers you left behind. Your agreement with—"

She grabbed Kendis' forearms, shaking them. "What did it say? Tell me again!"

"It said you and Miss Braun are to make an equal exchange: your mother's soul for Maria's biverse energy. There were very few details, Audri. It was signed on the night you tried 'tuh kill yourself—if that's what ya really tried 'tuh do. You left it in my studio."

The air was sucked out of the room. Another memory forced itself on Audrianna: Eva's words.

"I'm holding your beloved prize, in good faith, under guard, as promised. Should you be unable to fulfill the terms of our agreement you will not only forfeit said prize, but you will also ensure its wasting. Do not try me, Baroness von Traugott. I am unforgiving when someone breaks a contract with me."

"My God, Kendis." Audrianna clutched her chest. "Eva doesn't have Lorna. She has my mother! But how? I thought she was gone forever."

Kendis pulled her close. "Hush now, hush, honey. They're *soul traders*. All of them. Maria, too. I'm sorry to tell ya that—although, I think ya already knew. You just can't remember."

Hand to mouth, Audrianna searched inwardly for the missing pieces, as Kendis answered her thoughts. "Soul traders are profiteers within the Gavrilekian community dealin' in precious souls—aged souls, refined souls, souls to be savored rather than devoured. Where do ya think all their money comes from?" She gestured around the room. "Certainly not from the defunct German government."

The sound of the elevator engaging echoed through the shaft.

"Audrianna, come with me," Kendis urged. "Trust me. Lemme make everything okay. I will make everything okay. But you gotta trust me."

"I've heard that before," whispered Audrianna, numb.

Knock, knock, knock...

"Maria? I've come with the seal. May I enter?" It was Magda's voice.

"Kendis!" Audrianna hissed. "You have to hide! Quick, quick. Go into my closet and shut the door." She tried to shoo her off, but Kendis merely sat back on her haunches.

"Audri, I was invited here to negotiate in peace with Miss Orsic. Are you tellin' me I've been duped?"

"Maria?" Magda knocked again.

The lift gate opened and Maria stepped into the room. She saw Kendis on the floor and said, "Miss Lewis, it would behoove you to rise. My partners will look down on you, regardless, but you shouldn't make it quite so easy for them." She brushed by her, then waited for her to stand before opening the door. "*Wie geht es Ihnen*, Magda. Come inside, please. I apologize for the late hour, but I could not ratify this treaty without the seal."

Magda entered carrying a shiny gold box, ornately decorated with embossed panels. Two heavily armed Brownshirts accompanied her. She took one look at Kendis, then turned and dismissed them. "Thank you gentlemen. You may wait for me in the hall." She shut the door on their scrutiny. She remained with back turned for a moment, then pivoted and forced a smile. "Well, this is an unexpected...encounter."

A little unsettled, Kendis stepped forward without being introduced, extending a handshake. "Hello. I'm Kendis Lewis, representing the Naiad group."

"Indeed you are," Magda replied, softly, her eyes filling with bigoted contempt. She did not take Kendis' hand.

"Magda, Miss Lewis is joining us here under a truce to negotiate the surrend of her island on the Havel," Maria said.

A green apparition of Eva Braun appeared. "What is the meaning of summoning us here in the middle of the night?" she demanded, catching sight of Kendis. Immediately, she pulled a luminescent handle with a gilded knuckle guard—razored steel strands, five feet in length, were attached to the hilt. It seemed a ruthless weapon.

Kendis took a step backward.

"Put that away, Eva." Magda told her. "Miss Lewis is here to parley. We must honor that precept."

Furious, Eva turned on her and said, "Parley on what matter?"

"We were just getting to that," replied Magda. "Mr. Evans, may we expect you sometime today?" She called into the air.

Hiram's gauzy green image gradually appeared. "Yep, I'm here," he yawned. "Mornin' everyone." He squinted at his watch.

Magda placed the seal on Maria's desk and turned toward her. "You were saying, Maria?"

"Yes, thank you." Maria cleared her throat. "Miss Lewis' group has committed a minor infraction against us, which requires satisfaction on our part. Having opted out of a space scrimmage, she has agreed, instead, to surrender *most* of her property on the Havel to the German Third Reich; my team shall assume stewardship. I have allowed her to keep her nightclub, here in Berlin."

"What infraction?" Eva pressed, glancing at Audrianna.

"She has pilfered a small amount of the Vril from my irrigation system using a robotic pestilence of her group's design,"

Maria replied, levelly. "A small amount," she repeated. "Not enough to arm weapons, only enough to heat water, cook food, etcetera. She has many dependents to care for and cannot afford traditional electricity."

"Although, she had plenty of money to manufacture this robotic pestilence." Magda put in.

"Yes, and do you know how she came to acquire those *many* dependents?" Eva demanded. "Your leyonelle has been diverting children from her office, purposely subverting the racial hygiene laws, undermining my work—our work!"

Maria narrowed her eyes. "Interesting, you had that information, yet failed to act upon it. One cannot help but wonder what else you're withholding from the group."

"Enough." Magda said. "Let's keep to the purpose of this parley."

Ambling over to Maria's desk, Eva's ethereal figure opened the golden box and fingered the glowing green seal. "You're finished Miss Lewis," she glanced over her shoulder with a laugh. "We will bring the full weight of our firepower against your pathetic, conniving group, either here or in space—your choice. There will be no treaty. Enjoy this moment of peace between us while you can."

Maria stiffened. "This is my negotiation, not yours. I do not require your approval to proceed," she said.

"Magda! Are you going to allow this?" Eva shouted, slinging her green energy in the air. "This is an enormous transgression against our sovereignty. We must make a swift, deliberate example of these thieves—destroy them outright."

Magda said, "I tend to agree, Maria. We all know you have a generous disposition, but this treaty falls short of the mark. Theft of our super weapon is indeed an enormous transgression."

"However true that may be, my leyonelle has a special fondness for Miss Lewis and has invoked her liberties in her defense," Maria replied.

Audrianna's initial response was to shrink, but Maria's eye contact kept her steady. Somehow, she knew this was part of a larger scheme. This was Maria's set up.

"We're only bound to leyonelle liberties in regards to threats on their person or property," Magda calmly advised. "Not to the objects of their fondness."

"Lovers!" Eva shouted. "Plain language! Let's have that, at least."

Maria's eyelashes flitted briefly closed, but that was her only reaction to that shot.

"Baroness von Traugott," Magda spoke to her, "although you are *lovers* with this woman, you have no governance over her property."

"I do." Audrianna caught her stride, helped along by Maria's telepathic prompting. "I've used my independent—means to fund Miss … Lewellyn's—damn!" Audrianna cursed.

Maria rushed forward with a glowing green hand to Audrianna's head. She whispered, "Kendis Lewis," impressing the name into her mind.

Nodding a thank you, Audrianna then continued, "I've used my independent—means to fund Miss Lewis'—distillery. It is partially—mine. You cannot destroy it. Further, I—am offering Miss Lewis sanctuary on my—land in Sss … Saxony."

"This is preposterous." Eva shook her head disbelievingly. "Although," she laughed, "it boils down to yet another incompetence on your part, Maria. As if your negotiation of the Versailles Treaty hasn't set us back enough. Now, your leyonelle has us under the thumb of an insignificant, half-witted enemy. Can't you do anything right?"

Hiram spoke up for the first time, coming to Maria's defense. "Aww, it don't seem like this is Miss Orsic's fault, too much. B'sides, havin' them in exile seems a better alternative than blowin' that island up with all them feeble-minded kids on it."

"Please explain that reasoning, Mr. Evans," Magda invited.

"For one, it's a waste of ammunition. You're talkin, what? A minimum of two A-1 ballistic missiles, at a cost of—"

"Don't talk to me about ammunition, Mr. Evans," Eva sneered. "I am the Master of Military Operations, not you. If you have intelligence from your operation that's relevant to this parley, out with it. Otherwise, take some advice from your betters and *stay out of it.*"

Hiram shrugged. "All right. In case y'all didn't know, Hitler's bid for supreme authority isn't as credible as your informants would have ya believe. His toleration of y'all's luxury lifestyle when poor livin' standards still exist for most ordinary Germans is bein' heavily criticized. The racial hygiene program ain't that popular either. People get wind of the fact that the Party big-wigs," he pointed at them, "executed a group of defenseless jigaboos and a buncha' retards, there'll be a revolt. Count on it. It's just not a good idea, especially when there's no real purpose to it, b'sides provin' our superiority over a puny group of water nymphs. Let'um go to their prison in Saxony. That's what I think."

"Thank you, Mr. Evans," Magda said.

"Yes, thank you." Eva glared. "Did you get that from Canaris verbatim, or were you groomed beforehand?"

Maria started to respond, but Magda took control. "All right, I've heard enough. Let's draw up the treaty. Maria, where is your scribe?"

"Coming, presently," Maria replied.

"You're really going to allow this?" Eva asked with a scoff.

"Yes, and so are you. Mr. Evans has made a compelling argument, which I believe to be objective and without influence. We cannot afford to upset the general public—they'll shortly be called upon to do the unthinkable. Miss Lewis," Magda turned to her, "I do hope you'll advise your kinsmen that you are fully on our radar, so to speak. One wrong move and our benevolence will be retracted."

Kendis replied without emotion. "I've been warned."

"Master?" Zaldy peeked around the doorframe, leather box case slung on his shoulder

Maria went over to meet him. Protectively, she put her arm about his shoulder and escorted him inside. "Yes, Zaldy. Come in. I apologize for disrupting your sleep."

"He is yours to command. Is he not?" Eva asked as she paced the room.

Maria took him to her desk and sat him in her chair, keeping a hand on his shoulder for encouragement. "He may be mine to command," she replied, "but I am also considerate of his needs. Go ahead, Zaldy. Please." He opened his case and took out a piece of watermarked paper, a fountain pen and a portable inkwell. Telepathically, Maria directed his writing. Eva continued to grumble.

"This is absolutely unbelievable. We've been handled, we've been," she stuttered, "we've been…"

"Eva," Magda cut in. "Is this in any way likely to affect our state of play in European politics?"

"Of course not."

"Well, then," Magda smiled, "I suggest you find some other endeavor equal to this show of … zeal."

Annoyed by that statement, Eva lashed out at Zaldy. "Is that contract ready, yet, boy?" she barked.

Zaldy answered over his shoulder. "Yes, Master, we're finishing up now. If you'll just imbed your biverse signature, here." He shot up from his chair, pointing nervously to the paper.

"Thank you, Zaldy." Maria patted him on the back. "Grab your things and return to your bed. I'll finish up from here and file it in the morning."

"Oh. Okay. Thank you, Master." Zaldy quickly gathered his belongings and headed for the door.

"Zaldy," Maria called after him. "Manners please."

Mid-step, he about-faced and darted back to Audrianna, kissing her hand. "I apologize for that, Leyonelle. That's the second time I've ignored you. Isn't it?"

Audrianna looked down, embarrassed by the attention. "It's okay," she whispered.

"Okay, great. Goodnight Leyonelle. Goodnight Masters." He nodded at the others in the room, then sprinted out the door.

Eva came over and pressed her thumb into the paper. An iridescent print appeared. Sanctimonious as always, she turned and announced, "If we are to win this contest, we must avoid treaties of this nature. We are the Incubus. Mercy should not be on our menu." She looked down her nose at Kendis as her avatar faded to green dust.

The next endorsement was Magda's. Pressing her fingerprint into the paper, she said, "I do hope we've seen the last of this issue, Maria. Whatever's gone wrong between you and your leyonelle, please correct it." She walked over to Audrianna as Hiram came forward to make his mark, followed shortly by Maria. Magda kissed Audrianna's hand. "Baroness von Traugott, I'm pleased to see you recovering so well. Maria has accomplished a great miracle with you, I believe."

"One which I hope to repay," Audrianna whispered, glancing at Maria. "If she'll give me—chance."

"A chance to prove yourself. What a happy thought," Magda chimed.

Lifting her finger from the paper, Maria called behind her, "Miss Lewis? May we have your biverse signature here, please?" Aside to Hiram, she said, "I'd like to thank you for your objectivity, Mr. Evans—and your support. It's nice to have another voice of reason in the group. I shan't be so lonely, now." She flashed him her shy little smile.

"Call me Hiram," he said.

"Hiram. Right." Maria agreed.

He tipped his hat at her. "Your servant, ma'am," he said, and then his image disappeared.

Kendis rendered her fingerprint upon the document, then stepped aside for Magda as she dribbled wax on the paper, stamping it with the Incubus seal.

"There. It's done," she announced, replacing the seal in the box, and shutting the lid. She walked to the door and made a final remark. "Miss Lewis, I see no occasion for us to meet again, now that this matter has been settled—auspiciously settled in your favor, I might add. Maria has shown great spirit and generosity toward you in this and now I'll thank you to return the favor."

"If I can," Kendis offered.

"Stay away from Baroness von Traugott," Magda said, closing the door behind her.

***

"Dearest, it's late," said Maria, consulting her wristwatch. "I'll go and change into my nightclothes, then come back and help you." Telepathically, she added, "Use this time to say your farewells." She crossed the room to her bedroom door.

"Maria," Kendis blurted out her first name.

Maria stopped, head turned sideways.

"Thank you," Kendis said. "I get what ya did just now. You saved me from her."

"You forget yourself, Miss Lewis. I've done what I've done for my leyonelle. Not you." Maria went in her room and shut the door, leaving Audrianna and Kendis alone.

After a long moment of silence, Kendis spoke. She said, "Audri, I'm worried about ya stayin here. What if she finds out you were in on a trap to deliver her biverse energy to her partner?"

In a daze, Audrianna replied with her mind. "She's going to find out, because I'm going to tell her, Kendis. If she throws me out, so be it. If God is truly merciful, she'll forgive me for this vicious thing I've done and we can begin again."

"What about your mother?" Kendis asked. "You're gonna just let that go? Maria may not be directly culpable of sluicing your mother's soul to sell on the black market, but she's a soul trader, too, honey. She's done it to others."

Beads of sweat broke out across Audrianna's forehead as she processed that reckoning. Maria was a virgin. She'd never slept with anyone, so how did she accomplish the sluicing of human souls? Kissing? Could it be done that way?"

Kendis answered her thoughts. "I'm not sure how it's done, honey, much less how it's alchemized into liquid eyedrops. It's quite a protected covenant between those who do it."

"Eye drops," whispered Audrianna, conceptualizing that puzzle piece into place.

"Audrianna?"

"Yes?" Audrianna shook the glaze out of her eyes.

"You've already bonded with her. Haven't you?"

Audrianna recalled her momentary connection with Maria: the field of wheat, the blue tulips, the acid rain. Was that what bonding was? It certainly wasn't the euphoric experience Kendis had described to her before. Or were those details as twisted as the rest of her memories?

> *"Since we are exact replicas of our human's consciousness," Kendis explained, "it is possible to bond our biverse energy to our human's soul—tag along inside of them, if you will. I've seen it done before. It's a breathtaking ritual to watch, so I can only imagine how it must feel."*

Uncertainty hardened into conviction and resolve. "I'm not sure if we've bonded or not," Audrianna said in thought, "but I plan to make myself available to her in that way, however and whenever she needs me." She said it and it took. Her mind was now made up.

"Audri, I get that your opinion of Maria has changed, but she is still an Arbalest Master! Doesn't that matter anymore?"

Audrianna tracked the term to a remote recess of her memory:

> *"There are a dozen or so tyrannical groups of Gavrilekians who control the banks, the militaries, and the majority of the political offices on this planet, and they are the ones who wield most of the power in the game," said Kendis. "The rest of us have nicknamed 'um the Arbalest Groups, after the steel crossbow of the Middle Ages: the weapon that the Pope banned from*

the battlefield because of its brutality and the unfair
advantage it offered."

Anxiety pushed into Audrianna's thoughts. She looked around for Maria, wanting her back, forgetting the previous point.

"Audri." Kendis grabbed her hair in clumps. "She's inhumane!"

"She just saved—orphans," Audrianna came back, defensive.

Kendis shook her head. "Audrianna. She did that for you. She just said it. Had you not so obviously objected to Eva's racial hygiene program, she would still have little or no opinion about it. Honey, she's bewitchin', I get it, but she's also *misguided*."

"We have that in common," Audrianna croaked. "Perhaps we'll—beee…" She got stuck on the word.

"Perhaps we'll be better together." Maria opened the door in her white nightgown and cowboy boots. She wore an ankle length negligee over top, a cyan blue tulip in hand. "What a lovely sentiment, dearest," she said, starting Audrianna's way.

"You've been listening to us?" Kendis asked, eyes wide.

"Yes."

"Earlier, too?"

"Yes."

"How?" Kendis stammered. "I had a thought block up."

Maria presented Audrianna with her first tulip since the night of the Needle, then stood beside her, offering her hand to hold. Audrianna took it without hesitation. "You cannot block two mirrors in an open telepathic exchange, Miss Lewis. A device, such as the necklace Baroness von Traugott threw in the fire, must be crafted for such a purpose. You would've done better to employ a thought filter. Do you know the difference between the two?"

Kendis shook her head.

"No. I thought not," Maria chuckled. "Miss Lewis, not every master you engage with this contest will be as amused by you as I am—you've already experienced that reception from my partners. I encourage you to rethink your play-to-win objective. It seems a little *misguided* to me." She squeezed Audrianna's hand, then went and rang the servants bell, turning around afterwards. "I don't wish to be uncivil, madam, but you've outstayed your welcome. You may write to Baroness von Traugott, should it please you both, but neither you nor any member of your group will return to my house. If you or any of your team are discovered here, you will be captured on sight and sent to Sachsenhausen Concentration Camp to play out this series. Callum?"

Callum shuffled into the room. "Yes, Master?"

"Miss Lewis is leaving. Please show her to the car." Maria told him.

"Yes Master—Miss Lewis," he bowed to her, "if you'll please follow me. We'll get you back to your club."

Heaving a sigh of resignation, Kendis followed Callum out, catching her hand on the doorframe. "I'll write to ya, honey. Okay? I'll write," she said. Then, she was gone.

A sense of suspense hung over the place. Maria drifted to the fire, pulling a single hand-rolled cigarette from her pocket. She lit it up, taking a puff. The smell of marijuana filled the air.

A nervous tingle rushed through Audrianna. Averting her eyes, she managed a roundabout query. "I didn't know you smoked that sss...stuff."

"I smoke it when my heart gallops," Maria said, taking another hit.

"Oh?" Audrianna's pitch lifted. "Does it help?"

Maria glanced over her shoulder, laughing out her smoke. "I think so. Yes."

Audrianna scooted to the edge of her chair. "Are you sick?" she asked.

Maria shook her head. "This is an emotional manifestation of some variety, I'd say. I've felt it a time or two before, generally following some trying event." She reached above the hearth for Stephanie's secret ashtray and put her joint out in it. "Here's her next cover story," she said, replacing it in its hiding spot.

Audrianna chuckled at Maria's mild-mannered lampoon.

"Her magazine is full of drama of her own making," Maria muttered, falling into the chair next to Audrianna, stretching out her boots. She shook her head. "Showgirls? Ice fishing? I can't believe she left you alone with a gun, knowing you'd already attempted suicide once that way."

Audrianna's laughter petered out. Turning her head, she summoned Maria's eyes and telepathically said, "She doesn't know I tried to kill myself, Maria. I haven't told her. She thinks Lorna attacked me, same as everyone else. She knows nothing of my agreement with Eva, either. In many ways, she's just as confused by all this as you are."

Maria's expression softened. "Thank you for offering me that perspective, dearest. I don't want to dislike her, though, I wish she wouldn't lie to me. I wish you wouldn't lie to me, either," she said, flashing her shy smile. It was the first time she'd expressed vulnerability toward Audrianna.

"Is it so apparent?" Maria acknowledged that thought.

Audrianna answered with her mind. "It's only apparent if someone's paying close attention. I've been paying very close attention to you, *angel.*" She used a pet name with Maria, adding weight to her glove.

Maria catapulted up with a nervous laugh, leaning with both hands on the mantle. "No doubt you've engineered your trap of my biverse energy based upon some perceived vulnerability. It's lamentable that you have no memory of the details, dearest. It means we must tread very carefully with our courtship."

"We will tread in whatever way you want," Audrianna whispered, finding speech at that tone easier.

Maria nodded. "Yes, that's what I understood you to say. However, before you commit yourself entirely, I wish you to tell you—"

"Maria?" Audrianna called with her mind.

"Yes?"

"Suppose we turn our eyes to each other, rather than away?"

"Another beautiful sentiment," Maria cooed. "You're full of poetry tonight."

Audrianna softly chuckled. "I meant it literally, Maria. Turn around. I want to look at you."

Pivoting, Maria took a deep, apprehensive breath. She said, "I wish to tell you about a facet of my life, which has so far remained undisclosed. I intended to discuss it with you prior to our actual bonding; my timing has always been off where you're concerned. I've done a bad job of living without you."

Audrianna patted the armrest next to her. "Maria, come sit, please," she said, continuing with her mind. "I already know about the soul trading. Is that what's got you so uneasy?"

Maria came back and sat down. "Yes, although, in regard to your mother—my involvement, specifically. That's the conversation I wish to have."

Hair lifted on the back of Audrianna's neck. Even so she deflected Maria's innuendo. "I understand you must feel guilty by association, but you needn't—"

"It was me," Maria broke in, voice cracking. "I sold your mother's soul to Eva. I had her first and I sold her to Eva. There. It's said."

Silence brooded like a lonely spirit over a still and pulseless world—a weird world of morbid horrors. Audrianna forced a faint quivering smile. "Well," she whispered, "finally it's not so much a riddle why I—wanted you to—suffer."

"No." Maria admitted.

Audrianna's eyes swam as events became demystified: the dance card given to her, dated three days before her mother's death. The final entry was Wilhelm Canaris: Maria's Captain Canaris. Eva gave her that card to showcase Maria's responsibility.

"So, did he do it, or did you?" Audrianna carried on telepathically, tilting her head back to keep the tears in her eyes. "Or, did he do it for you? I'm not sure how this all goes?" A single rogue tear escaped.

Maria rose and stood above her, looking down. "He brought her to me," she said, sweeping the tear onto her forefinger. "May I have this," she asked, flicking it into the air: *flick flick*. The room was immediately sponged with a glowing blue light.

Easily incensed by Gavrilekian tricks, Audrianna tested Maria's temper. "Captain Canaris brought her to you and *you* killed her," she declared. "You killed my mother."

"No, I did not." replied Maria

"Did you sleep with her, too?" Audrianna landed a punch.

Maria's nostrils flared. "I did not, Audrianna. I've been intimate with no one other than myself, as you well know."

"Then, how did you her get her soul out?" Audrianna wiped both eyes with alternating hands, angry.

Maria captured her wrists. "Don't smear," she said. "Just let them fall."

A sudden premonition of fear held Audrianna in its vice "What are you doing?" She began to struggle.

Maria gritted her teeth, forcing Audrianna back in the wheelchair. "I'm showing you what I did to your mother. That's what you wished to know. Right?"

Audrianna felt her bladder go loose. She slung tears off her chin, side-to-side, teeth chattering a response. "I don't…" She couldn't even think what to say.

"Shh…" Maria pulled her forward by the back of the neck, fingers sifting through her sweaty hair.

Shelves in the room began to shape shift, toppling books onto the floor—clouds of tinkling letters shattered into the air. The room filled with floating words.

"Oh, God." Audrianna gripped the armrests.

"I apologize for frightening you." Maria kissed the top of her head. "But, you've taken the position and deserve a response."

The floorboards squeaked and relaxed with groans of tortured pleasure. Audrianna closed her eyes in a panic, sucking air in and out through bared teeth. "What's happening, Maria?" she asked in thought.

"Keep your eyes closed, please. I want to talk to you while your memoir is being written." Maria snapped her fingers, gluing Audrianna's eyelids shut. Bucking with initial panic, Audrianna eventually succumbed to reconciliation, clinging to Maria as she held her comfortingly, breathing in her face. "You're quite a paradox," she whispered. "Believing me capable of destroying your mother, yet embracing me for safety."

Audrianna pawed at her, daring her, drunk on love. "Yes? What else?"

Maria did not hold back. She said, "I've worked hard to fill the time, to make possible what I am waiting for. I've told myself that I will only be apart from you for one day more, for that is as much as I can bear. I want to feel your breath upon my face; I want to feel you gazing at me. I want to fill my senses with you. But, how can I do that when you doubt my very character? I did not kill your mother, Audrianna. She *cried* for me. That is all."

"What?" Audrianna lifted her eyelids and this time they opened. Maria stood before her, book in one hand, a tiny glass vial in the other. She offered Audrianna the book first: it smoked with blue energy.

"Here is the memoir of your soul: past, present and future," she said. "Normally, I require payment with tears. There are trace amounts of one's soul in tears—this is how I came about your mother's soul. Captain Canaris brought her here to read her soul's memoir, and I read it to her. While I read, she cried for me. I did not kill her, Leyonelle. Her death came days afterward."

Audrianna floated a hand to her throat, mouth agape. "Okay," she choked, pushing the book away, rejecting the vial, too. "I don't want—read this," she said, blathering.

"Why?" Maria asked, tilting her chin up, fishing out a handkerchief to clean up her nose.

"I'd rather—read this." Audrianna reached over and pulled *Sense and Sensibility* from the pocket of her wheelchair, showing it to her, wanting unanimity. Maria was exonerated from the worst crime. Everything else was immediately unimportant.

Reaching into the pocket of her negligee, Maria pulled out and unfolded papers Kuniko had transcribed from Audrianna's speech lesson. She read through them quickly, then stopped on the last page, taking *Sense and Sensibility* from Audrianna's hands. She snapped her fingers and the room reverted to normal.

"This is the page we were on. Shall we start from here?" Maria asked, looking up.

Audrianna licked her lips, sighing with an elated, hopeful peace. She said, "No. Let's begin again."